THE AQUARIANS

THE AQUARIANS

2012 - A NEW ERA BEGINS

ERIC RANKIN

iUniverse Star

New York   Bloomington

THE AQUARIANS
2012 - A NEW ERA BEGINS

This is a work of fiction. All of the characters, names, incidents, organizations, and dialogue in this novel are either the products of the author's imagination or are used fictitiously.

iUniverse Star
an iUniverse, Inc. imprint

iUniverse books may be ordered through booksellers or by contacting:

iUniverse
1663 Liberty Drive
Bloomington, IN 47403
www.iuniverse.com
1-800-Authors (1-800-288-4677)

Because of the dynamic nature of the Internet, any Web addresses or links contained in this book may have changed since publication and may no longer be valid. The views expressed in this work are solely those of the author and do not necessarily reflect the views of the publisher, and the publisher hereby disclaims any responsibility for them.

ISBN: 978-1-935-27882-5 (sc)
ISBN: 978-1-935-27883-2 (ebook)

Printed in the United States of America

iUniverse Rev Date: 10/12/09

This book is dedicated to my wife, Elena, and my son, Ryan. I love you both more than words could ever express.

Acknowledgments

I must acknowledge Candi Sary, Peter Kalionzes, and Dr. Jim Turrell, each of whom came into my life at just the right moment to keep this project moving forward. This book would not have existed without them.

Special thanks are also in order to the following people and organizations:

Alfred Publishing, for permission to use lyrics from the song *Aquarius;*
the Mayan Studies staff at Millsaps College in Mississippi;
the brave men and women who served aboard the destroyer *USS Nicholas;*
Vern of the Newport Beach, CA, dory fishing fleet;
Dr. John Lilly, who posed the most intriguing questions about dolphins;
Dr. David Nathansen, for his pioneering work with dolphin-assisted healing;
the dedicated staff of dolphin behaviorists at SeaWorld, San Diego;
MK Mendoza, for her perfectly timed words of hope and encouragement;
Bob Weil and the rest of the *South Coast Safari* video production crew;
Dr. Wayne Dyer, for reminding me that we are all spiritual beings leading temporarily earthbound lives;
my parents, Glen and Jill, for always supporting my unusual endeavors;
Jimmy Buffet, for inspiring me to go out and live my own exotic adventures;
the Hawaii Institute of Marine Biology, for their groundbreaking ultrasonic imaging research with dolphins;
the warm and friendly people of Tortola, British Virgin Islands;
the staff at Cigarette Offshore Racing Boats, Miami, FL;
the staff at Lido Dry Stack storage in Newport Beach, CA;

Finally, I owe an incalculable debt of gratitude to my editor, Cheri Laser. From fact-checking to story-arc issues, Cheri did a phenomenal job of helping me shape *The Aquarians* into the book I'd always hoped I could write.

Preface

Mayans of the classic period (250 to 900 AD) were prolific writers of books. Tragically, those books, which conveyed precise information about the culture's history, mathematics, astronomy, and prophecy, were burned by the thousands at the hand of Hernan Cortez and his fellow Spanish Conquistadores in the early 1500s.

Along with more valuable plunder, four of those ancient manuscripts, or codices, were spared and sent to the King of Spain as novelty gifts, where they were displayed in various locations throughout Europe. Eventually, one of the rare books found its way to Vienna, where it was procured by a private collector and donated in 1740 to the Royal Saxon Library of Dresden, Germany.

The 800-year-old Dresden Codex, as that particular Mayan textbook is now called, is best known for its incredibly accurate astronomical predictions and dire prophetic visions of the future. On the last page of the codex—a page symbolized by the arrival of a celestial water-bearer—the Mayans wrote of a day when time as we know it would cease to exist.

That day is almost here.

Prologue

Four Moments in Time

August 28, 1945—Sagami Bay, Japan

Under the glow of a nearly full moon, Senior Mess Officer Vern Becket leaned against the starboard railing of the destroyer *USS Nicholas*. Scanning the anchored vessels of Task Force 38, his eyes stopped at the hulking silhouette of *USS Missouri*, the fleet's battleship. In the morning, *Missouri* was scheduled to sail into Tokyo Harbor, where she would serve as host to Japan's unconditional surrender. World War II, at least in the Pacific Theater, was over.

Out of the darkness, Vern's best friend, Ensign Johnny Lane, sidled up to the rail and lit a cigarette. The match's flame illuminated similar expressions of numb fatigue on the two young men's faces. "Damn, if I'd known you were out here, I wouldn't have had to wear this stupid vest."

Vern was not in the mood for idle conversation. "Fall off the deck at midnight and you'd be plenty glad you had that thing on." He gave a sharp tug on his own vest's straps.

"Yeah, I suppose you're right." Johnny turned his back to the slight breeze blowing across the bay and flipped up the collar of his jacket. "Say, have you noticed any strange sounds coming from inside the ship in the last hour or two?"

"Can't say as I have. Why?"

"I dunno. Kept wakin' up thinkin' I heard something, but maybe I'm just imagining things." He took a long drag on the cigarette, holding the smoke deep in his lungs before letting it stream out with his next words. "So, you think the war with the Japs is really over?"

Vern did not respond.

"Sure it's over," Johnny said, answering himself. "I don't think they want another city getting A-bombed to smithereens."

"Not to mention another hundred thousand civilians being incinerated," Vern added, his voice constricting as the unspeakable images flashed across his mind.

Since the dropping of the two nuclear bombs over Hiroshima and Nagasaki three weeks ago, he had been left with a sickening feeling in his gut that would not go away.

The lull in the conversation was awkward, but not awkward enough to shut Johnny up.

"Hey, I hear we might be one of Missouri's escorts when she ties up in Tokyo tomorrow. Probably get to rub elbows with some Navy brass, don't you figure? Maybe even get our picture in the papers back home with ol' Emperor Hirohito kissing our asses!"

From the bridge, twelve clanging strikes on the ship's bell interrupted Johnny's diatribe and announced the start of a new day.

Vern glanced down at his wristwatch. "Zero hundred. Guess I'd better get a little shut-eye before startin' breakfast. G'night, Johnny."

Oddly, Johnny's only response was a frozen, wide-eyed stare into space.

"I said, good night there, buddy—"

Johnny cut Vern off, his voice raised in urgency. "*There*, Vern! There it is *again!*"

There was no mistaking the sudden sound of flexing metal emanating from inside the ship. The groaning noise was common enough whenever the destroyer rolled over storm swells, but never at anchor in calm waters like this.

"What the hell *is* that?" Johnny gulped as the mournful twisting intensified.

They were about to find out. Just aft of the galley, the ship's auxiliary boiler was straining to contain an enormous overload of pressurized steam that had built up behind a corroded safety valve.

Without warning and with a thunderous roar, the thousand-gallon boiler blew apart, blasting a hole in the starboard bulkhead. The rupturing metal and screaming rush of scalding air hurled the two men over the railing and into the frigid waters of Sagami Bay.

Within minutes, every ship in the fleet would be standing at full alert in a frenzy of sirens and searchlights, but for the moment, all was quiet once again. Except for the roughly seven-foot hole in the upper deck of the *Nicholas*, and the two lone souls adrift in the midnight sea, the scene appeared untouched from just seconds earlier.

Dazed and bobbing on the surface, kept afloat by only his life vest, Vern began to regain his focus and assess what had just happened. Until this moment, he'd survived four years of active duty on a warship without sustaining a single injury.

Gazing up at a glittering ceiling of stars, the irony of the situation did not escape him. *What will the Navy consider me?* he wondered. *A casualty of peace?*

Illuminated by the moonlight, a deep red slick of blood confirmed his fear that he and Johnny had, indeed, been severely injured.

"Johnny!" Vern coughed through the saltwater filling his lungs. "Johnny! You okay?"

Vern managed to paddle a couple of flailing strokes toward his friend. Then he slowed with stunned horror when he got close enough to see that Johnny's throat had been sliced wide open, a jagged piece of metal still lodged deep in his neck.

"Oh, God, please," Vern whispered, knowing without a doubt that his friend was already dead.

High above, someone up on the bridge of the *Nicholas* began scanning the ocean's surface with a hand-held flashlight.

Vern managed to wave both arms once over his head to try and draw attention to himself. After taking quick stock of his own condition, however, he doubted that he had any better chance than Johnny of being pulled out of the water alive. Though he had not suffered a direct hit from any flying metal or debris, he was certain he had sustained extensive internal injuries. There was a severe burning sensation in his torso, which led him to believe he was hemorrhaging somewhere near his kidney. Placing a hand on the lower left side of his abdomen, he could feel the firm bulge of blood beginning to push up hard against the underside of his skin.

In the enveloping blackness, Vern took a labored breath and surrendered to the likelihood of death by reciting the only prayer he ever knew.

"Now I lay me down to sleep," he said out loud, his weak voice trembling. "Lord, I pray my soul to keep. And if I die ..."

He stopped when an unexpected thought came to him. "I mean, *before* I die, I want to talk to my guardian angel… if I have one."

Treading water, he could hear hurried footsteps and muffled shouting as his shipmates scrambled onto the decks of the *Nicholas*. But drifting in behind these familiar noises was something else— something distant and quiet. Concentrating on the sound, he realized that what he was hearing was a voice, soft and feminine, repeating an indecipherable string of words.

"Hello?" Vern called out into the night. "Is someone there?"

Now he could hear the words clearly, as they somehow seemed to be emanating from both the far distance and inside his head at the same time.

"I'm here, Vern," was all the voice said, and he realized that these were the words he'd heard repeated over and over.

His rational mind lurched to the conclusion that he must be hallucinating or, at the very least, talking to himself. Even so, he could not help but respond to the alluring voice.

"Who … who are you?"

"I am the one you asked for."

"My guardian angel?"

There was a long pause.

"If this designation brings you comfort, you are welcome to refer to me as such," the voice finally replied.

The brief response convinced Vern that he was not generating both sides of the conversation, for he knew he would not respond to anyone, much less himself, with words like *designation* or *as such*.

"You're here because I'm dying, aren't you?"

Another moment of silence.

"I am here because you invited me here."

Because I invited you here? You mean that's all I've ever had to do? "All right, then, I'll ask it another way: *Am* I going to die tonight?" The question made him wince because he believed he already knew the answer

"No, Vern, you will not die tonight. No one leaves this life, no matter how long or short it may be, without accomplishing what they were meant to accomplish here on earth."

The cryptic statement triggered as much confusion as it did relief. "I don't understand."

"I need you to do something for me."

"I ..." he gulped. "I need to do something for *you?*"

"Yes, I need you to deliver a message."

"A message? What message? To who?"

"At this moment, I do not have the answers to those questions," the voice replied. "But I *can* tell you this: when the time is right, the sea will deliver both the message and its recipient to you. As such, I'm asking you to always stay near the water to receive them both."

Disoriented and confused, Vern realized that the conversation—or maybe it *was* a hallucination—was coming to an end.

"Wait!" he called out desperately into the night. "Will you ever be with me again?"

Thankfully, he heard an answer. "Vern, I have always been with you, and I always will be."

With these last words echoing through his head, a tingling sensation began to flow through him—a pulse of energy—causing his body to shudder in violent convulsions and his eyes to roll involuntarily up in their sockets.

◆　　　◆　　　◆

A small motor launch was being hoisted down the sheer hull sides of the *Nicholas*. Inside were the launch's skipper, two crew members, and the ship's medical officer, who barked orders to the sailors up on deck.

"Come on! Hurry up and lower this thing! And get that searchlight turned on!"

"Yes, *sir!*" the light operator acknowledged. "It's already warming up."

"Do we know how many men might be out there?" the medical officer called out to anyone.

"We just finished emergency roll call," answered one of the seamen standing at the railing of the destroyer, "and everyone's accounted for except Mess Officer Becket and Ensign Lane. We're still looking for them inside, but they might have come out on deck in between their shifts."

Just then, the massive searchlight switched on and began scanning the dark surface of the sea.

"Over there!" the light operator shouted, holding the light steady on a motionless floating form.

The skipper navigated the motor launch inside the illuminated area.

"Good God!" the medical officer exclaimed, looking at the body lying face up with eyes wide open. The jagged piece of metal lodged in Johnny's neck had almost completely severed his head. "One fatality!" he shouted up to the deck, then redirected his attention to the crew. "Quick, grab that blanket and help me pull him over the side—*carefully.*"

Once Johnny was in the boat and covered up, the searchlight's beam slowly began scanning the water nearby. Moments later, the light operator's throat constricted in terror. From his post high on the bridge, he could see a swarm of gray fins moving into the glaring circle of light.

"Sharks!" he gulped before screaming the warning out loud. *"Sharks!"*

A group of gray, torpedo-shaped figures, seven or eight in all, surrounded Vern's lifeless body.

"Looks like they found this sailor before we did," the medical officer said, shaking his head at the apparent futility of the rescue. "Sharks can smell blood from a hell of a long way off."

Then, in an incredible display of coordination, the animals gathered around Vern in a tight circle, aiming their pointed snouts toward his body. They appeared to be waiting for just the right moment to mount a unified attack.

Strangely, though, even with the launch moving cautiously in their direction, the animals never moved from their positions.

"What the hell is going on here?" the skipper stammered as the boat glided into the midst of the eerily stationary creatures floating at the surface.

From this close, the men could hear an occasional, staccato-sharp *whoosh* piercing the darkness.

The ship's doctor could not begin to make sense of what was happening, but he did know one thing. "These are *not* sharks," he said, recognizing the loud exhalations of air. "They're *dolphins.*"

"Dolphins?" the skipper challenged. "What in God's name are they doing?"

"I'm not even going to try and guess. But I don't think they'll bother us. Let's just hurry up and get this man out of the water."

Once the launch was close enough, the two crew members reached over and heaved Vern into the boat, readying another blanket for his body. Purely as a formality, the medical officer placed two fingers on Vern's neck to confirm the second fatality. His eyes widened. "Wait! I've got a pulse!"

Hurriedly shifting gears, the doctor ripped open the mess officer's uniform to check for any wounds while one of the seamen waved smelling salts under his nose.

Slowly regaining consciousness, Vern looked up at the four men leaning over him with a vacant expression in his eyes. "Sorry for making you guys come out here," he said with a weak cough, "'cause I don't think there's anything you can do. I'm all busted up inside."

The medical officer ran his hands across the skin of Vern's abdomen, gently probing with the tips of his fingers for signs of internal damage. "Is that right, sailor? Do you know something I don't?" he asked, elated yet puzzled after determining that Mess Officer Vern Becket had inexplicably come through the horrific explosion without sustaining a single serious injury.

Thereafter, news of Vern's mysterious survival spread quickly and was the main topic of conversation for days among the crew of the *Nicholas.* But what held everyone's attention far longer was the story about the group of wild dolphins that had visited and surrounded Vern in such a protective manner. Omens like that were not taken lightly by sailors, and Vern was subsequently regarded as a man possessing a special affinity not only for the sea, but for the creatures living within.

◆   ◆   ◆

August 17, 1989—Tortola, British Virgin Islands

At the end of a palm-shrouded dirt road, a rusting metal sign announced the research facility. The sign's hand-painted letters, crooked and unevenly spaced, notified the two young entrepreneurs that they had arrived at the Institute of Dolphin Ultrasonic Imaging. Taking note of the moniker, they raised a skeptical eyebrow at each other as the Jeep forged ahead through the sweltering jungle.

"You sure this was worth the trip?" asked Chad Hanover, cofounder of Shipwreck Salvage, a lucrative treasure-hunting firm based in Miami. Past the sign, the road degenerated into nothing more than a pair of parallel ruts following the island's scalloped shoreline.

"Am I *sure?*" Calvin Brooks grunted, wiping his sweaty brow with the sleeve of his shirt. "Hell no, I'm not sure. But like I've said before, if this guy's for real, we'd be crazy not to see what he could do for us." There was no hiding the eagerness in Calvin's voice while he replayed in his head the phone call that had lured them to this remote corner of the British Virgin Islands. "Look. There it is up ahead."

"Oh, Jesus. You've got to be kidding me," Chad moaned at the underwhelming sight of a crude rock-and-cement shack, not more than twenty feet square, covered with a roof of overlapping tin scraps. Behind the shack, the waters of a small, man-made lagoon, roughly two hundred feet in diameter, lapped at the shore. "That's it? That's the high-tech research institute you've been telling me about?"

"Hey, at least we know the guy's not wasting any money on a fancy building."

When the Jeep pulled up to the front of the structure, a welcoming committee consisting of three adults and one small boy piled out of the shack and eagerly converged upon the visitors.

Dr. Troy Wallace, founder of the Institute, thrust out his hand to each of them. "Welcome to Tortola!" he beamed. Dressed in crisp white linen pants and shirt, Wallace could have passed for an activities director at some posh resort hotel. "And to our humble little research facility."

With a firm grip and shake that instantly telegraphed confidence and enthusiasm, Dr. Wallace commenced with the introductions. "I'm Troy, resident mad scientist here on the island, and this is my assistant, Jerry Spears."

Calvin and Chad took quick note of the contrast between their two hosts. Appearing to be in his mid-to-late fifties, with bright blue eyes and a thick head of chestnut hair, Troy carried his lean frame with the poise of someone half his age. Conversely, though probably just over twenty, Jerry was bloated and wheezing, an unkempt testament to a likely over-consumption of both food and liquor. And, if the vapid expression on his face was any clue, he had also indulged regularly, and recently, in the potent marijuana that could be procured quite easily throughout the Caribbean.

Taking off his thick glasses and wiping them with the edge of his T-shirt, Jerry let a slight nod take the place of a handshake—a gesture that caused the bangs of his long red hair to fall into his sweaty face.

Calvin turned his attempted handshake into an awkward wave. "Um, nice to meet you, Jerry. I'm Calvin Brooks, and this is my business partner, Chad Hanover. Dr. Wallace tells me that you're the real brains behind this operation."

Jerry barely acknowledged the compliment. "Well, Troy's the guy with the bright ideas," he conceded, brushing back his hair. "But it's going to take some radical computer hardware to tap into what he thinks dolphins can do. And that's the stuff I know. Computers."

"Computers," Chad said with a disdainful snort. "Everybody's talkin' about computers these days. I mean, come on. Aren't they really just fancy typewriters?"

Jerry bristled at Chad's ignorant statement. "Mr. Hanover, someday the personal computer will replace every piece of information-sharing technology you've ever used—the telephone, radio, television, you name it."

"Yeah, right. As long as no one minds watching television on a tiny little black and green screen."

"Trust me. All computer monitors will be full-color soon," Jerry predicted with a sneer.

Troy stepped in before the exchange could get any more prickly. "Yes, well, while I hate to interrupt, I would like to introduce you to two other people who are very important to our operation. It is my pleasure to present Mr. Haden Turrell—and this little fellow here is his son, Randi."

Haden, a native of the island, lunged forward enthusiastically and gave Chad and Calvin each a quick and unexpected hug. With equal warmth and passion, and with a smile full of perfect teeth nearly glowing against his ebony skin, he informed them of his duties at the compound.

"My job is keepin' dat fish fed," he said proudly as he looked over his shoulder toward the lagoon.

Everyone's attention shifted to the shallow lagoon, where a lone bottlenose dolphin could be seen gliding just beneath the placid surface.

"That's Notchy," Dr. Wallace said. "He's our most recent guinea pig here at the compound."

"Notchy?" Calvin queried.

"I named 'im," the boy volunteered eagerly, his dark skin glistening in the sun. "'Cuz de Dolphin Mon here said I could and 'cuz dat dolphin's got a big notch missin' outta' de fin on 'is back. Dolphin Mon tinks a boat hit 'im, but I bet he got in a fight wid a giant sea monster!"

Troy blushed slightly at being called the Dolphin Man, the name a visiting class of schoolchildren had bestowed upon him during a field trip to his facility.

"It's a shame you're so shy," Calvin joked. "What's your name again?"

"Randi. I'm twelve years old and I'm already in de sixth grade."

"Nice to meet you, Randi," Calvin said before giving Troy a quizzical glance. "Hey, Doc? Is it okay if Randi takes us over to meet your dolphin?"

"I think that's a great idea," Troy enthused. He motioned for the boy to lead the way down to the lagoon.

As the group shuffled through powdery white sand, Troy began to lay the groundwork for his presentation. "Calvin, I've read all about your recent success salvaging the wreck of the galleon *Finisterra.*"

"Yeah. A lot of homework, not to mention a lucky hunch of mine, found us that one," Calvin boasted. His words and tone relayed, in no uncertain terms, that he considered his hunch far more valuable than the research. "Every Spanish document we found said she sank nearly fifty miles southeast off the tip of Florida, which would've put her in water so deep we'd have had to use remote subs to salvage her."

Chad jumped into the story.

"Turns out she was only *five* miles off the coast of Miami in water shallow enough that we could have almost used snorkels," he chuckled. "Twelve million dollars of gold at a depth of twenty feet, and nobody found her for nearly four hundred years."

Troy let them bask in their story of good fortune for a moment before dropping his bombshell. "What if I told you that I could have found that wreck in less than a week?" he asked.

With his brow furrowed, Calvin pondered the outlandish statement. "Dr. Wallace, I'd say that if you could prove your claim, we'd like to offer you an immediate advance on your research."

"Did you bring the pieces-of-eight that I requested?" Dr. Wallace asked.

With a puzzled expression, Calvin reached into his shirt pocket, pulled out two of the gold Spanish coins that had been retrieved from the *Finisterra,* and placed them in Troy's waiting hand.

Troy admired the irregularly shaped coins for a moment then casually flung one of them far out into the middle of the lagoon.

Chad was stunned. "What the hell are you doing?"

In silent reply, Troy kicked off his leather sandals, waded a few steps into the lagoon and smiled as Notchy rushed toward him like an exuberant puppy. With an open mouth full of conical teeth, the dolphin poked its head out of the water and emitted a long string of loud squawks and chirping whistles.

"Notchy?" Troy said, stooping down and opening his hand to reveal the other coin to the dolphin. "Go find same." Once the command was given, Troy then pulled what looked like a small aquarium net out from his pants pocket and placed the net's wooden handle in the dolphin's clenched mouth.

Appearing familiar with the exercise, the dolphin peeled away with a splashing twist of its muscular body and dove below the surface.

"Wait a minute. You're not expecting him to find that tiny little coin way out there," Chad sputtered.

"No, he's not *going* to find it." Troy said with a shake of his head. "He's *already* found it."

In an astonishing display that took no more than a few seconds, Notchy was back at Troy's feet, offering him the scoop that now contained the golden coin.

Calvin and Chad could hardly believe their eyes.

"Oh, come on," Chad exclaimed, slapping his partner on the shoulder. "It has to be a trick."

Calvin stewed in silence while the ramifications of Troy's display took shape in his head. When he finally spoke, he was serious and to the point. "Could your dolphin do that in the open ocean?"

"Of course. All you have to do is show a properly trained dolphin what you're looking for, and then you just sit back while the most sophisticated biological sonar-scanning device in the world roams the ocean searching for it."

"You must be kidding," Chad responded, looking as skeptical as he sounded.

But Calvin wasn't listening to his friend. Instead, his mind raced to the next most obvious question. "So what do you need us for? Why wouldn't you just open up your own salvage operation?"

Troy directed his attention inward, recalling more than three decades worth of research with dolphins. "Well, as I told you over the phone, this work requires a steady influx of cash to keep going. But the real reason ..." he began, his tone heavy with portent. Then he allowed himself a long pause.

"Yes?" Calvin prodded.

"The real reason is that this research seems to be leading to something far more exciting," Troy said, barely above a whisper. "Because, if my guess is right, some day we won't need to tell the dolphin what to look for. Rather, the dolphin will describe to us, or more accurately, *show* us, objects it has already seen."

Troy's terse and deliberate words were sinking deep into Calvin's consciousness. "And just how, pray tell, would a dolphin do this?"

One thought ahead of his intrigued guests, Troy was already leading the group back up to the building, where he was prepared to let Jerry take over the second half of their presentation.

The inside of the shack caught Chad and Calvin by surprise, for while its exterior looked no different than many of the half-finished, ramshackle structures on the island, the interior was spotlessly clean and filled with stacks of expensive electronic equipment.

Jerry ambled over to a large mainframe computer sitting on a shelf and hoisted himself up onto a stool in front of it. "Let me get you up to speed on how a dolphin senses its surroundings," he began, his thick fingers moving nimbly over the keyboard. "In addition to eyesight, dolphins use an incredibly precise form of echolocation to experience their environment. You've both seen ultra-sound images of a baby in the womb, right? Well, those are primitive compared to what a dolphin can visualize using a biological version of the same technology."

"How would you know that?" Chad challenged.

"Because we know that dolphins emit ultrasonic pulses at over 65,000 hertz, while most imaging equipment we use today is never more than 40,000. Here, take a look at this. It's a sonogram of a German U-boat that sank in World War II. Troy was on the team that helped find it three years ago."

On the computer's monitor, a green, three-dimensional submarine filled the screen.

"Hey, I remember that sub!" Chad said. "It's the *U-534* that the Sharkhunter Diving Club found off of Denmark."

"That's right," Troy said proudly. "They knew about my work with high-resolution equipment, and they hired me to generate this sonogram. We scanned the sub at 50,000 hertz."

Chad studied the monitor. "The detail's amazing. It's like you could reach out and touch it."

"I know," Troy said. "Everyone involved, including the salvage company and the Danish sponsor who paid for the whole operation, was quite pleased with the result."

"Yeah. So pleased that they decided to give this to Troy as a gift," Jerry added and withdrew an ornate wooden box sitting on the shelf beside the monitor. He opened the lid of the box, exposing a pristine Luger P08 pistol resting on a bed of crumpled red satin. "This was found in the sub and presented to Troy as a token of their appreciation."

Calvin's eyes opened wide at the sight of the large black pistol. "This was actually on *U-534*? It's in perfect condition!"

"The whole boat was," Troy answered. "It was preserved by a film of oil that had been leaking out of its tanks for over forty years."

"May I?" Calvin asked, already reaching into the box. "It's not loaded, is it?"

"Of course not," Troy laughed. "I don't think anyone would want to fire a gun that has been submerged for more than four decades."

Cradling the hefty gun with both hands, Calvin redirected his attention to the facsimile of the submarine on the screen. "Okay, so where were we?"

Troy took over the presentation.

"As Jerry was saying, we believe that dolphins not only receive these same sorts of ultrasonic images, but that they are capable of *re-transmitting* them as well."

Calvin's mind was barely able to fathom what he was hearing. "You mean to other dolphins?"

"Yes, but also to anyone capable of intercepting and decoding their transmissions."

"You're not suggestion humans, are you?" Chad asked, his cynicism mounting.

"Humans possessing the right technology, yes," Troy confirmed.

"Expensive technology," Jerry added and tapped the side of his computer monitor.

It was instantly clear to Calvin how such a breakthrough would facilitate his company's treasure-salvaging endeavors. Then, without even glancing over to see if his partner concurred, he uttered the words that he realized would probably cost them millions, but could also earn them *billions* of dollars in salvage revenue.

"We're in," was all he said, disregarding Chad's pessimism. And with that, he delicately placed the Luger back in the box, pulled a checkbook out of his shirt pocket, and started writing.

◆   ◆   ◆

April 7, 1993—Key Largo, Florida

Tapping her fingers to the classic rock blaring over the stereo, Rebecca Larson looked at herself in the rearview mirror of her VW camper van and smiled. A long and bitter winter had driven her into a melancholic funk, and she knew that a week in the sun with her girlfriends was just what she needed to break the spell.

She rolled down the driver's side window and let the warm morning air blow through her long mane of blonde hair.

Her three passengers, all Duke University sophomores like Rebecca, bobbed their heads in unison to the music.

A wood-paneled station wagon full of teenage boys passed from the left as both vehicles headed south on Florida's Highway One. "Spring break!" they shouted and pumped their fists in the air.

"Spring break!" Rebecca and her friends hooted in return.

"Where you comin' from?" one of the boys asked.

"North Carolina," Rebecca answered. "How about you?"

"Michigan. Goin' to Key West?" he yelled right before the station wagon accelerated to make room for an oncoming truck.

Rebecca nodded with a wave then rolled her eyes when another boy suddenly yanked his pants down and pressed his naked posterior against the car's rear window.

When the girls drove across the bridge connecting the continental United States to Key Largo, she whooped and did a drum roll on the van's steering wheel. "This is it, ladies. We're officially off the mainland and in the Florida Keys."

From the passenger seat, Penny, who was Rebecca's roommate at Duke, raised her hands and slapped them against the roof. "Only a hundred more miles before our first margarita at Sloppy Joe's."

"Duval Street, here we come," squealed another from the back.

Resting her sunglasses on top of her head, Rebecca took in the wide-open expanses of mangrove trees, white sand, and deep turquoise water all around her.

"Wow, this place is beautiful. And there's so much *space* between everything."

The other girls, who had all grown up on the eastern seaboard and made numerous trips to the Keys, were less impressed.

"Is it really that crowded in California?" Penny asked. "On *Baywatch*, the whole place looks like a picture postcard."

"Are you kidding? That's only because they film that show in front of a protected marine preserve." Though her information was firsthand,

Rebecca chose not to mention that her knowledge came from personal experience as a bikini-clad extra in many episodes of the popular television program. "Seriously," she continued, "California oceanfront property like this would be crammed with shopping malls and million-dollar McMansions. That's why I ended up going to Duke. I just had to get away from the whole Southern California cliché for a while."

"Oh, I thought you went to Duke because it's the *best damn college* in the whole United States! Go Blue Devils, *yeah!*" Penny hooted.

"Well, that, too," Rebecca laughed. "And their psych department *is* awesome."

"Psych," Penny clucked and lowered the radio's volume during a commercial. "How's that going, anyway?"

The question blew like a sudden squall over Rebecca's brightening mood. Her deep brown eyes—uniquely dabbled with irregular flecks of brilliant gold—became fixed on the open road. "It's going fine, I guess," she sighed, slumping her shoulders. "But I don't know. I'm just not sure that psychology is really my thing anymore. And if it isn't, then I honestly have no clue what I want my major to be."

"Listen," Penny interjected. *"None* of us are sure if we're going to stick with our majors. Besides, what do you care? With your looks and that body, you're just going to marry some rich movie producer or stockbroker back in California and be set for life anyway."

Penny's remark did nothing to lift Rebecca's sagging spirit.

"Hey, look," came a shout from the backseat. "Dolphins!"

Rebecca had seen dolphins many times while surfing back home in California. Instinctively, she began to scan the ocean's horizon for telltale dorsal fins slicing through the surface of the water.

"No, over there," Penny said, pointing to the opposite side of the highway where a gigantic and gaudy billboard urged, *"Come Swim with Our Dolphins. Everyone Welcome!"*

"Pull over," Penny ordered. "I want to check it out."

Rebecca downshifted and veered the van into a gravel driveway directly below the sign. Before she knew it, the other girls had shepherded her through the doors of a small, white stucco building that served as headquarters for the Human-Dolphin Swim Foundation.

"Are you serious? How much is it?" Rebecca asked no one in particular.

Penny nudged her up to the sales counter to sign up for a swim. "Don't worry about it," she said, whipping out a credit card and slapping it down onto the counter. "Dad gave me this card for just this type of unexpected emergency."

After reading and signing the foundation's reliability-release forms, the four girls followed a young woman to a small lagoon at the back of the building.

Roughly one hundred yards square, the lagoon was divided by floating boardwalks into four separate enclosures. Each one contained a water-level platform that provided access to the dolphins.

Rebecca took note of the other tourists who had come to swim with the dolphins while making her way over to her group's assigned platform. In the first pool, three elderly women frolicked with a pair of midsize bottlenoses. In the second pen, another group of college-aged students donned masks and snorkels in preparation for going in.

But the group occupying the enclosure adjacent to where she and her friends would be swimming caught and held her attention the most. Rebecca studied the people gathered on the platform: a middle-aged man, two young women, and a young boy about eight or nine years old. The child's hands were bent down toward his forearms and his eyes were fixed in a stare of unfocused detachment.

The boy sat in swimming trunks—his frail body contorting and twitching—while a man and a woman Rebecca presumed were his parents anxiously watched from a bench behind the platform.

"What's going on over there?" Rebecca asked the woman in charge of her group's session.

"Oh, that's Dr. Davidson," the guide replied. "He works with autistic kids and the dolphins here a few days a week."

Doctor? Autistic kids? Dolphins? What could those three things possibly have in common? With increasing intrigue, Rebecca monitored the activity as the boy, Dr. Davidson, and his two assistants interacted with a lone bottlenose dolphin answering to the name of Bea.

"Bea's happy to see you again today, Tommy," Dr. Davidson said with a broad, compassionate smile. "Isn't that right, Bea?"

Responding to a nearly imperceptible twitch of Dr. Davidson's index finger, the dolphin lifted her head out of the water and nodded enthusiastically.

"And I'll bet you're ready to go back in the water with Bea, aren't you, Tommy?"

The boy began twisting his body with sudden agitation and spewing unintelligible, guttural noises.

His mother sprang from the bench and rushed toward the platform. "Dr. Davidson, you know that Tommy can't speak," she pleaded in a heavy British accent. "Please don't upset him so!"

"We are all quite aware of Tommy's limitations," Davidson replied. He gently cradled Tommy's head between his large hands then looked directly into his eyes. "Tommy, do you want to swim with Bea?"

Again, the boy produced nothing more than frantic, garbled sounds.

"I'll take that as a yes," Dr. Davidson replied.

With the help of his two assistants, the doctor slowly eased the boy into the warm, shallow section of the lagoon. The three held him there securely in a face-up floating position.

Seemingly on cue, the large dolphin approached Tommy. When she got close enough for the knuckles of his clenched hand to make contact with her taut, rubbery skin, she stopped and hovered motionless at the surface.

Not caring that she had fallen behind her group, Rebecca felt herself being pulled into the surreal interaction.

"Bea loves being touched like that," Dr. Davidson said quietly to Tommy, but otherwise let the encounter unfold on its own.

After a few minutes spent floating at Tommy's side, the dolphin eventually maneuvered herself so that the tip of her snout rested gently against the top of his head.

As they watched, Tommy's parents were noticeably unnerved by what they were seeing.

"Is…is this what's supposed to be happening?" his mother queried with more than a trace of alarm in her voice.

Dr. Davidson placed a finger on his closed lips, and in the ensuing quiet, they could all hear the steady, high-pitched hum Bea was emitting into the child's skull.

Rebecca froze in awe.

As he lay there floating in the water, an undeniable expression of joy began to take hold of Tommy. His gaping mouth curled upward at the edges, and his eyes no longer appeared to be staring at nothing, but rather at something only he could see.

But it was the boy's hands that made Rebecca gasp. "Oh my God," she mouthed silently, stunned by the sight of the boy's clenched fingers slowly beginning to open and relax.

"This can't be happening," Tommy's mother said, the color draining from her face.

Not long thereafter, Bea unceremoniously terminated the session by swimming off to the far corner of the enclosure, though no one else moved for a long time.

With a knowing smile, Dr. Davidson took in a deep breath and then exhaled slowly. "I'd call that a productive short session," he said to no one in particular. "How 'bout you, Tommy?"

To everyone's shock and dismay, Tommy began to writhe once more in the arms of his assistants. Pained grunts and moans erupted from deep inside him.

Tommy's mother bolted to the edge of the platform. "Dr. Davidson, what's wrong?" she begged. "Why is he so upset?"

The growling, indecipherable vocalization started like every other he'd ever made. But this time something was different. With the sound forming deep in his throat, Tommy pressed his lips tightly together in an obvious effort to shape it. He closed his eyes with forced concentration, and with the veins in his neck bulging, he pushed the word out.

"Buh, Buh … Bea!" he wailed at the top of his lungs. "Bea!"

Rebecca felt suddenly weak.

"Bea!" Tommy yelled again ferociously, slapping the water with his open hands. "Bea!"

The dolphin, responding to his call, casually resumed her place at his side.

"Bea," Tommy said with an immediate sense of calm and relief. "Mmmmy Bea."

In shock, Rebecca lowered herself unsteadily into a sitting position on the dock, holding her face in her hands as tears began to stream down her cheeks.

Oblivious to the events that had just transpired, Penny doubled back to find her friend. "Rebecca! What's going on? Are you okay?" she asked, sitting down and wrapping her arms around Rebecca's trembling shoulders.

Rebecca could not find the words to express what had just taken place, but one point had suddenly become patently clear to her. "Penny," she said, slowly lifting her head. "You know how we were just talking about me not knowing what I wanted my major to be?"

"Yeah?" Penny replied in complete confusion.

"Well," she paused, "now I do."

Uttering those three little words, Rebecca knew she had just committed herself to a future she could not have even imagined less than an hour ago.

◆   ◆   ◆

July 20, 1999—Newport Beach, California

Born into a family dynasty that owned the largest yacht brokerage in Newport Harbor, Ryan Ericson had lived a charmed life—a life his friends and family were convinced he was about to throw away.

"You can't be serious," his father, Glen, scoffed over his mid-afternoon martini. The two men sat at their usual table in the Pirate's Den, Newport Harbor Yacht Club's private bar.

"Listen, Dad," Ryan began, his blue eyes dancing with confidence. "You know I love the marine industry and that I'll never completely leave it, but I'm almost thirty years old. I need to know that I can make a success of myself on my own."

"But you *have* done it on your own, Ryan. You think just anybody can sell fifteen million dollars worth of boats a year? Christ, we're talking over half a million dollars in commissions. Don't tell me you're willing to walk away from that for some cockamamie scheme."

Ryan leaned back in his chair and sighed while their waitress delivered two identical orders of club sandwiches and fries. "I realize this doesn't make much sense to you right now, but I got that journalism degree at USC for a reason."

"I know that, and your writing's worked out great as a sideline. Don't you sell every article you've ever written for all those magazines?"

"Yeah, but writing articles for boating magazines doesn't require a whole lot of creativity. I need to do something that I can really sink my teeth into," Ryan explained. He took a huge bite out of the triple-decker sandwich.

"You don't have to quit the brokerage to do that. Can't you ease yourself into this new thing without totally abandoning your only source of income?"

"Listen, I know I won't be making the kind of money I've made in the boat business, but I don't plan on this being a loser, either."

"Plan? How can you even talk about a goddamn plan when you don't know the first thing about producing a television show?" His father slammed the martini glass down hard enough to chip its delicate base. Had there been any other members in the dark, rustic bar, they would have been privy to some prime yacht-club gossip.

"Come on, Dad. It's local cable. *Anything* I do is going to be better than the homemade crap on there now, right?" Standing his ground, Ryan gave his thick mahogany hair a flip. "Besides, the charm of the show is that it's not *supposed* to be too polished."

Glen could see he was getting nowhere. "All right," he acquiesced. "Let's hear the whole thing one more time."

Disarmed by Glen's sudden willingness to listen, Ryan took a big gulp of his martini, bit off half of the olive skewered on a plastic mini pirate cutlass, and began his presentation. "Okay, here's the pitch: I'm going to host a local entertainment program that'll showcase all the things there are to do in Orange County—the fine dining, shopping, yachting, surfing, whatever—and I'm going to air it on all the individual local cable networks up and down the coast."

"Sort of like those infomercials we do for the brokerage," Glen said.

"Exactly."

"The ones where we pay for our own air time."

"Right."

"So I'm still not getting it. If it takes your own money to both produce *and* air the show, how do you make a profit?"

"From sponsors. I'll hit up a few selective hotels or car dealerships for a commercial, and they'll pay every time their ad airs on the show.

You think I couldn't get Fletcher to put an ad together for his Mercedes dealership? Or Hans for all his restaurants?"

"Only because you know those guys," Glen grumbled.

"Dad, I know everybody in this town! That's why this is going to work. I could make ten calls right now and have ten sponsors lined up before I shot the first episode."

"And you think there'll be enough margin between your outlay and sponsor revenue to actually make some money? And if that's true, then why hasn't anybody done this before?"

"They have, but only in a half-assed way. The difference is I'll be producing a better-looking and more interesting show than anyone's used to seeing on public access. On top of that, I happen to be really good at separating rich people from their money."

Glen raised his glass and winked. "That's true. You definitely have the gift of persuasion. But aren't you going to miss all this?" He gestured toward the luxurious boats tied up to the club's docks and moorings. "I mean, you've become a real player here in the harbor. The girlfriends, the parties, the beachfront house—you're going to jeopardize all that on some whim?"

"Well, I don't foresee this being a permanent move down the ladder. In fact, if it's as successful as I think it's going to be, I'll bet it'd only be a couple of years before I could sell the program to a major network."

Glen stared down through his drink to the bottom of the glass. "And what was the show's name again?"

"*South Coast Safari.*"

"That's right, and you're like some jungle tour guide."

"Exactly. Khaki hunting clothes, pith helmet, zebra-striped Jeep, the whole adventure-guide shtick." The words had become sort of a mantra for expressing his vision to anyone willing to listen.

"And the safari theme is what's going to make it popular."

"You got it."

Glen stewed in silence as their waitress came over.

A leggy brunette as attractive as she was flirtatious, the young woman appeared to be about twenty-five years old. "Can I get you gentlemen another martini?" she asked, her attention and smile overtly fixed on Ryan.

Glen watched the instant chemistry spark between his son and the waitress, admitting to himself that the improbable scheme he'd just heard could have real potential. Ryan's only job to date had been selling something nobody needed in the first place to people with more money than they knew what to do with. In that moment, Glen began to believe that *South Coast Safari* might actually become a hit.

Chapter 1

October 2004 Ordinarily filled with sightseers bound for Cancun, Tulum, or Chichen Itza, the bus was empty except for its sleeping driver. Parked at the far end of Cancun International Airport's pickup zone, the dirty white vehicle had a piece of paper taped to the side door. On the makeshift sign, two names—*Fletcher* and *Tac-Mol*—had been scribbled crudely with a red marker.

Socio-astronomer Mick Fletcher arrived first, exhausted from the flight from Washington, D.C., which stopped in Mexico City and then continued down to the state of Quintana Roo. Lean, fair-skinned, and still blond and boyish at thirty-five, Fletcher dragged his carry-on bag behind him. He appeared weighed down by his heavy backpack, which was full of celestial reference papers and star charts. Making his way to the bus and confirming his name on the rudimentary sign, he rapped on the windshield with his knuckles.

The driver—a frowning man with weathered brown skin and blue-black hair—woke up and yanked the door open with an exaggerated grunt.

"*Buenos tardes,*" Fletcher smiled through his weariness.

"Good afternoon," the driver replied in curt, perfect English.

Fletcher blinked through the sweat dripping down his face and climbed into the vehicle. He had forgotten how oppressively hot and humid the Yucatan could be. "I thought it started to cool down here by October," he said with a grin, attempting to lighten the mood.

After receiving a barely perceptible shrug in response, Fletcher headed to the back of the bus and chose a seat next to a window, which he unlocked and slid down for some ventilation. Then he noticed another man making his way through the bustling herd of tourists.

At first glance, the man, short and thick, looked like he could have been the driver's twin. But as he neared, Fletcher could make out the differences: the wide, hooked nose, the high cheekbones and

25

round face. By comparison, the driver seemed to be a blend of Native American and European ancestry, while the person entering the bus looked like a full-blooded Mayan.

With almost regal dignity, the distinguished traveler stepped into the broiling vehicle, paused for a moment, then said something quietly to the *busero*, whose dour expression instantly turned to respect and reverence. After ambling down the aisle and taking the seat directly across from Fletcher, the Mayan looked deep into Mick's eyes and nodded.

A little uncomfortable with the stranger's stare, Fletcher rummaged for an appropriate greeting. "What, may I ask, did you just say to the driver?"

Appearing to be at least seventy years old, the neatly dressed Mayan sat motionless as stone. "I thanked him for the work he does." His soft and tonal reply had a lulling effect. "I acknowledged his dedication in providing for his family. I reassured him that his life was full of meaning."

Fletcher sat up straighter in his seat. "Why would you say that?"

"Say what?"

"That his life was full of meaning. Do you know him?"

The Mayan arched his eyebrows. "No, but I do know much *about* him. I noticed the picture of his children taped to the dashboard. I noticed the simple wedding ring on his finger. I noticed that his hands were callused and dirty, meaning that he probably has a job working in the fields when he's not driving this bus. Besides, my friend, whether I know him or not, *every* person's life has meaning."

Fletcher turned to look out the window again as the bus lurched onto the two-lane highway. Watching the verdant landscape of palms and tall grasses blur past, he knew he was in for quite an adventure. "I suppose I should've read your bio more closely back in Washington," he said, still looking out the window rather than at the Mayan. "It's unusual that people with such differing backgrounds would be invited to the same archaeological dig."

"Yes, it is rather unusual, but science and spirit are not always two dogs yanking at opposite ends of a rope. They can be like two oxen working together, pulling the truth further along with each tug of the yoke."

Fletcher shifted in his seat to face the man. "Spoken like a true shaman," he surmised with a subtle tilt of his head. "By the way, my name's Mick Fletcher. I've been studying the Mayan calendar for some time now." He extended a hand in greeting.

Tac-Mol reached out and held Fletcher's hand in a firm grip. "I am aware of that, as I did read the information your government sent me about *you*. And I must say that I am quite impressed by your depth of understanding about our ancient calendar." A relaxed smile spread across his weathered face. "My name is Arturo Tac-Mol, and yes, I am a shaman, albeit one with a specialty of sorts. I am known as a *daykeeper*, or *ajq'ij* in my native tongue. Are you familiar with the term?"

Mick slowly disengaged his hand and attempted to mimic Tac-Mol's guttural inflection. *"Ahk-eeh?* Sorry, but I am far from fluent in ancient Mayan." For the first time since leaving the US Naval Observatory in Washington, Fletcher was apprehensive, suddenly feeling like an amateur in the company of a seasoned professional. "You know," he said, still pondering why an astronomer such as himself had been included in an archaeological team excavating the ruins of Tulum, "there aren't many secrets left to the calendar. There's a good chance that I won't have anything new to offer."

Tac-Mol nodded. "Mr. Fletcher, we both know the calendar's most baffling mystery is not that it tracks time so accurately, but that it tells of the day—a day concerning a rare planetary alignment—when time itself will stop."

Even in the heat, Mick felt a chill wash over him at the sound of those words. "Well, yes," he replied, no longer comfortable with the probing eye contact. He shifted his attention back to the bus window. "I suppose I am one of the few scientists in the world willing to even entertain such a preposterous notion."

Through the reflection in the window glass, Mick watched Tac-Mol's face become fixed with concern behind him.

◆   ◆   ◆

In the final violet moments of twilight, the bus finally pulled up to the gates fronting the temple complex of Tulum.

Fletcher looked out at the modest assemblage of bleached and crumbling ruins perched at the rim of a cliff overlooking the glittering Caribbean Sea. "Gee, I haven't been here since college." His eyes scanned the small array of stepped pyramids and rectangular housing structures clustered closely together. "And yet it doesn't look any different than it did twenty years ago."

Tac-Mol looked intent and impressed. "Yet something *must* be different for us to have been invited here."

With the dust settling from the bus' arrival on the dirt parking lot, a middle-aged man—tan and sporting a curious bowl-cut of thick brown hair—emerged from a small guard shack at the edge of the lot. He stepped forward and embraced each of his guests. "Señor Arturo and Mr. Fletcher! Welcome back to Tulum, both of you!" he beamed. "I'm George Baylor, and on behalf of the proud state of Mississippi and Millsaps College, I'd like to thank you both for coming and offering your expertise to our project."

Tac-Mol smiled and wrapped his arms around their host. "It is my honor to be here at your service."

"That goes double for me," Fletcher chimed in. "I've always admired Millsaps' Department of Mesoamerican Studies. It's a pleasure to be included in this expedition."

"Ah, yes, our mighty expedition!" Baylor let out a satirical belly-laugh. "Can you believe it? Every day this place is overrun with thousands of tourists, and yet Tulum is still offering up new secrets." Then he leaned in toward his visitors, shifted his eyes back and forth, and lowered his voice. "Shall I show some of them to you?" he asked, reaching into a vinyl tote and handing yellow plastic flashlights to his two guests.

"We'd like nothing more," Fletcher responded, his expectations quickening.

"Excellent," Baylor said. "Please just leave your things on the bus. Later on you'll be driven to your hotel, where I've made reservations for dinner tonight. I hope you don't mind."

"On the contrary," Tac-Mol answered politely, "it is much appreciated."

Fletcher nodded in agreement.

"Very good, then," Baylor said, marching off in front of the two visitors and motioning for them to follow him. "Come quickly. You must see this."

◆   ◆   ◆

Activated by a slight yet invigorating drop in temperature, the jungle surrounding the complex was coming alive in the encroaching darkness. With an exotic cacophony of sound, the resident frogs, birds, and insects combined to provide an unsettling ambiance for the newcomers.

Aware that his imagination was being stoked by the chorus of eerie cries and squawks, Fletcher tried to ignore his sense of brewing danger. But as he pushed forward into the thick growth with Baylor and Tac-Mol, he became convinced that their three-person excavation team was being followed. Swinging his flashlight toward the sound of a snapping twig, he froze when the light's narrow beam landed on a pair of eyes that did not belong to any person in the group.

"George! Someone's following us!" he called out, freezing in place.

Baylor gave a casual glance back, noticed the eyes—black, squinting, old—peeking from behind a tree trunk, and moved on.

"Ah, yes, I should have told you about her. She's a regular here at Tulum. Homeless, rarely talks, and when she does, it's in some virtually indecipherable Mayan dialect. Calls herself Ixchel. Quite harmless, I assure you."

"But why is she following us?"

"Because this is her trail that we are on. She sleeps out here in the jungle during the day, then sneaks back into the temple complex every night."

Tac-Mol slowed his pace. "She's the reason we're here, isn't it? She's the one who discovered whatever it is you're about to show us."

Baylor stopped the procession and momentarily shined his light upon Tac-Mol's face. "Your intuition serves you well, my friend. It was less than a month ago, when a security guard from the temple followed her back into the jungle one morning. Upon his return, he said he had watched her duck into an opening—an opening no one had ever noticed before—cut into the hillside."

Before Tac-Mol or Fletcher could consider Baylor's explanation, they found themselves standing in front of an unassuming archway made up of irregularly stacked stones. The portal was all but hidden behind a tangle of hulking palms and enormous philodendron vines.

Taking their cue from Baylor, the two men entered the archway and proceeded through a low and narrow tunnel that Fletcher accurately guessed was guiding them back toward the temple grounds. Stooped over as they walked along the dark, dank passageway, their movement was slow and labored. When the tunnel finally widened into a subterranean earthen chamber roughly ten feet square and eight feet high, Baylor halted his wheezing guests with a raised hand.

"Where are we?" Fletcher asked. On the far side of the chamber, he could make out an unadorned door comprised of a single slab of polished stone.

Baylor's voice was filled with hushed excitement. "We are in an antechamber. Behind that door is a room situated directly below Tulum's Temple of the Descending God."

"He's referring to the stepped pyramid right above us," Tac-Mol said, addressing his explanation to Mick. "It's a small structure topped with a stucco-relief image of a winged human falling headfirst from the heavens."

Growing more anxious by the minute, Fletcher could not contain himself any longer. "So, what's in the hidden room?"

Baylor stepped aside. "Mr. Fletcher, I give you the honor of going in first."

"Me?" Fletcher gulped, assessing the heavy door. "But how am I supposed to open it? That slab must weigh at least a ton."

In an instructional reply, Baylor used the index finger of his left hand to make a gentle sideways pushing motion in the air.

Fletcher approached the threshold and pressed a single finger against the upper left corner of the door, which then pivoted effortlessly on its axis. When the door stopped moving, two identical entrances roughly three feet wide and six feet tall were created on either side of the slab.

"Incredible!" Tac-Mol exclaimed. "Such precise engineering is extraordinary!"

The men stepped single file through one of the openings. When the beams of their lights fell upon the room's walls, both Tac-Mol and Fletcher's jaws dropped open in unison.

"What—what *is* this place?" Fletcher stammered.

"I'm not sure," Baylor replied. "I was hoping you two might be able to help discover the answer to that question."

Tac-Mol stood in the exact center of the room—a perfect circle capped by a shallow dome—and marveled at the murals painted over every inch of the surrounding stone's smooth surface. "I have never seen anything like this in my life!" he enthused, gesturing toward the life-sized human figures depicted in various poses on the wall. Then, when he looked directly overhead, he appeared stunned to see the unique interlocking ring design of the Mayan calendar painted on the inside of the dome. Around the calendar, stars were strategically arranged in an illustrated sky of deep indigo blue. "Mr. Fletcher," he said, his head still tilted back, "I think I know why you and I were invited to come here."

Quickly shifting his focus to the ceiling, Mick let his light catch every amazing detail of the calendar. "This can't be real," was all he said at first. Then, shuffling toward the center of the cylindrical chamber, he began discerning the placement of particular groupings of stars. "Wait a minute. I know this sky!" he said, his eyes widening in recognition.

Baylor held his breath. He had made some educated guesses of his own, but he needed to hear the conclusion of an expert in the field of astronomy. "Is it ... *December?*" he asked.

Fletcher studied the complex calendar and star positions in the sky. Aware of the calendar's incredible accuracy and ability to foretell every eclipse, solstice, and equinox since its creation, he felt his skin tighten as he considered the device's final and most astounding prediction: that the procession of time would stop at a specific date in the future.

"It *is* December," he confirmed. "And, as you have probably guessed, not just *any* December. We are looking at the night sky of the winter solstice, December 21st, 2012—the final day of the Mayan time-system. You can tell the date by two things: the placement of the constellation Aquarius on the eastern horizon and the perfect alignment of all the visible planets on that night."

Tac-Mol shuddered. With focused attention, he lowered his flashlight and studied the colorful frescoes—an orgy of deep red, turquoise, ochre, and black—painted on the walls. "In all my years of studying Mayan artwork," he said, his voice barely rising above a whisper, "I have never seen anything like these images."

"I've had weeks to ponder the meaning behind the figures," Baylor said, directing his words to Tac-Mol, "and now I'm anxious to hear your thoughts about them. I find myself drawn to these two in particular," he added, pointing to an illustration of a squatting woman delivering a baby, while right next to her was another woman stabbing herself in the abdomen with a long-handled knife.

Tac-Mol pored over the drawings and began to detect a theme. Situated next to a gaunt and sickly old man, a young, healthy farmer harvested fruit from a tree. Side by side, a smiling child shared space with a gruesome skeleton of similar size. In another part of the room, the familiar Descending God, the winged figure gracing the temple above, was plummeting, just as a similar winged figure a few feet away was ascending majestically upward. Lastly, a fierce warrior stood beside a naked and empty-handed man. "It's as if each scene represents a polarity of conditions," Tac-Mol said before turning his attention back to the doorway. Taking a few steps toward the opening, he appeared absorbed in the paintings gracing both sides of the threshold. "And what of this?" he asked himself aloud, rubbing his chin as he stared at two tall, white columns portrayed on either side of the door. Accenting each pair of columns was a cascade of falling water and a figure of an upright dolphin bowing its body toward the opening.

The columns intrigued Baylor as well. "I would hardly attribute this artwork to the Mayans," he said, "had I not seen it here myself. And did you notice the images painted on the edge of the door? Two circles—sun and moon—stacked vertically on top of each other."

"Day and night," Fletcher volunteered. "Kind of goes with the rest of the polarized imagery in the chamber," he added, pulling out a small digital camera and snapping a picture of each mural in the room. "Don't you agree, Arturo?"

But Arturo Tac-Mol had grown silent. Long seconds passed while he cocked his head to one side and then the other, softening his focus and letting his eyes absorb the entire design: the open doorway, the paired columns on either side of it, the stacked circles. When he finally spoke, his voice was low and pensive. "It is a symbol," he said.

Fletcher stared intently at the artwork. "A symbol? What kind of symbol?"

Arturo Tac-Mol, the shaman capable of seeing things that most people never noticed, showed no shame in admitting the truth. "I do not know," he replied without taking his eyes away from the odd assembly of geometric forms. "However ..." he mused, seeming to follow some obscure idea.

"However ...?" Fletcher prodded.

"However, there are people who do. I can feel them when I look into the doorway. I can sense the way they are holding this very image in their consciousness."

Baylor looked confused. "All right, then. How do I go about finding one of these people?"

"You don't," Tac-Mol replied, peering into the darkness on the other side of the door. "Right now, seemingly by accident, they are finding each other. And eventually, as their numbers multiply, one of them is bound to find you."

Chapter 2

The clear October morning was laced with an invigorating chill that announced autumn's arrival in San Diego, California.

Dr. Troy Wallace paced around the perimeter of the Marine Mammal Research facility's pool, an area off limits to the public at SeaWorld Amusement Park, rubbing his hands together to keep them warm.

Rebecca Larson, Senior Dolphin Behaviorist at the park, was treading water alongside a pair of bottlenose dolphins.

This was not the first time their paths had crossed.

For Troy, the events leading to their recent reunion had begun in Tortola in 1991. After spending a total of two years on his ultrasonic research, with the financial backing of Calvin and Chad, he had not made any real progress. Dolphin-generated sonograms remained elusive.

Anxious to continue pursuing his vision in a different environment, Troy had approached both the Scripps Institute of Marine Biology at the University of California San Diego as well as the Woods Hole Oceanographic Institute in Massachusetts, seeking a position that would pay him to teach while also conducting his research. Since his findings to date were widely published and respected, both institutions offered him a position as an adjunct professor, along with laboratory space and access to the marine facilities. After much consideration, Troy chose Scripps, preferring the Southern California climate to that of the Northeast.

But making the break from Tortola turned out to be anything but easy. His young apprentice, Jerry Spears, made it quite clear that he considered Troy's departure an act nothing short of abject abandonment.

Doing his best to explain that any hope of success required going out on his own into a different surrounding, Troy placated Jerry by agreeing to let him stay at the Tortola facility, which Troy owned outright. Troy also left behind one computer and a few pieces of equipment that Jerry could use for his own research, which Troy felt was more than equitable.

In the years that followed, Troy's research continued to be impressive, and his professional reputation grew in stature. Yet all the while, the breakthrough moment he had worked so hard to achieve never came to pass. Whether it was because his access to captive dolphins was far more limited at Scripps or because technology always seemed to lag two steps behind his hardware requirements, his scientific objectives remained elusive.

Then, thirteen years after he left Tortola, digital-imaging capabilities finally caught up with Troy's notion of what he had long theorized dolphins could do with ultrasound. That's when he approached SeaWorld about the possibility of giving him a small laboratory space and letting him work with one or two of their resident dolphins. With his prominent reputation and work at Scripps preceding him, Troy was well-received by the SeaWorld authorities.

By the time he arrived, Rebecca had already been at SeaWorld for six years, having worked her way up to Senior Dolphin Behaviorist. Along the way, she performed various jobs throughout the park: she fed the animals, maintained the facilities and conducted educational lectures to visiting tour groups. When she was informed that Dr. Troy Wallace would be a guest member of the staff and that she had been selected to be his assistant, she understood without a doubt that this was where her life had been leading her.

Following the incredible experience in Key West when she'd watched Bea the dolphin transform an autistic boy, Rebecca had finished up her sophomore year at Duke and then transferred to Scripps in San Diego, where she changed her major to Marine Biology. That was also where she and Dr. Troy Wallace met for the first time. Now, suddenly, here he was back in her life, and this time she was going to be his assistant—his *paid* assistant—in a job that hundreds of people just like her would have lined up to perform for free. As far as she was concerned, fortune and destiny had definitely conspired to reunite them.

Three days after she and Dr. Wallace had begun working together, Rebecca and two of the park's dolphins, Sandi and Echo, waited in the water for his instructions.

"You ready to try it again?" she asked optimistically, even though the last three days of research had not given them much cause for optimism.

Dr. Wallace stoically tinkered with an array of computer equipment stacked near the pool. "Sure, come on out," he sighed. "Let's get on with this mission of proving that I'm a complete failure."

With the surface of her turquoise wetsuit steaming as she climbed out of the water and reached for a towel, Rebecca conveyed that she was nowhere near ready to accept defeat. "Listen, Dr. Wallace," she began after unleashing her hair from the requisite ponytail and towel-drying the golden strands.

"Troy," he interrupted. "Calling me Dr. Wallace makes me feel like your college professor all over again."

"Okay, Troy," she smiled. "For starters, let's get over this talk about you being any kind of failure. The research you've conducted with dolphins over the years is the stuff of legend, and just because ..."

"Just because I've spent millions of dollars of someone else's money without being able to prove a single one of my theories, I shouldn't let that get me down?" he interjected, the heavy dose of sarcasm impossible to conceal.

"No, I was going to say that, just because there's no hard evidence to support your sonic-imaging theory, it doesn't mean you haven't made a huge impact on other great research. I mean, look at all the work they're doing at Hawaii's Institute of Marine Biology. That's a direct result of your ultrasonic studies."

"Now you're just trying to be nice," Troy said with a limp swat at the air.

"Nice? Don't you realize that it was your lectures that got me through my two years at Scripps? And now look at me—the youngest senior dolphin behaviorist ever employed at SeaWorld. How much more impact on a person's life do you need to make to consider yourself a success?"

With a smile of surrender, Troy turned back toward the imaging equipment and began flipping a few switches. "You certainly make it hard for me to throw a pity party for myself, don't you?"

Rebecca just smiled.

"All right, then, I guess you may as well bring Sandi back, and we'll take another stab at it."

Following a drill they had repeated dozens of times already during the last few days, Rebecca leaned over the lip of the pool and motioned for Sandi, the larger of the two dolphins, to approach and rest the rounded melon of his head against her open palm. Once the dolphin was in position, Rebecca then instructed him with a gentle tap on the snout to remain stationary in front of a submerged transducing device. The black transducer, roughly the diameter and depth of a pie tin, was connected by a thick cable to a computer sitting just a few feet away.

Troy fine-tuned the equipment. "Do you know that this computer is nearly a thousand times more powerful than what I started out with back on Tortola?" he told her, awed that such an advanced piece of equipment could even exist. "I mean, that was barely fifteen years ago, and we thought we were the cat's pajamas with our five-inch floppy disks and whopping two hundred and fifty-six bits of RAM."

His use of such antiquated terms as *cat's pajamas* reminded Rebecca that Troy was in his seventies. His athletic build, alert blue eyes, and firm skin belonged to someone at least twenty years younger.

"Computer technology *has* come a long way in the last few years, hasn't it?" she replied, happy to hear a touch of enthusiasm in his voice. "I remember my first so-called portable computer," she laughed, framing the word *portable* with quotation mark gestures. "I brought that dinosaur along with me when I transferred out here to Scripps from Duke. It was this giant Kaypro—as big and heavy as a microwave oven."

"I remember those! Of course, I'm old enough to remember when the first portable calculators came out. That was in the late sixties—probably a few years before you were even born," he mused.

"Just a few. Nineteen seventy-three, to be exact."

"Oh my God, I *am* as old as the hills, aren't I? I was just finishing my work with John right around your first birthday."

"John?"

"Lilly," he clarified.

Rebecca's eyes flew open. "Are you kidding? You *worked* with John Lilly? Oh my gosh! Do you know that he's been my hero ever since I took my first cetacean physiology class? I know we talked about him in your lectures, but I had no idea that you actually *knew* him or *worked* with him."

Her reaction reminded Troy once again of the mystical spell the late Dr. John C. Lilly had been able to cast over anyone even remotely interested in dolphins. An American physician and psychoanalyst, Lilly had been a pioneer in dolphin physiology in the 1950s and '60s.

Troy let his mind wander back five decades to the small research facility and magical memories he and Lilly had shared on the gulf coast of Florida. "He was my hero, too—for a while, anyway," Troy said. "I interned for him after I graduated, which was an experience that set the tone for the rest of my life."

"I've devoured every one of his books," Rebecca gushed. "My favorite is the one where he discovers that dolphins aren't automatic breathers."

Rebecca's words caused Troy to revisit another era and a younger version of himself that he had not considered for a very long time. "Believe it or not, I was there when he made that discovery," he said, halting his work at the computer and pulling up an aluminum chair. "It was 1955, and it happened quite by accident. We were sedating a healthy dolphin with a general anesthetic to do some blood work when—all of a sudden—the animal just died. That's the moment when John realized that every single breath a dolphin takes, from birth to death, is a breath it has to think about taking."

With her lips parted in awe, Rebecca sat down crossed-legged on the smooth cement directly in front of Troy. "You...you were there? Do you have any idea how important that discovery has been to me? I mean, that's when it hit me how *in the moment* a dolphin must be throughout its whole life. To this day, whenever I get stressed out, it helps me so much if I just do what dolphins do—stop and become aware of every breath going in and out of my body."

"It does seem like dolphins were the original Zen masters, doesn't it?" Troy concurred. "Which is, of course, what John Lilly came to believe. I'm sure you know that the ultimate meditation device ever created, the sensory isolation tank, was an invention of Lilly's."

Rebecca still could hardly believe she was having this conversation, for while the more metaphysical dimension of dolphin research had always fascinated her, she knew the scientific community regarded it as nothing more than incalculable nonsense. This realization also made it clear why Troy had never mentioned his personal association with the controversial Lilly in any of his lectures. "I did know that," she replied. "But I'm not so sure I completely understood his reasoning."

"I'm not so sure *he* did, either," Troy chuckled. "But at the root of it all, John was just trying to figure out what dolphins do with those big, complex brains of theirs in the relatively low-stimulus environment of the ocean."

Rebecca was catching on fast. "So that's why he invented the isolation tank. He wanted to know what the human brain, which is very similar in size and design to a dolphin's, would do in the same type of environment."

"Exactly. And that's when things started getting dicey with his studies, because when you put a person in a dark tank full of warm sea water—with no visual, auditory, or tactile stimulation—that person's brain starts behaving in a way which does not easily fall into the realm of quantifiable research."

"I remember reading about some of those experiments. Didn't people start hallucinating like crazy?"

"Indeed they did, which led John to the thought that, since the dolphin brain *is* so similar in size and structure to a human's, maybe dolphins spend much of their time living in a kind of awakened dream-state... a realm they can create for themselves whenever they want."

Rebecca rubbed her forehead with her fingertips, trying to wrap her mind around Lilly's suppositions. "And if I remember right, he also started conducting those studies on himself ..."

"Which was the beginning of the end for his scientific career," Troy ruminated. "The whole idea of being able to exist in a self-created reality took hold of him, and before long he was experimenting with hallucinogenic drugs while immersed in one of his sensory isolation tanks. It nearly drove him mad."

Troy's voice grew wistful. "After that, it didn't take me long to realize that our research days together were numbered. Besides, his dolphin communication work, which is what I was most interested in, was always slanted toward getting dolphins to 'speak' audible English to humans. I can't tell you how bothered I was by his repeated efforts to get a dolphin to mimic human speech using its blowhole as a mouthpiece."

"And that's when you went off on your own with your ultrasonic research?"

"That's right. Of course, I haven't had much more success than John did, but I still believe I'm on the right track."

"That's obvious," she surmised, scanning the stacks of electronic equipment bordering the pool. "You wouldn't be here if you didn't think you were making progress."

"You know, there have been times when I let the work rest for a while, like when I left Tortola. But whenever digital technology took a leap in the direction of my research, I just had to get back into it. Fortunately, Calvin and Chad believed in what I was doing enough to keep funding me."

"Which is how you ended up here at SeaWorld."

"Well, I still own my little research facility on the island, but it would have been a major undertaking to try and get everything up and running there again. And when the folks here at SeaWorld volunteered their facilities and dolphins, not to mention *you*, I realized it was too good an offer to pass up. Imagine my surprise when they told me that Rebecca Larson, my favorite student, would be my personal assistant!"

"Oh, come on," Rebecca blushed. "That was twelve years ago. I'm sure I wasn't your favorite."

"Oh, yes you were, and do you know why?"

Rebecca shrugged, inviting him to answer his own question.

"It's because you were always open to the possibility that solving the mysteries about the dolphin species would somehow help humanity as a whole. You never forgot that dolphins don't just represent a *compilation* of fascinating facts ..."

"They represent an *integration* of fascinating facts!" she said, finishing the thought for him, unable to forget the words he had repeated so often in class.

"And it's the integration that we still cannot figure out. Sure, we know dolphins use ultrasound. Yes, we know they live in cooperative societies. Of course we know how big and complex their brains are. But it is only when we start combining all these individual facts together that we realize we are beholding something truly incredible." He paused, giving Rebecca a look of fatherly pride. "And you seem to have always known that."

Troy's words accessed a place deep within her and her eyes, all amber glitter, moistened as she collected her feelings. "I ... I had a very special introduction to dolphins years ago in Florida," she said, sharing a bit of the story that she had intentionally kept out of her official biography. "And no amount of empirical data or scientific jargon could ever take that away from me," she added with a sniff, recalling that amazing day in Key Largo.

Feeling the effect of those gold-flecked eyes, Troy stood up and walked defiantly back to one of the computers. "I know what you mean," he said with newfound hope. "So let's try it again, shall we?"

Rebecca leapt into action, motioning for Sandi to swim closer to the transducer hanging just below the water line.

It was a ritual that had been repeated thousands of times with various assistants and numerous dolphins over the past two decades. However, Troy could still feel his heart skip a beat in anticipation of what it would mean should his revolutionary theories prove true. "Well," he said anxiously, "here goes nothing."

While Troy tapped the computer's keys with one hand and crossed his fingers on the other, Rebecca found herself affirming something completely different.

"No," she said with conviction. "Here goes *everything.*"

Chapter 3

The *USS Nicholas'* tour of duty ended in San Pedro, California, on November 1, 1945. Immediately following the destroyer's return from Japan, the ship was decommissioned and scheduled to be mothballed.

Vern Becket, who had stayed with the boat for its final voyage from Tokyo to California and then through the first phases of decommissioning, walked off the ship's rusting gangway for the last time on Sunday, February 3, 1946. With just over three hundred dollars in his pocket and only one clear directive in his head, he boarded the first available public transportation out of San Pedro, which happened to be a rickety old red trolley, and rode it as far away from the naval base as it would take him.

When the conductor of the southbound trolley announced the last stop on the route, a sleepy little harbor town called Newport Beach, Vern stepped off, eager to get a closer look at the place where he'd ended up. The streets were filled with day tourists from Los Angeles and Orange County who had flocked to the coast to enjoy the sunny midwinter weather. Ambling among those crowds for a while, he eventually found himself in the middle of the city's quaint commercial hub of hotels, snack bars, and local fish vendors, all clustered around the base of Newport's municipal pier. This, Vern figured, would be as good a place as any, and probably better than most, to try and make a living by the sea.

It did not seem particularly fateful to him that a suitable business proposition would present itself so quickly, but that was only because he didn't realize how rare it was for a fishermen to sell his stake in a local enterprise known as the dory fishing fleet. The fact that a dozen little wooden boats, a few clapboard shacks and a couple of old Jeeps were even called a "fleet" at first seemed almost laughable. But watching the operation, located directly upon Newport's sandy shore, he found himself admiring the way the hearty men launched their boats directly into the open surf to fish the deep waters of the Pacific. It was a place where people who worked hard could eke out a living, and Vern had never been put off by the idea of hard work.

As it happened, one of the senior members of the group—a cantankerous old codger who could recall the days when the boats were retrieved from the surf by horse instead of four-wheel-drive vehicles—had decided that he'd finally had enough of the place and hung a *For Sale* sign on his shack to prove it. That sign caught Vern's eye like a fishing lure, and as he hovered around the dory village, absorbing the rustic existence the fish-catching men and their fish-selling wives had forged for themselves, his intuition told him that he had found exactly the right place to settle down. So with a handshake, the whole enterprise—a sixteen foot, flat-bottomed boat with a ten-horsepower motor, an eight-foot-square wooden shack, an army surplus Jeep, and a host of heavy fishing lines—was sold to Vern for a grand total of two hundred fifty dollars and seventy-five cents. The seventy-five cents was for the resident cat, a fat tabby named Mabel, who was tacked onto the deal at the last minute.

On that same Sunday evening, over an outdoor dinner of fresh steamed crab and barbecued cod, Vern Becket was formally inducted into the tight-knit community of men and women of the fleet—a group he would come to know and love as his family.

◆   ◆   ◆

Vern often thought about the remarkable weekend and happenstance that had so surely set the course of his life, and he never failed to be grateful for his good fortune. On a day more than half a century later, he forged through the same routine he'd done thousands of times before. With the morning sun just beginning to peek over the horizon, he rubbed his hands together vigorously to keep the stinging cold away. While monitoring the GPS coordinates of his haul-in site, he keyed the VHF radio's microphone.

"Hunky Dory here," he announced to any of the other fishermen in the fleet. "Anybody pullin' up anything worthwhile?" His voice had grown thick and raspy over the years, yet there was an eagerness in his tone that showed how much he still enjoyed being a doryman.

"Goose egg at the Fourteen Mile Bank," came one crackling reply over the radio's speaker.

"Not much better at the flats," chimed another.

Hearing these reports, Vern felt all the luckier to be straddling the mound of bright red rock cod and green sea trout flopping on the floor of his boat. "Guess mid-channel was the place to be today, boys," he said with a smile. "Probably hauled in four hundred pounds."

"Then the coffee's on you," another tossed into the open conversation. "Again."

"Roger that," Vern replied. "I've still got one more haul-up. See you boys back home in about an hour. *Hunky Dory* out."

Vern throttled the sturdy flat-bottomed boat—his third over the last five decades—up on plane, the one hundred horsepower, fuel-injected outboard motor pushing the little craft briskly across the surface of the calm sea. In minutes, the GPS unit began to beep, alerting him that he was nearing his final pre-plotted destination, and the bright morning sunlight illuminated the bobbing orange float he had placed there the day before to mark the heavy fishing line beneath it.

In a concert of fluid coordination between man and machine, Vern slowed the dory, leaned over, and grabbed the float with a grappling hook. Then, after hauling in the float and wrapping the line attached to it around a heavy metal pulley atop the starboard gunwale, he flipped a switch that set the wheel in motion with a furious clatter. Knowing that the two-thousand-foot lines used to be hauled in by hand, he said a quiet *thank you* once again to the hydraulically-driven wheel pulling the line into the boat.

The pulley's motor ground steadily along, reeling in the long, non-baited section of line as Vern peered over the boat's edge to see if his luck had held. Soon, coming up through the blue depths, he spotted the first bright flash of vermilion, a big rock cod, followed by a steady parade of others behind it. When the fish finally arrived at the rail of the boat—its eyes and tongue bulging grotesquely from the rapid ascent out of the pressurized depths—Vern quickly unhooked it and tossed it to the floor to get ready for the next one.

After the last of the roughly two dozen cod, sculpin, and trout were hoisted over the side of the dory, Vern could barely summon the energy to gather up and drop the next day's pre-baited line. With a wheeze rattling through his aching lungs and the muscles in his arms and shoulders burning with fatigue, he slung the heavy black clump of twisted nylon cord overboard then all but collapsed with a muffled groan onto the wooden bench at the stern of the boat.

Following habit, he decided to allow himself a few minutes of rest before heading back to shore. Lying there as the dory swayed gently back and forth like a cradle being rocked by a loving mother ocean, sleep overtook him in rapid fashion.

Lulled ever deeper by the soothing sound of water lapping against the boat's hull, it wasn't long before the same dream, the flying dream, came to him again. Repeating a sequence that had played out in his subconscious mind uncountable times over the years, he awoke with a start and sprang to his feet in a state of panic. He wondered how far off course he may have drifted, and after anxiously surveying his location, the first thing to grab his attention was the startling vision of *himself* still asleep on the bench. *Who was this weathered old man?* Moving in closer, he studied the thickly gnarled hands and wrinkled face with curiosity, unable to make the connection that he and this craggy fisherman were one and the same.

He could have pondered the person lying there for a much longer time, but, like always, something hovering far above the ocean caught his eye. It was a row of lights spread in a straight line across the heavens, and as he stood there, he became aware that the lights were blinking on and off at precisely-timed intervals, similar to the Morse Code system from his days in the Navy. The strange lights in the heavens flickered in a series of two long dashes, then two dots, and then two long dashes before repeating the sequence all over again.

Mesmerized by the phenomenon, he found himself longing to be closer to the lights, which was all the motivation his body seemed to need to begin levitating toward the luminescent pearls in the sky.

Vern had never been in an airplane before, so the receding view below him was nearly as breathtaking as the undulating lights above. From his ever-higher vantage point in the sky, the first thing he noticed was his tiny boat floating upon the open expanse of sparkling ocean, then the beautiful aqua-white-brown modulations of the sea crashing against Newport's shoreline. With increasing altitude, the vista soon included all of California and the jagged peaks of the Sierra Nevadas dividing the state from the rest of the country to the east. Seconds later, the panorama stretched far enough to include the entire continent of North America until it ended abruptly at the edge of the Atlantic Ocean.

Now traveling away from the earth faster than the speed of sound, of light, of even thought, he streaked upward, looking back just long enough to see the entire planet getting smaller behind him. There was a twinge of longing as he watched the world recede from view, yet it could not dampen the sheer exhilaration of getting ever closer to the string of jewels blinking brightly ahead of him.

But then, just like always, he began to lose momentum. Stalling like a race car that had run out of fuel right before crossing the finish line, he was crushed once again by his failure to reach his final destination. Even worse, he realized that he was now in full reverse, free-falling in silent protest back to earth.

This time, however, something *did* happen differently. In this particular repeat of the dream, he was allowed a moment to hover in a place equidistant between earth and the flashing lights overhead. He had no idea why this was happening, but floating there between these two realms, he somehow knew that he was about to receive the message that he had been told would come one day.

With a clarity of thought and a sense of awareness unlike anything he'd experienced before, he found himself glancing down, marveling at the planet's swirling cloud patterns, then up toward the pulsating gems: *dash, dash—dot, dot—dash, dash.*

When his gaze turned downward once again, he was shocked to find the orb of the earth shrouded in darkness.

Long, long—short, short—long, long, the lights above replied.

Another look back, and the familiar blues, greens, and browns of the planet appeared, brighter than ever before.

Dash, dash. Dot, dot. Dash, dash.

Incredibly, Vern knew what it all meant.

"Vern!" a voice shouted from far below.

"Vern!" another echoed, this time directly into his ear.

He awoke, wide-eyed and gasping, as he simultaneously bolted up and reached for the VHF radio's microphone. Disoriented and shaken, he keyed the mic to respond.

"*Hunky Dory* here," he panted.

"You okay?"

"Yeah—yeah, I'm okay," he said, regaining control of his voice.

"Thought you said you'd be back in an hour."

"I did. I mean, I *will*..." He could not hide the confusion in his voice. "What time is it, anyway?" he asked with a quick look at his tide-chart wristwatch. The large digital numbers revealed that he had been asleep for over two hours.

"Hell, it's almost nine!"

"But I was only gone for a few seconds," Vern bleated accidentally into the open microphone.

"What do you mean, *gone?* You sure you're all right?"

"I meant *out*. Out for a few seconds. Must've fallen asleep, that's all."

"Well, hurry the hell up before them fish start stinkin'."

"Roger that," Vern answered, the startling vision in his dream repeating over and over in his fully awakened mind.

Chapter 4

Against all odds, Ryan Ericson's career in television had followed the improbably optimistic scenario he had presented to his father five years earlier in 1999. His video entertainment guide, *South Coast Safari*, had become a Southern California phenomenon. Debuting on local cable stations in Orange County, the program not only attracted network attention, but in a deal sweeter than Ryan would have ever thought possible, the show was sold to Fox Network's Los Angeles affiliate for a lump sum of five million dollars in cash, plus ten percent of all syndication royalties and the guarantee that he would continue to host the show. Gone forever were the days when he would personally book a local story in the morning, tape a stationary-camera interview by midday, and have most of an episode edited in the same afternoon. Now, to his amazement, over thirty people were on *South Coast Safari's* staff: bookers, writers, production assistants, sound and lighting technicians, cameramen, and a host of personnel who handled every aspect of the giant-sized, prime-time version of the program he once had hoped would attract a few thousand cable viewers.

Success, however, had not come without a price, and that price seemed to be going up by the day.

♦   ♦   ♦

Like an invading army, the *South Coast Safari* convoy of vehicles—production trucks, craft-service trailer, honey wagon, motor-home lounge, and auto carriage toting the show's trademark zebra-striped Jeep—descended upon the Aquarium of the Pacific at exactly six o'clock in the morning. The Long Beach attraction was celebrating the grand opening of its newest exhibit, *Shark Lagoon*, and Ryan knew this high-profile event would be a perfect fit for the show's weeklong series of entertaining things to do and see along California's coast.

The befuddled security guard at the park's entrance took off his cap and scratched his balding head. Leaning down to talk with the driver of the Lexus leading the parade, he asked, "Now, who is it you're supposed to see?"

The show's director, Jen Rutledge, jammed the car into park, opened her PDA, and scrolled through the screen with agitation. "So much for the red carpet treatment," she huffed at Ryan, seated on the passenger side of the car. "Here it is. Libby. Libby Cohen."

The guard flipped through the pages on his clipboard. "Ahh, here we go. *South Coast Safari.* I got you coming in at two o'clock this afternoon."

"That's when the *interview* is scheduled," Jen replied, rolling her eyes behind her dark Gucci sunglasses. "Doesn't it make sense to you that we would need to be set up *before* then?"

"But it's six in the morning. Park doesn't even open until eight."

"Jesus, do you believe this guy?" she grumbled, not completely under her breath.

Ryan just sat back and waited for the fireworks to begin.

"Listen, Mr. Security Guard Man," Jen said, ratcheting up the volume of her voice with each word. "Do you have any idea how long it takes to unpack all the equipment in those trucks behind me? No, of course you don't, so why don't you call up a supervisor and ..."

"No supervisor here 'til after eight," the guard calmly interrupted.

"Is there somebody you can call?" Ryan leaned over Jen's lap and aimed his question politely through her open window.

"Hey!" the guard exclaimed in a flash of recognition. "You're *him!* It's you!"

"Wouldn't be *South Coast Safari* without our fearless Funhunter," Jen scowled.

Ryan gave her a quick, strong pinch on the leg. "Do you watch the show?"

"Sure do," the guard chirped. "Say, would it be asking too much to get an autograph?"

"That depends. Would it be asking too much to let us in?"

The officer held up one finger, then ducked back into his booth to make a phone call. After receiving a couple of autographed headshots, he happily waved the convoy through the opened gate.

"Nice way to start the day," Jen fumed, checking herself out in the rearview mirror and scrunching up her short, jet-black hair.

"It wasn't his fault," Ryan replied, noting to himself that the altercation was just another reminder of how bloated the show had become. "Besides, he's right. Why *are* we here at the crack of dawn? When I was doing this show on public-access, I could've been in and out of here in two hours with more footage than I needed."

"Here we go again with the public-access," she groaned. "When are you going to get it—that this isn't your low-budget little piece-of-crap show anymore? It takes a lot of time and effort to make a network-quality program!"

He slumped into the seat. "Relax, will you? I'm just saying that maybe not every assignment has to be this full-blown extravaganza."

"Yeah? Well, Fox seems to think otherwise. And why the hell are you complaining? All you have to do is sit around in the motor-home and come up with a few pithy things to say until we're ready to shoot." As the only person who could speak so candidly to Ryan, Jen made sure he never forgot who signed their paychecks.

"Okay, okay," he said, raising his hands in surrender. "And I'm not really complaining. I'm just stating the fact that the show has become something completely different than what it used to be."

"You say that like it's a bad thing."

"Very funny," he bristled. "Maybe you're forgetting that it was Safari's *spontaneity* that got it noticed by Fox in the first place, and now, *spontaneous* would be the last word I'd use to describe it." He let out a muffled laugh at the irony as it struck him. "It's like the punch line to a joke… This whole fun-hunting thing just isn't that much fun anymore."

"Oh, come off it," Jen shot back. "You're getting paid and laid like a rock star for doing this gig. If I were you, I'd just show up for work and *pretend* I was having fun. This *is* Hollywood, after all. People on TV are supposed to be able to act."

Her logic was abrasively accurate.

"Fine," Ryan allowed. "But just so you know, I never had to fake enjoying myself when it was just my little cable-access program."

"Would you stop it already?" she nearly screamed, skidding to a stop in front of the shark exhibit. "Just stop it! And before you get me really pissed off, why don't you run along and make yourself comfortable in the make-up trailer. I'll let you know when it's time to come out and act like you might actually enjoy being an adored celebrity."

"You know what?" he snapped, slamming the car door behind him. "I don't need this."

Leaning over the car's console and looking at him through the open passenger window, Jen raised her sunglasses to more effectively stare him down. "You're right, Ryan. No one *needs* this. You just got lucky enough to *have* it. Now get moving. I'll go over the pre-interview with you as soon as you're done in makeup."

Not wanting to make a scene in front of the production crew, Ryan walked off in silence toward the trailer. Passing the auto transport truck, he gave a slight nod to the Jeep's off-camera wrangler.

"Morning, Mr. Ericson," the young man called out while pulling down the truck's rear door ramp, revealing the show's famous zebra-striped Jeep.

"Morning," Ryan replied, forcing a strained smile to his face. He paused to watch the driver climb up into the Jeep and carefully back it out of the transport. "You know, I used to have a lot of fun cruising around in that thing."

◆   ◆   ◆

The day unfolded according to the precisely timed production schedule. The set crew had erected an elaborate interview platform while the lighting, camera, and sound crews each went about their duties prior to the one o'clock rehearsal.

"Sound check in ten minutes, Ryan," Jen's voice crackled over his walkie-talkie.

Ryan was just finishing up in the wardrobe trailer, being helped into his safari hunter vest by an obviously smitten wardrobe girl. "Ready in ten," he answered back into the radio. Emerging from the trailer, he was instantly barraged by various staff-members.

"Here's the shooting schedule," one assistant said, thrusting a few pages into his hand.

"Hold still for some touch-up," another added while dabbing some foundation onto his nose.

Jen marched up beside him to review the segment's key points. "Okay, the main reason we're here today is to talk about the grand opening of Shark Lagoon. Sharks are open water predators. Sharks are endangered. Man is more of a threat to sharks than sharks are to man. Seals and sea lions are a common source of food for larger sharks."

Ryan stopped, pulled out a tablet and pen that he always kept in his pocket, and began to write. "So," he asked while scribbling down a few notes, "why are wetsuits black?"

"What? What are you talking about?"

"If seals are a common source of food for sharks, then why are wetsuits the color of seals? I mean, surfers and scuba divers may as well just hang a big 'Eat Me' sign around their necks."

"That's funny," she said. "Use that somewhere during the interview. Now, here's how it's going to go down today. After the sound check, we'll shoot the intro for this episode and the teaser for the next day's show. Then we'll wander around the exhibit for a while before heading back here to the platform for the interview with Libby. Got that?"

"Got it," he said while glancing down at the notes in his hand and stepping up onto the platform. "I'm ready whenever everybody else is."

After a final flurry of activity and last-minute lighting adjustments, Ryan got the countdown from Jen.

"Long Beach Shark Lagoon intro in five, four," she called out before silently lowering the remaining three fingers on her upraised right hand.

"Hi again, everybody. Ryan Ericson here, reporting from the shark-infested waters of Long Beach! But don't panic—the sharks I'm talking about aren't in the ocean. They're at the brand new Shark Lagoon exhibit here at the beautiful Aquarium of the Pacific, the latest stop on our harbor-to-harbor jaunt down California's shoreline. Anyway, stay tuned for another thrilling episode of *South Coast Safari!*" Ryan held his perfect smile until he was sure the cameraman had finished taping.

Following a silent pause, Jen yelled, "Cut!" then nodded at his smooth delivery. "I'm okay with that unless you want another go at it."

"Naw, let's just go straight to the dory fleet teaser."

"All right. Everybody ready? Newport dory fleet teaser, take one."

"Hey, Ryan the Funhunter here. Don't miss our next episode, where we'll be stopping by my hometown of Newport Beach to visit a real, live dory fishing fleet. Don't know what a dory is? Well, tune in and I'll fill you in on a hundred-year-old bit of living history right in the middle of Orange County. Until then, don't forget that if you've got to have something, you may as well have fun!"

"Perfect," Jen said after the pause. "And where'd you come up with that *living history* stuff?"

"Are you kidding? Everybody in Newport knows the dory guys. And you're going to love their funky little village. It looks like a *Cannery Row* movie set."

"Sounds good," she said, pulling out her PDA and tapping its keys with a stylus. "Let's see, the interview's scheduled for three. You want to just meet there tomorrow around eleven?"

Ryan gave Jen an exaggerated double-take. "Excuse me? You're actually giving me permission to sleep in?"

"Well, since you live in Newport, I can't see any reason to make you come to the studio first. But I'm warning you! You'd better be ready to shoot the interview at two or you're dead," she said, then walked away to scout their next location at the aquarium.

"Don't worry, I'll be ready," he said.

But he was wrong. He would not be at all ready for the events about to unfold.

Chapter 5

Returning home from another productive morning of fishing the day after his disquieting dream experience, Vern spotted a large pod of dolphins swimming a perfect intercept course toward his boat. With a smile spreading across his craggy face, he pulled the throttle back and reduced the dory's cruising speed to a comfortable twelve knots. Through trial and error over the years, he had come to know the exact speed for dolphin bow-surfing.

Just as he anticipated, a small group soon broke away from the pod and swooped in front of his boat like an aquatic fighter squadron, lunging in precision just beneath the bow to surf the pressure wave of water created by the boat's forward momentum.

"Good morning, my friends!" Vern shouted with glee. "Haven't seen you in a couple of days!"

The dolphins responded with loud, millisecond breaths rushing in and out of their blowholes. It never ceased to amaze him that, according to an old *National Geographic* magazine he had read numerous times, the dolphins were exchanging over 80 percent of the air in their lungs with each one of those lightning-fast respirations.

Knowing that all the variables—smooth ocean surface, compass course aligned with the pod's direction, boat speed of precisely twelve knots—were right for an extended encounter, Vern lashed the steering wheel to the helm's handrail with a short piece of line and made his way forward.

He leaned over the bow and watched them glide in the water. "Come witness the dolphins, the lads that live before the wind!" he recited from *Moby Dick*, one of his favorite books. "For they are accounted a lucky omen!" Seemingly in response to Vern's enthusiastic oration, one of the dolphins let out a long, shrill whistle as it surfaced. "For if you can withstand the urge to cheer at beholding these vivacious fish, then heaven help ye; the spirit of godliness is not in ye!" He used to be able to quote the lines verbatim, but even after all these years he was not far off.

The first squadron of dolphins darted away, allowing another flank to move immediately into its place, and for nearly half an hour, one gang after another approached to ride the perpetual wave beneath *Hunky Dory's* bow.

When the last group had taken their turns, Vern made his way back to the helm, untied the wheel, and corrected his course for home. "See you soon!" he called over his shoulder, steering the dory toward the fleet's home base in Newport.

Eight nautical miles and twenty minutes later, the boat made a gentle arc around the end of Newport's municipal pier, where Vern pulled the throttle handle back to idle and considered his approach through the breakers. Sometimes the strip of beach just west of the pier was teeming with surfers who didn't always know it was their responsibility to get out of his way. Other days produced tricky wave-sets that had to be precisely timed so as not to stuff the dory's bow into the sand.

But this day offered optimal conditions for driving a boat directly onto shore. The cold October sea was flat and free of surfers. Even better, the tide was low, exposing a gradual incline of sand perfect for the flat-bottomed dory to skid upon.

Vern revved the motor and accelerated briskly toward the beach. It was a sight that even the most jaded local resident would still stop to watch as the sturdy little boat pushed full-speed through the surf before grounding on the tightly compacted inter-tidal sand.

The moment the dory came to a full stop, Vern switched off the outboard motor and stiffly climbed out of his beached boat. Looking up toward the village, he noticed One-Arm Eddy, the second oldest member of the fleet, shuffling briskly toward him with a look of agitated befuddlement on his face.

"Look what's goin' on up at your locker," Eddy announced.

"What *is* all that up there?" Vern raised his chin toward the mass of trucks, trailers and production equipment, not to mention the growing crowd of onlookers perched overhead behind the western rail of the pier

"Don't you remember?" Eddy replied. "Today's the day you're doin' that interview for TV."

"Oh, that's right," Vern said, recalling the telephone conversation he'd had with the show's booking agent. "All that for some silly interview? And why are they here now? I thought it wasn't 'til this afternoon."

"That's what *we* said! But then they started flashin' all kinds of papers and permits from the city. Before we knew what was goin' on, they were settin' all that stuff up right in everybody's way."

Still jubilant from his encounter with the dolphins, Vern sloughed off the minor inconvenience of *South Coast Safari's* invasion. "So we'll work around 'em for a day. We can live with that, can't we? Besides, think of all the free advertising we'll get."

"Like we need advertising. We already got more customers than fish to sell 'em as it is."

"Aw, let it go, Eddy." Vern patted his friend squarely on the shoulder that used to have an arm attached to it. "And how about giving me a hand getting *Hunky* up on the trailer? Then we'll ditch out of here for a minute and go grab a cup of coffee."

Eddy refocused his attention and trudged over to the rusting Chevy pickup and trailer he and Vern shared to launch and load their boats. Working efficiently together, the two men hand-winched the boat onto the trailer, then transferred the day's catch from *Hunky Dory* to one of the eight permanently retired boats, now serving as sales counters, parked between the two rows of lockers in the village.

"Are you getting this?" Jen asked the show's lead cameraman. Hired for her keen eye, she was always on the alert for the perfect shot, and she knew the image of two rugged old men laboriously unloading the day's catch would provide some great voice-over footage.

Tyler, one of two permanent camera operators on the show, bristled at her question. "You see the little blinking red light, don't you?"

"Listen, I just want to make sure we get some good establishing shots, okay? And I really don't need the attitude."

"That's for sure," Ryan agreed while sauntering up behind them. "Because you've definitely got enough for all of us."

"Well, would you look at this?" Jen gaped, noticing that he had already been to makeup and wardrobe. "Mr. Ericson is actually ready ahead of schedule!"

"Hey, if we shot every episode this close to my house, I'd never be late."

"Hmm," she pretended to consider while tapping her chin. "*Newport Beach Safari.* You know, that *is* a great idea! After all, who could ever get bored watching a bunch of trust-fund debutantes shopping at Fashion Island all day long?"

"Listen, sister, you're on the wrong side of the Orange Curtain to be talking trash about Newport."

"Hey," Tyler piped in. "Instead of fighting, how 'bout we make the most of Ryan being here early?" he suggested, tilting his head over to the two dorymen.

"Good call," Jen replied. "What do you think, Ryan? Feel like jumping into the shot? It'd make a good lead-in for the interview."

"Sure, why not? You want me at a distance, or should I go in and introduce myself?"

"Well, the one with both arms is Vern Becket, the guy you'll be interviewing later, so I'd say go ahead and get yourself acquainted with him."

"Gotcha. You ready, Tyler?"

Tyler hoisted the camera onto his shoulder. "Good to go, chief."

Eddy stiffened as Ryan approached. "Uh-oh. Looks like we got company."

Vern turned and was caught off guard by the bizarre sight of a safari hunter plodding his way through the sand toward them. "Looks like we do at that."

Ryan switched on his radiant smile and extended a hand to both of them in turn. "Good morning, fellas!" he beamed. "I'm Ryan Ericson, and I believe I've got an interview with one of you two gentlemen for my television show."

One-Arm Eddy was the first to shake hands, but he made no attempt at returning Ryan's congeniality. "I'm Eddy, and I thought you guys weren't supposed to be here 'til this afternoon."

Ryan knew just how to handle Eddy's unenthusiastic greeting. "Yeah, we are a bit early, and I apologize for that. But that's the way my boss works. If she tells me we're shooting at three o'clock in the afternoon, what she really means is that I better be ready by eleven in the morning—or else! I'm not late, am I?" He gave a worried look back at Jen.

Vern glanced at his watch. "Not too," he said with a shake of his head. "It's just a few minutes after." Then with a nervous twitch, he looked immediately back down at the large digital numerals. "To be exact," the old sailor said in a barely audible whisper, "it's eleven minutes after."

Ryan was ready to keep up the casual banter, but his timing was thrown off by Vern's suddenly odd behavior. "Um, excuse me. Is everything okay?"

Vern did not even seem to hear the question. *The lights went Dash-dash, dot-dot, dash-dash. Lay these numbers on their sides and you get the exact same thing,* he thought, never lifting his eyes from his watch. *Long-long, short-short, long-long, just like in the dream.* Raising his head, he turned his gaze from the watch to Ryan. Their eyes, almost the same crystal blue, locked long enough for Ryan to feel uncomfortable. "Well, I'll be," Vern clucked, his face reflecting a distinct look of discovery.

Having no idea what the man was talking about, Ryan felt himself fumbling for something, anything, to say that would somehow bring this exchange back into a two-way conversation. Finally he came up with, "Well, am I late or not?"

Without taking his eyes off Ryan, Vern said with a sly smile, "No, you're not late. As a matter of fact, it seems to me that you're right on time."

Chapter 6

During their talk about John Lilly, Rebecca had been able to revive Troy's fading hope for success. But after two excruciatingly unproductive days of fine-tuning the transducer's sequencing parameters and going over every last detail of his equipment's design, he finally threw up his hands in disgust. Sweating heavily, he stomped away from the computer as if he never wanted to look at it again. "Well, here we are," he sighed, slumping onto a bench near the pool. "The beginning of the end." There was a dimness in his eyes that Rebecca had not seen before.

She put on a brave face, but respected him too much to placate him with words of hollow optimism. She understood that this last round of tests had been a fruitless exercise, and that, more likely than not, there weren't going to be any more experiments in the future. Joining him on the bench, she asked, "So, when are they supposed to be here?"

Troy looked at his watch. It was three o'clock. "Any minute."

"Do you think they'll be mad?"

"No, they won't be mad. They've always known the risks involved with this work." He slouched deeper. "But that still doesn't make this any easier."

Their conversation was interrupted by the sound of approaching footsteps as Calvin Brooks and Chad Hanover made their way into the gated training area.

"Anybody here?" Calvin called out.

Rebecca stood to greet their guests. "Just us," she said with a wave then gestured to the two dolphins cruising the perimeter the pool. "Well, us and *them*, of course."

Troy got up slowly. Though he had practiced what he thought he was going to say, his pre-planned speech was replaced by a spontaneous admission. Extending a hand to both of them, he said, "Gentlemen, I wish I had better news to report, but the truth is..."

"Whoa, hold on just a second," Calvin interrupted, his voice reverberating off the training area's cinder block walls. "First things first. You haven't even introduced us to your assistant here."

Troy apologized for his lack of etiquette. "Of course. Calvin, Chad, this is Rebecca Larson. She was a student of mine years ago, and now she's the head dolphin behaviorist here at SeaWorld. She's been helping me test the new transducer."

"Pleasure to meet you," Calvin replied, smiling as he shook her hand. "And I must tell you that you're quite an improvement over the assistant Troy had back in Tortola."

"I'll say," Chad chimed in. "What was that guy's name again?"

Troy's body tensed at Calvin's question. "Jerry. Jerry Spears," was all he said.

"That's right, Jerry the computer whiz. Whatever happened to him?"

Troy nervously rubbed the back of his neck. "I … well, I'm not sure."

Rebecca was confounded by the exchange. How odd that Troy had never mentioned having an assistant during his years in the Caribbean. She waited to hear more.

"You don't stay in touch with him?" Chad asked. "Back then you said he was the real brains behind your ultrasonic research."

Troy made a lame attempt at diverting the subject. "Well, that was a long time ago. As you know, I've become pretty adept with computers myself since then."

The encounter was becoming increasingly awkward.

Rebecca, though curious about Troy's odd behavior, sensed that this was not the time to pry. "I can vouch for that. I've never met anyone who knew more about digital imaging than Dr. Wallace."

At that, Troy's body language shifted from tense defensiveness to one of dejection, his shoulders slumping in surrender. "Not that it's helped." He cleared his throat. "Calvin, Chad. I don't know a better way to say this so I'll just come right out and say it: Even with the new transducer, we're still not getting any recognizable sonograms."

Though they had been apprised of the transducer's disappointing preliminary results, Troy's desperate words caught his benefactors by surprise.

"Hey, you've only had the new 'ducer for a few days," Calvin replied. "You're not giving up on it already, are you?"

"I'm afraid so."

"But why?"

Troy looked over at the dolphins in the pool. "Because it actually functions better than I could have ever imagined, but we're still not getting any usable imagery."

Calvin pushed his fingers into his temples as if he was suffering from a sudden migraine. "Okay, stop right there. Let's go through this one step at a time. First, tell me about the part where it works."

Troy shuffled over to the stack of computers and picked up the transducer. "I finally got the paint to stick, that's all." He placed the disc-shaped device delicately in Calvin's open palm. "Ever heard of powder-coat painting?" he asked.

"Sure," Calvin answered, though obviously confused by Troy's reference to paint. "We have stuff powder-coated all the time on our dive boats."

"And do you know how the process is done?"

"Not exactly."

"Well, basically, it's a magnetic process. You apply a negative electrical charge to the item you want to paint and a positive charge to the dry paint powder in your spray gun. This electrostatic attraction draws the airborne powder to the object and holds it there until the paint can be baked on in an oven."

"Okay, so now I know how powder-coating works."

"Which means that you now also know how this new transducer works. When a dolphin's sonic transmissions pass through it, it assigns a virtual negative polarity to those signals before sending them to this computer."

Calvin's eyes opened a little wider. "I think I get where you're going with this," he said and walked over to the monitor. "What I'm looking at here is a green mist of digital paint particles floating around behind the screen... kind of like a spray booth at an auto shop."

"Well said," Troy nodded.

"And whenever a dolphin makes a sound, the *pattern* of that sound is sent into this spray booth, where it then gets painted by all these positively-charged particles of light."

"Exactly right," Troy affirmed. "And that's the piece of the puzzle I've been missing all these years. The sound-shapes were always there, but the computer's digital paint wouldn't stick until I created a polarized attraction between them."

Troy rotated the transducer in Calvin's hand then instructed him to hold it up to his mouth like a microphone. "Here. Say something into it."

Calvin spoke the first words that came to mind. "Sunken treasure," he said, and was taken aback when a three-dimensional object shaped somewhat like an undulating kidney bean flashed on the screen. "Sunken treasure!" he sputtered again and watched with amazement as the exact same image appeared on the monitor.

"Now try this one," Troy instructed. "Say *Mississippi* over and over, as quickly as you can."

"Let me," Chad said, grabbing the transducer from Calvin's hand. "Mississippi-mississippi-mississippi!"

Incredibly, the cadence created a smoothly animated form—a green, wormlike image—that pulsed and slithered across the screen.

"*That* was a surprise," Troy intoned with a hint of wonder. "I never expected the transducer to be able to process sound into a *moving* picture."

Calvin was flabbergasted. "My God, Troy, this is incredible! So what happens when you use it on the dolphins?"

With a pensive frown, Troy took the transducer from Chad's hand and placed it back on top of the monitor. "Nothing. Nothing useful, anyway. All we get are the same type of random patterns you just saw."

Troy's terse pronouncement left little room for further optimism.

"So that's it?" Calvin stammered, finally beginning to comprehend the fine line separating scientific success and real-world failure.

"That's it," Troy admitted. "I just can't think of anything else to try."

Calvin did not know what to say. After fifteen years of funding this research, he could not believe that Troy was giving up. He was too shocked, too dismayed for any immediate response.

Chad, on the other hand, had never shared his partner's uncompromising belief in dolphin sonic-imaging. Skeptical from the beginning, he wasn't surprised that this moment had finally arrived. Fixing a wicked glare on Calvin, Chad said, "I always knew this was a wild goose chase. But did you ever listen to me? No! You just kept throwing money at him like we were printing it in the basement. Well, you know what? This time *I'm* making the decision." Walking away from the group and heading toward the facility's gate, Chad turned back to Troy. "I'm genuinely sorry, Dr. Wallace. For all of us. But unless you *can* think of something else to try by this time next week, I'm going to arrange for the equipment to be picked up and sold to the highest bidder. At least then we'll get *some* kind of return on our investment. I'll be calling you within the next couple of days."

At that, Chad spun back around and stormed through the gate, not looking to see if his partner was following him.

Chapter 7

The afternoon sun hung low in the sky, illuminating the ramshackle dory fishing village in a soft amber glow.

Ryan replayed in his head some of the shots they had gotten earlier in the day. Sitting down on the beach's cold sand, he ran through a mental rehearsal for the segment's lead-in.

"Do you get what I'm after here?" Jen asked. "I want to convey a sense of what the beach feels like during the off-season."

"Yeah, yeah—that lonely, abandoned tourist destination right?"

"You got it. Any idea what you're going to say?"

"Do I ever?" he replied, only half joking. "Just give me a minute to jot down a couple of ideas," he said, taking the tablet from his shirt pocket.

"All right." Jen turned toward the cameraman: "Tyler, just go ahead and start taping whenever he's ready. Dory fleet teaser, take one." She stepped aside to let Ryan collect his thoughts.

Less than three minutes later, Ryan raised a hand in silence and counted down the lead-in on his own fingers. *Three, two, one.*

With the camera rolling, he sat cross-legged on the sand, pulled up the collar of his vest, and gave a slight shiver. After a glance at the wind-tossed Pacific for dramatic effect, he turned to stare directly into the lens. His delivery was quiet and subdued, minus his trademark smile. "Hello again, everybody. Ryan Ericson here, and today I'm going to tell you about a historic enterprise in Newport Beach that's been around longer than the city itself. So stick around, won't you? We'll be back right after these words."

Jen could see that Ryan was on a roll, so she just let him move into the segment without a new countdown.

"You know," he continued. "I've heard it said that Southern California doesn't experience a change of seasons from summer to fall, but that's not true. Come down to the beach and feel for yourself how the delicate afternoon breeze picks up and laces through the still-warm days of October. Stroll for miles on an empty beach that in July would be layered with thousands of tourists. Listen! Instead of boom boxes and screaming kids, all you hear is the boom of crashing waves and the lonely scream of the seagull. Look out over the ocean, and what do you see? Not an armada of jet skis and pleasure yachts, but a few solitary workboats braving the windswept swells.

"Those workboats, and the people who earn their living in them, are our story." Ryan finished the narrative with a slow, reflective turn back toward the ocean and held that pose until Jen cut the shot.

"Damn, that's good stuff!" Tyler exulted after getting the nod from Jen that the take was over. "How the hell do you think up crap like that so fast?"

Crude as Tyler's accolade was, Ryan knew the words of praise were genuine. "Hey, I've been writing a lot longer than I've been acting, so it helps to jot down a few key points that I can run with once I'm in front of the camera. And speaking of being on camera, aren't we supposed to be doing the interview about now?"

Jen looked down at her watch. "It *is* after three," she acknowledged while simultaneously picking up her walkie-talkie. "How we doin' up there?" she asked into the radio.

"Mr. Becket's ready whenever you are," the production assistant's crackling voice replied.

"Okay, go ahead and get him positioned in front of his shack, and we'll be there in just a couple of minutes."

"Roger that."

Leading the way up the beach, Jen gave Ryan his usual pre-interview rundown. "All right, the dory fleet's been here since 1898. Dories are flat-bottomed fishing skiffs. The usual catch is deepwater cod. Vern Becket's been fishing here for over fifty years. That enough to get you started?"

"More than enough."

"All right then, Mr. Lonely-scream-of-the-seagull—get over there and weave some of that magic of yours."

Ryan gave her a flippant look before heading over to the locker and taking a seat on a barrel next to Vern. With minimal wardrobe fussing and just a quick touch of makeup, he was ready to pick up from where he had left off with his narration.

Jen counted down, and Tyler gave Ryan his cue.

Ryan cleared his throat. "Plying the local waters of the Pacific, dory fishermen rely on their intimate knowledge of the sea to earn a living. But just what is a dory, and when did this fishing village first show up in Newport Beach? To answer these questions and more, we've invited Vern Becket, senior member of the fleet, to clue us in." Ryan turned away from the camera and made casual eye contact with Vern. "Thanks for taking the time to talk about this historical landmark."

Vern laughed at the introduction. "More like a *hysterical* landmark, if you were to ask anybody that works here."

Smiling with relief at Vern's ease in front of the camera, Jen sat back comfortably in her folding director's chair and let Ryan take control.

◆   ◆   ◆

During the course of the interview, Ryan and the rest of *South Coast Safari's* crew learned much about the daily operations of the fleet. And while it was interesting at first to hear that the boats used to be hauled up by horses, or that there used to be a steam-train terminal up on the pier facilitating the transport of fresh fish to inland markets, at some point the interview went into information overload.

Impatiently tapping her toe in the sand, Jen motioned to Ryan by spinning a finger in the air that it was time to wrap things up.

Picking up on her cue, Ryan eased the conversation toward a natural end. "So, Vern, you definitely seem to know everything there is to know about being a doryman. But I'm curious: What was it that brought you here in the first place?"

Although he had been quick-witted during the interview, the question caused Vern to become suddenly meditative and withdrawn. He took off his hat and scratched his head as he searched for an answer. Then after a pause so long that Jen nearly gave the call to cut, he looked at Ryan and gave a response incongruous with his previous banter. "You know, I don't think I can explain it very well."

Momentarily caught off-guard by Vern's reply, Ryan tried to steer the conversation back into something usable for the show. "Well, maybe you just liked fishing and decided to make a career out of it."

"That's not a bad guess, but the truth is that before I started fishing here in '46, I'd never fished a day in my life." He let his eyes make an even deeper connection with Ryan's and his words took on an almost mysterious tone. "No, it was something bigger—deeper—than that. Fifty-eight years ago, it was like the ocean just called me to be here, and I knew I had no choice but to answer that call."

Jen groaned under her breath.

Though he knew a sarcastic eye-roll would play best for the camera, Ryan could not divert his eyes away from the old man's piercing stare. "Some people call that the lure of the sea," he replied.

"I guess that might explain it," Vern nodded. "But have you ever wondered why *humans* would feel such a thing?" He collected his thoughts before continuing. "I mean, we're warm-blooded mammals living on land. How do you begin to explain the inescapable draw some of us feel for the ocean?"

Ryan shifted uncomfortably on the barrel. And while his Funhunter character quickly generated a host of superficial quips, he realized that there was an authentic voice within him that had something else to say. "I grew up around boats, and I can remember how disconnected I would feel from … from *everything* if I went too long without being out on the water." He couldn't believe he was saying this in front of the camera.

"Then you know what I'm talking about." Vern smiled.

A part of Ryan knew exactly what Vern was talking about, and though any content that wasn't strictly upbeat had no place on this lighthearted television program, he felt compelled to say what was on his mind. "I miss it," he said and looked down at the sand. "You're lucky that you've been able make a living being out on the water." The quiet reverence in his voice sounded odd even to himself.

Vern agreed. "I *am* lucky. So maybe there's something to that old superstition after all."

Ryan caught himself drifting and rebounded. "Yeah? What superstition is that?"

"Well, an old fishermen's legend says that whenever you see dolphins, you're going to have good luck. And, heck, I'm on the water so much I get to see 'em all the time. I'd say that *does* make me pretty lucky, wouldn't you?"

The word *dolphins* jolted Jen to attention.

"Cut!" she said with a slap to her forehead. "Dammit, Ryan, dolphins! We still gotta shoot the SeaWorld teaser, and our light's almost gone. Come on. Snap out of it and think of something quick before we lose that sunset." In a huff, she grabbed Ryan's arm and hurriedly dragged him back down toward the breaking waves.

The flaming orange ball of the sun was already half-hidden behind the ocean's horizon, leaving them only minutes to get the shot.

"Just go whenever you're ready."

The camera's light jolted Ryan to his senses. "Hey, Ryan Ericson here. Be sure to stick with us as we coast our way down to SeaWorld in San Diego, where we'll meet up with the park's head trainer—"

"Behaviorist!" Jen barked. "SeaWorld won't let us use the word *trainer*. Now take it from the top, and hurry up."

"Hey, Ryan Ericson here, reminding you to stick with us tomorrow as we coast on down to SeaWorld in San Diego, where we'll meet up with the park's top behaviorist. Until then, don't forget that if you've gotta have something, you may as well have fun!" He smiled and held his finger pointed at the camera until he knew the tape had stopped.

"Cut. Guess that'll have to do," Jen sighed in exasperation while already plodding back up the beach.

The camera's light and Ryan's smile dimmed in unison. With the late afternoon breeze tousling his hair, he stuffed his hands deep into his safari vest and just stood there surveying the windswept ocean.

Vern ambled up next to him. "Quite a sunset, isn't it?"

Ryan did not answer right away, and when he did, his eyes did not leave the blazing panorama. "Yeah. Looks like we might even get a green flash out of it."

Ryan's assessment drew a quizzical stare. "What's that now?"

"You know, the green flash. I've seen it a few times, and whenever I did, the sun looked just like it does now: super bright orange with that weird shimmer at the bottom. I've heard it's an optical illusion the light plays on your eyes—that for a millisecond, you see the exact *opposite* color of orange—which is green—right after the sun sets."

Vern pursed his lips and shrugged. "I suppose that might explain it."

"Oh boy, here we go," Ryan groaned. "Obviously you've got some other idea."

"Well, mariners consider it a sign of changing fortune. They say that when you see the green flash, something profound is about to happen in your life."

"Why am I not surprised? Sounds like everything that happens to a fisherman is some kind of omen."

"We *can* be a superstitious lot," Vern agreed with a wink then redirected his attention toward the setting sun.

At that moment, the last speck of orange dipped behind the ocean, and a brilliant green spark did indeed appear to flash in its place on the horizon.

Hearing Vern gasp slightly at the sight, Ryan did not move or look away, holding his own reaction in check. "Optical illusion," he stated without emotion.

"Whatever you say," Vern quipped, marveling at the last golden shafts before nightfall.

Chapter 8

Ryan knew the park's lead dolphin behaviorist was a young woman, and since she was also a public performer, he figured she was probably in good shape and at least somewhat pleasant to look at. His mind began conjuring up a few possibilities.

"So, where is she?" he asked as he and the crew made their way into SeaWorld's main dolphin show arena.

Jen looked down into the pool's sparkling water, noticing three figures approaching from below. "Well, either there are two dolphins and a mermaid coming up, or that's her now."

Ryan leaned over the lip of the pool then stepped back quickly to avoid being splashed by the trio. The moment could not have been more perfectly staged.

"That was awesome, you two!" Rebecca enthused before blowing a shrill metal whistle. "Now go ahead and play for a while on your own, okay?" She swam over to a ladder and dipped her head backwards in the water before climbing out.

Watching her exit the water, Ryan could not help but notice the way Rebecca exceeded every one of his nearly impossible ideals of feminine beauty. Her wet, golden hair fell around what he considered to be a perfectly proportioned face, and every curve of her toned body was accentuated by the turquoise SeaWorld swimsuit.

"Uh-oh," Jen whispered to Tyler. "Looks like this one's got all the qualities Ryan appreciates in a woman."

"She's certainly got a few *I* can appreciate!" Tyler whispered back, never taking his eyes off Rebecca.

Jen elbowed him sharply in the ribs. "Gee, it's nice to know that Ryan's got an understudy picking up on all the commendable ways he values women."

"Hey, I've seen a lot more crude behavior from chicks chasing *him* than the other way around," Tyler said. That truth temporarily quieted Jen.

Rebecca walked over to a fiberglass utility box, took out a towel, and languidly dried herself off. Not oblivious to Ryan's eyes upon her, she then slipped on a loose sweatshirt before making her way over to introduce herself. With a smile and a piercing flash from those liquid-amber eyes, she reached out to shake his hand. "Hi, I'm Rebecca."

Ryan cleared his throat and wrapped both hands around one of hers. "And I'm available," he grinned with a wink of smarmy confidence. The come-on, a favorite of his, worked 99 percent of the time.

Unfortunately, he had just met someone from the 1 percent category.

Though caught off guard for a moment by his audaciousness, she recovered quickly. "Umm, thanks for sharing?" she said while retracting her hand. Then, almost as if he had simply vaporized in front of her, she sidled past him to go meet the rest of the crew.

"Welcome to our little corner of SeaWorld," she said graciously to Jen and Tyler. "I'm Rebecca Larson."

"Hi Rebecca. Thanks for having us," Jen replied. "And please accept my apology on behalf of *him*," she added, lifting an eyebrow in Ryan's direction.

With light-hearted candor, Rebecca relayed that it wasn't the first time she'd been approached in such a manner. "Hey, when your uniform is two ounces of wet Spandex, it kind of goes with the job." Taking notice of the sound and lighting crews starting to file into the pool area with all of their equipment, she asked, "Is all that stuff for my interview?"

Ryan stepped back into the conversation, his ego and libido no less diminished. "You know, some people would call it *my* interview, since it *is* my show, but why quibble over details? By the way, my name's Ryan." His smug tone implied that he knew he needed no introduction. "Ryan Ericson."

"I know who you are and I've seen your program," Rebecca replied, unaffected by his celebrity. "It's actually pretty good sometimes."

Despite the initial rebuff, Ryan was nowhere near ready to abandon the hunt. "Yeah, well, that's no accident. There's a whole lot of work that goes into a show like this. Isn't that right, Jen? Wouldn't you say that it's all the time and *preparation* we put into the show that makes it the number one entertainment guide in California?"

At first, Jen was baffled by his emphasis on the word *preparation,* but then she realized where he was going.

"Oh, that's right, Ryan," she deadpanned. "It's all about the *preparation.*"

"And you know, I was just thinking to myself how little I know about dolphins. Now, I ask you: How can I conduct a quality interview with Rebecca here if I don't know anything about the subject?"

"Sometimes you do a pre-interview," Tyler suggested, casually assuming the role of strategic facilitator.

"Hey, you know what? That's true. I *do* often pre-interview a guest, don't I? Of course, if Rebecca doesn't have the time, I would understand completely."

"Really smooth, guys," Jen cut in, exasperated. "Listen, Rebecca, if you think you can handle this legend-in-his-own-mind, it actually would help to do a pre-interview."

"Um, hello. I can hear you," Ryan interjected. "And I have feelings, you know."

Jen pulled Ryan a few feet back and whispered sternly, "Maybe between your legs you do. But even so, I agree that the pre-interview's a good idea. Just remember to actually get some useful information… which means more than just her phone number, got it?"

"Did you hear that, Becky?" Ryan called out to Rebecca. "Jen thinks it's a good idea for us to go off on our own and get better acquainted!"

Rebecca had made the complete personal shift needed to deal with Ryan. "That's fine with me. There's a research pool just around the corner that we can use until your crew's ready." She then set the tone for their exchange. "Oh, and here's one thing you should know. My name is Rebecca. Call me Becky again, and your *preparation* will be over."

◆   ◆   ◆

Rebecca led Ryan to the closest semiprivate area, which happened to be the enclosed research pool she and Troy had been utilizing for their sonic-imaging experiments. She motioned for him to have a seat in a white plastic patio chair, which was surrounded by stacks of the doctor's equipment.

Ryan recognized a few of the video-processing components. "This looks like some kind of giant outdoor editing bay," he said, clearly intrigued.

Rebecca rummaged for the right words. "It's something like that. SeaWorld is working with a marine biologist who's doing some experiments with dolphins. I've been assisting him after hours."

Lucky guy, Ryan thought. "So, what's all this stuff do?"

Dr. Wallace had told Rebecca not to share information about his experiments with anyone, so this was one topic she and Ryan would not be discussing. "Unfortunately, nothing. And even if it did, I'm not really supposed to talk about it."

"Ooh, top secret, huh?" he teased. "Okay, then I guess it's on to my dolphin lesson."

Taking the lead, Rebecca squatted down at the edge of the pool and slapped her hands against the water's surface. In seconds, two sinewy gray shapes bolted in through a narrow underwater passage that connected the pool to another holding area. "These two are Sandi and Echo, our star performers here at SeaWorld, San Diego," she said. "Get it? Sandi-Echo?"

The dolphins hovered next to her with their perpetually smiling faces poking out of the water. "Their Latin name is *Tursiops truncatus*, and they are two of the smartest animals here at the park—and that includes people!"

"Yeah, right. SeaWorld probably pays you to say that."

"Well, their brains *are* roughly 30 percent larger than ours. In fact, these guys have the largest brain-to-body weight ratio of any animal that has ever lived."

Ryan pulled the tablet and pen out of his shirt pocket and scribbled a few notes. "Okay, that's an interesting fact," he said. "But does that automatically mean they're smart?"

"No. However, a large, intricately-folded brain like theirs—and ours—*does* seem to be a prerequisite for higher thought and communication."

"Communication? So now you're saying that they talk to each other?" he asked and kept writing.

Peeling off her sweatshirt, hoping this time that Ryan would have the tact to keep his eyes to himself, she sat at the rim of the pool. Dangling her legs and running her hands back and forth through the chilly water, she recounted a still-vivid memory. "Let me tell you about two young dolphins I worked with a few years ago. I was teaching one of them to retrieve a ring and place it over a floating pylon, and the other one to grasp a baton in its mouth and push a button with it at the side of the pool. Now here's the important part: Those dolphins were always separated during their training sessions, meaning that neither of them ever saw what the other had been trained to do. Well they both got very proficient at their individual behaviors, until one day everything just kind of fell apart. During two consecutive sessions, they each struggled with their designated tasks. And while they both did eventually manage to complete the behaviors, their performance was sloppy and erratic."

When she stopped, Ryan interjected the obvious question. "So, did you ever find out what the problem was?"

"Yes. Somehow, their handler had gotten the two dolphins mixed up and brought the wrong one to each session."

Ryan was slow to catch on. "I'm not following."

"Don't you get it? Without any training, the button-pusher accomplished the hoop sequence and vice versa! For this to happen, they must have had a prior conversation discussing what each of them had been taught to do!"

"Hmm, I guess that *is* pretty amazing," Ryan had to agree.

"And here's another interesting fact you might want to write down. Did you know that dolphins have hands?" she asked.

Ryan flashed her a quizzical look. "What do you mean, they have hands? Where?"

"Inside their pectorals, or side fins, there are the bones of a five-fingered hand."

Ryan had never heard anything like this before. "Why?"

"Believe it or not, millions of years ago, dolphins used to live on land. Then, for some reason, they went back to the oceans, which is quite a strange evolutionary move for an air-breathing mammal to make. Don't you think?"

When he didn't respond, she looked over her shoulder and was surprised by his troubled expression. "Is something wrong?" she asked.

"Huh? Oh, I, uh ..." Remembering his encounter with Vern the day before, Ryan couldn't summon the words for what he was thinking. It was somehow unnerving that, within twenty-four hours, he had heard two different references about land-dwelling creatures being drawn to the ocean. "I was just thinking about an interview I did with this old fisherman yesterday. He said some things that remind me of what you're talking about."

Rebecca seemed to perceive the sudden shift in his mood. "I'm not surprised. A lot of fishermen are really into dolphins. Did he mention that spotting them is a sign of good luck?"

Ryan gave her a perplexed look. "Yeah, he might've said something like that. Listen, can we just get back to some simple facts that I can use for the show?"

Rebecca, ever more confused by his behavior, tried to coax whatever was troubling him to the surface. "Is something the matter?"

"I... I'm not sure," was all he said. His tone had become oddly neutral, his expression vague and troubled—all very out of character for the glib, vivacious television personality she'd just met.

"Are you feeling okay?"

Ryan rose up from the chair, walked over to the edge of the pool, and stared vacantly down at the water and dolphins for a long while. "You know, *okay* is probably not the first word that comes to mind."

But he was feeling something, something different from anything he'd ever felt before.

Chapter 9

Driving home from the SeaWorld taping, Ryan tried to make sense of his thoughts about Rebecca, dolphins, the stacks of video editing equipment, and Vern. He'd been grateful that the shoot had settled into the usual routine for the rest of the day, but at the same time he could not deny that it felt like he was being drawn into some strange web of coincidence. He pulled his black Mercedes SL500 convertible over to the side of Interstate 5 and dialed Fox Studios in Los Angeles. Soon he was being patched through to the archive department.

"Ryan Ericson?" the voice—young, male, enthusiastic—asked in disbelief. "*South Coast Safari's* Ryan Ericson?"

"Why the surprise? I call the studio all the time," Ryan said with a laugh.

"Yeah, but you never call us in Archives. What can I do for you?"

"Here's the deal. We were shooting a segment about dolphins over at SeaWorld today, and I need a little extra research material. Does Fox have any old documentaries in their library? You know, Jacques Cousteau? That type of stuff?"

"Probably. When do you need it?"

Ryan took a deep breath, aware of his own urgency. "Right now," he answered as calmly as possible.

There was a hesitation on the other end of the line, then, "What do you mean, right now?"

"I mean that if you can find something, I'd like you to e-mail the video file to me right away." He had never asked such a favor before, and he felt the need to justify it. "We're thinking about re-shooting a couple of scenes, and any information that'd keep me from sounding like a total idiot would be helpful."

The archivist accepted that readily. "Gotcha. Let me just take a look at what we have," he said, probably scrolling through all related program titles in Fox's archives. "Let's see, there are a few old documentaries from the seventies and eighties: *Whales and Dolphins, Dolphin Diaries.* Hey, how about this one, it's one of those *In Quest Of* shows: *Dolphins, Humans of the Sea.* That sounds pretty interesting."

"Humans of the Sea? That's really the name of it?"

"Says right here."

Ryan feigned indifference. "Sure, that's probably as good as any. Do you have my e-mail address?"

"Yes. You must have one of those new wireless internet connections. I can hear the cars in the background."

"Yep, so go ahead and send it on over. I'll find a place to pull off and grab a bite while the file's downloading. Oh, and thanks for your help," he said and flipped the phone shut.

After exiting the freeway in Encinitas and making a left turn toward the ocean, he remembered his way to Swami's, a little sandwich shop on Pacific Coast Highway. He ordered their specialty turkey burger and date shake combo then grabbed a table on the restaurant's outdoor patio. Allowing himself the amount of time he thought the download would take, he ate while watching the sun begin its descent toward the horizon. Roughly a half hour later, he got back in the car, settled into the driver's seat and logged onto his laptop.

The e-mail from Fox Studios had just finished downloading. With the lowering angle of the sun bouncing a sharp glare off the car's hood, the tinted windows and upraised soft-top provided just enough shade for the laptop's monitor to be seen clearly. Ryan shifted in the firm leather seat and opened the attachment.

Soon a deep and eerie tone came from the car's stereo, which was linked to the computer via an FM transmitter. The show's opening shot of Einstein's famous $E=MC2$ formula appeared on the screen. Accompanying the image, an echoed voice announced, "This is *In Quest Of*, where the science fiction of today becomes the science *reality* of tomorrow."

Ryan chuckled at the program's crude graphics, haunted-house soundtrack, and overly melodramatic narration.

"In this episode, join us as we explore mankind's aquatic alter-ego in …" the voice paused for effect, "Dolphins, Humans of the Sea." The narrator then explained that this title was based on the book *Lilly on Dolphins, Humans of the Sea,* by Dr. John C. Lilly.

Ryan stopped mocking the show's primitive technical quality shortly after the opening comments, for in its commercial-free run time of twenty-two minutes, he learned more amazing facts about dolphins than he would have thought possible.

"This is, or, to be more precise, was a dolphin," the narrator intoned as the image of a small, hippo-like creature appeared on the screen. "Sixty million years ago, these quadrupeds were climbing up Darwin's ladder of survival amidst a vast array of other land-dwelling mammals and reptiles. But dolphins made a peculiar detour on their evolutionary journey. As we now know, approximately forty million years ago, prehistoric dolphins headed *back* into the sea from which they had evolved eons earlier. One can only speculate as to why the ancestors of the modern dolphin would do such a thing, but it is likely that competition for sustenance was a factor. Life on *terra firma* was getting more difficult by the day as increasing populations of animals competed for limited resources, while the ocean would have provided a much more stable and abundant supply of food.

"Today, dolphins offer proof of their transition from land to water in the form of a no-longer-needed *hand* hidden within the muscle and skin of their pectoral fins." Accompanying the voiceover was an X-ray revealing a startling image: the five-fingered appendage that Rebecca had described. Another portion of the program discussed the importance of brain size and structure when considering intelligence. At a weight of 1600 grams, the commentator noted, a bottle-nose dolphin's brain is roughly 30 percent larger than a human brain.

Finding himself being drawn further into the show's revelations, Ryan's eyebrows rose with each new piece of information. But it was when the narrator addressed a dolphins' ability to echolocate that intrigued him the most.

"It has been known for years," the voice continued, "that dolphins use a highly keen sense of echolocation to construct a sonic hologram, or sonogram, of their surroundings in their minds. This form of acoustic awareness is a biological version of the same technology we call ultrasonic imaging. For instance, when doctors scan a pregnant woman with ultrasound, they employ equipment that can translate the echoes of high frequency sound waves into a three-dimensional display of her unborn fetus. And while this electronic technology is quite amazing, the visual clarity it provides doctors with is no match for the imagery some experts believe dolphins create using a biological form of this same technology.

"Today, scientists are quite sure that dolphins use this natural form of ultrasound to not only look *at* each other, but also *into* each other, where a cancerous growth or an irregular heartbeat would be easily and instantly detected."

The program ended with a recap of its facts: Dolphins *re-evolved* into air-breathing ocean dwellers, they appear capable of higher thought, seem to share a complex language with each other, live in highly organized societal groups called pods, and possess an ultrasonic-imaging capability that would challenge the most sophisticated echo-sensing equipment mankind has ever made.

As the computer monitor faded to black, Ryan was left wondering why this information about dolphins was not more widely known. He recalled a magazine article written by a creationist who denounced the theory of evolution, remembering the theologian's key point that if evolution was correct, Africa would be littered with the skeletons of short-necked giraffes. This argument forced Ryan to similarly consider that if dolphins ever really walked the earth, they might still have the hands to prove it—which he now knew they did!

The tires of his Mercedes squealed as the car peeled out of the parking lot. Upon his arrival at the 5 Freeway intersection, he stopped at a traffic light. Idling there, he knew it made no sense to turn south and head back toward San Diego. SeaWorld would be closed, and Rebecca would most likely be gone by the time he returned.

It didn't matter. He had to go back.

When the light turned green, he cranked the wheel to the right and gunned the powerful Mercedes up the southbound onramp.

Chapter 10

Usually, Rebecca's favorite time at SeaWorld was the special, lingering moment just after closing—when the sea lions, walruses, killer whales, and dolphins scattered throughout the park would join their voices together in a chorus as if to celebrate the retreat of another day's army of tourists.

This night, however, the animals' song of echoing squeals and growls sounded mournful and sad to her, and she wondered how much her mood was coloring her perception. On a bench beside the pool, with bare legs tucked under her sweatshirt, she watched as Dr. Wallace packed up the equipment.

There was not much to talk about except the bleak reality at hand.

"So, what will you do now?" she asked.

Troy paused. Stupefied, he said, "I have absolutely no clue."

Rebecca winced. To hear Troy admit that he didn't have a single new idea to hang his hopes upon was like hearing him deliver his own death sentence.

"You could always go back to teaching," she volunteered.

That idea did nothing to boost his spirits. "Teach? Teach what—my flawed hypothesis about dolphin communication? Or maybe I could teach a course on how to waste fifteen years and millions of dollars on a crazy pipe dream."

"This was not a pipe dream," she said. "Your research picked up where John Lilly's left off, and he would have been proud of the advances you made."

Troy sank wearily down beside her on the bench. With his hands resting on his knees, he breathed out a groaning sigh.

Her heart ached for his pain, and she reached out to comfort him, placing a hand on top of his. "I'm so sorry it has to end like this."

Exhausted, Troy momentarily surrendered to her soft touch. "I'm not. I mean, of course, I'm devastated, but this would have been so much harder to endure if you hadn't been here to help me through it." With tears beginning to well up in his tired eyes, he turned away from her. "Your genuine concern for my work, and for me, has meant more than you could ever realize."

Crying would only add to his desolation, so she fought back her own tears. "Dr. Wallace—Troy, it has been my honor to be your student and assistant. I will never forget the amazing things I have learned from you."

Into this sorrowful and private moment came an intruder, the sound of hurried footsteps drawing ever closer to the pool enclosure's gate.

"Knock, knock," Ryan's voice called out. "Anybody home?" he asked while sauntering through the gate to the research area.

His arrival could not have been more unexpected, or more unwelcome.

"What are you doing here?" Rebecca shot up off the bench and charged at him as if she was warding off an actual threat. "There'd better be a good reason for this, or I swear I'll call security!"

Though he hadn't been a perfect gentleman earlier that day, Ryan didn't feel he warranted such antagonism. "Whoa, calm down. I just came back to talk to you a little more about dolphins, that's all," he replied, confused by her anger. "Besides, since it was the security staff who let me in, it probably wouldn't do much good to call them." Taking a few steps closer, he reached into the lining of his coat and pulled out a glossy promotional photograph of him standing next to the zebra-striped Jeep. "You'd be surprised what an autograph or two will get you."

Rebecca yanked the photo out of his hand and tossed it to the ground. "Well, let me assure you that we are not interested in your autograph."

"We?" Ryan asked, not seeing Troy in the dimly-lit background. "You mean you and ..." he paused and tilted his head toward the two dolphins swimming in the pool, "them?"

Her eyes followed his glance toward the dolphins. "What are you talking about? Of course I don't mean them," she scoffed.

"She means me." Dr. Wallace stepped out of the shadows, holding out a hand in greeting. "My name's Troy. Troy Wallace." Then his eyes opened wide in recognition. "And you're Ryan Ericson from *South Coast Safari*. What are you doing here in San Diego?"

The fact that Rebecca hadn't deemed their interview worth mentioning threw Ryan slightly off balance. "Well, I was down here shooting a segment for the show this afternoon, and Rebecca was my guest." Recalling the events of the day, he remembered that she had been assisting with some kind of experiments. "Hey, you must be the scientist who owns all this equipment."

Rebecca glared at Ryan then turned back to Troy, alarmed. "Dr. Wallace, I swear I didn't tell him anything! We only met back here to get out of his crew's way."

Troy did not seem the least bit concerned. "Rebecca," he reminded her, "it's not like we have to keep this a secret anymore."

Ryan was baffled by their exchange. "Keep *what* a secret anymore?"

Rebecca was growing impatient. "I'm sure it's nothing that would interest you."

"Oh, yeah? Care to try me?"

She looked up, crossed her arms, and tapped her bare foot rapidly on the ground. "Well, first, you'd have to have a basic understanding of how dolphins echolocate, which I know you don't, so I—"

"You mean how they translate ultrasonic echoes into three-dimensional images?" Ryan interrupted with TV-perfect timing, remembering almost verbatim the narrator's words from the *In Quest Of* program.

With Troy nodding approvingly beside her, she found herself struggling to respond. "Okay, how do you know that, when you barely knew that dolphins were mammals just a few hours ago?"

"A reporter has his sources." Ryan returned his smugness for her sneer. "Anyway, as you were saying ..."

Troy took over the conversation. "In a nutshell, Ryan, what we've been trying to prove is that dolphins not only *receive* ultrasonic images, but that they are capable of *sending* them to other dolphins as well."

Ryan's blank stare showed that he was not grasping the profundity of Troy's simple explanation. "So, you're saying they might send pictures to each other."

"Not just pictures, but exact duplications of their ultrasonic echograms. Let me give you an example. Let's say we're all dolphins and that a week ago I fired my sonar signal at, oh, I don't know, a giant sea turtle. After receiving the ultrasonic echoes that bounced off the turtle's body, I instantly *digitized* and translated them into a perfect, three-dimensional image of it in my mind."

"I'm with you so far," Ryan said with questionable confidence.

"Okay, here's where it gets really interesting. Imagine that I could store in my memory this turtle-image, like a digital file is stored in a computer's memory, and then send you that file like an ultrasonic e-mail any time I wished."

"So the image I'd *see*," Ryan responded, using his fingers to form quotation marks in the air, "would be an exact copy of what you sounded against?"

"Just as if that turtle was right there in front of you."

The full impact of Troy's theory was beginning to materialize in Ryan's mind. "Does that mean that *I* could then e-mail this turtle-file to Rebecca?"

Watching Ryan immersed in Troy's explanation, Rebecca felt as if she were with someone entirely different from the man who'd repulsed her earlier.

"It means *exactly* that," Troy affirmed with newfound enthusiasm. "Now, imagine this digital file not only making its way from dolphin to dolphin, but from generation to generation of dolphins!"

"Which happens to cover about forty million years," Rebecca interjected.

Ryan swallowed hard. "Are you saying that if a dolphin scanned a dinosaur forty million years ago, the file it created could still be circulating today?"

Troy allowed a lingering silence to relay the magnitude of his theory. "That's precisely what I'm saying. And that's what this equipment was designed to do—intercept and display those images. Can you imagine being the first human to know for certain what an ichthyosaur actually looked like? Or, for that matter, a prehistoric human?"

"Wait, though—how would dolphins know that if they live in water and we live on land?" But the instant Ryan asked this, the answer came to him.

"Ever go swimming?" Rebecca teased.

Dazed and exhilarated, Ryan sat down on the bench. "So, what *have* you seen so far?"

His question instantly quelled the flow of excitement that had built between them.

"Unfortunately, nothing," Troy admitted. "Which, by process of elimination, leads me to three logical conclusions. One, my theory is completely wrong, and dolphins do not send ultrasonic images to each other. Two, my equipment is still incapable of decoding their transmissions. Or, three ..." There Troy stopped.

Rebecca had never heard of a third possibility. "Three?" she prodded.

"Or, three, Sandi and Echo here have not felt like cooperating— meaning that they simply have not been sending each other the type of transmissions my equipment is designed to translate."

Rebecca was confused. "Why would they not cooperate?" she wondered aloud. "*How* could they not cooperate?"

"You know as well as I do that captive dolphins often behave differently than those in the wild," Troy speculated. "Maybe there's a reason why they don't use this imaging ability in isolation."

"So why don't you get yourself a boat and do the tests out in the open ocean?" Ryan asked the obvious.

"If I had had more time and money, that's exactly what I would have done," Troy explained. "But it's too late for that now. You can't just make a pod of dolphins materialize out in the wild, and my benefactors are not about to pay for me to bob around in an expensive research vessel for days on end."

Ryan remembered all the times he had encountered dolphins while conducting sea-trials during his years as a yacht broker—how easy it had been to find them if that's what his guests wanted to see. Still, he couldn't believe what he was about to propose. "What if I could get you out on a boat, no charge? I've got a thirty-eight footer back in Newport that's always fueled up and ready to go."

Rebecca, slack-jawed, could not have been more shocked by what she was hearing.

"That's very generous of you, Ryan. And if things were different, I might have even taken you up on that offer. Unfortunately, the equipment is being picked up early next week."

"Then let's go this weekend. I'm free if you are."

Troy appeared to make a transit from despair to last-ditch optimism. "Are you serious?"

"Not very often," Ryan smiled and winked. "But right now I am."

"I—I don't know what to say. Rebecca, what do you think?"

Rebecca cautiously lowered the protective shield she had erected against Ryan. "I think you'd be crazy not to take Mr. Ericson up on his offer."

Hearing this, Troy clapped his hands with a loud whoop and launched into a fit of euphoric activity. He began pacing the length of the pool, making mental notes of which components he would need to conduct an open-water experiment.

Ryan seized the opportunity to speak with Rebecca in private, nudging her away from Troy's anxious movements. "So, does this mean that you *don't* hate me?" he asked.

Taken aback by his assumption, Rebecca stopped and stared deep into Ryan's eyes. "Ryan, let me tell you something about me: I don't hate anything, or anyone, including you. But that doesn't mean I appreciated the way you acted toward me today."

Ryan felt a strangely alien response forcing its way out of his mouth "I'm...sorry," he said. "Can we just kind of forget this morning and start over from here?"

Rebecca crossed her arms and studied him. "And just how do you see us starting over?"

"How about as friends? Friends having a casual dinner together. Tonight."

She shook her head, laughing at his determination. "You know what? To prove I'm not a person who holds a grudge, I'll take you up on that offer. We'll just need to swing by my place first so I can clean up a little. Is that okay with you?"

"Hmmm, that sounds a little suspicious. How do I know you're not planning on attacking me once we're alone?"

"Trust me. I think I'll be able to control myself."

He nodded thoughtfully, drooping with exaggerated disappointment. "I was afraid you'd say that."

Chapter 11

In many ways, the first fifteen years of Ixchel's life, which began in 1950, could not have been more predictable. Born into an impoverished but happy family, the raven-haired child grew up like most other Mayan girls. She played and worked in the fields her mother and father farmed for food, milked the family's cow, and constantly explored the dense tropical landscape surrounding her meager home in Quintana Roo, Mexico.

The striking difference was her family's allegiance to the ancient Mayan ways. She was not allowed to speak Spanish at home—only the difficult language of her ancestors. Nor could she play with children of mixed-blood lineage. She was taught to read Mayan hieroglyphics, and most of her family's excursions away from home involved touring the abundant ruins dotting the nearby area—her favorite being the seaside temple complex of Tulum.

The pride of her father's life, Ixchel had grown into a beautiful young teenager. With a sculptured, classical beauty worthy of her namesake, the ancient Mayan Goddess of the Moon, she carried herself with a dignified bearing that often drew comments and compliments.

Despite her exceptional promise and the suspicion that she might even have a future as a shaman *day keeper*, the first turn of a permanent, spiraling descent occurred on her sixteenth birthday. This was an especially significant moment to a Mayan girl, based on the legendary belief that this particular day marked the point where the gods converged in the heavenly realm to determine the fate of her remaining earthly life. Garbed in a colorful embroidered dress that her mother had made just for this occasion, she sat at the head of the family's outdoor dining table and graciously received the gifts presented to her: a corn-husk doll made by her younger sister, a jar of honey her mother had gleaned from a nearby hive, and a host of other handcrafted items from visiting friends and relatives.

When the time came for her father to present his gift, the most significant of the day, she was so excited she could hardly breathe. The present was about the size of a small adobe brick and wrapped in a sheet of hand-painted newspaper. Taking it from his thickly callused hands, Ixchel expressed her heartfelt gratitude to her father for whatever was inside.

As she slowly unwrapped the box, a hush of anticipation fell upon the people crowded around her. Lifting the last flap of paper, she looked down at the miraculous gift in wide-eyed wonder.

A collective gasp erupted from the group when she held up the printed box depicting an all-electric, simulated-wood-grained, *Illuminated for Night-Time Viewing!* digital clock.

"It is the future of time-keeping," her father said with noble flair. "Just as you are the future of this family and our ancestors."

Despite their primitive living conditions, Ixchel and her family were not ignorant of the outside world. They'd heard about this magic called electricity, which brought light to darkness without moon or flame. But never would her imagination have allowed her to think that any aspect of that world, however small, would be given to her as a gift. With her hands trembling, she lifted the box's lid and tugged at the tissue paper surrounding the appliance, slowly extracting it as if the technological wonder might self-destruct from the slightest jostling. "Oh, Father, where did you get this?"

His chest swelled with pride while he recounted the story. "Remember the trip I took to Merida last year to visit my brother? Believe it or not, I found a store there filled with such modern wonders."

Ixchel ran her fingers over the appliance's plastic casing.

"This clock," her father added proudly, "has the ability to tell you exactly what time it is."

"But how, Father? It has no gears or wheels to calculate the passage of time." Ixchel was referring to the workings of one of the most accurate timepieces ever invented, the Mayan calendar, which her ancestors had created over one thousand years ago. Familiar with the gear-within-gear design of the ancient device, she had come to believe that any instrument gauging the movement of time would be similarly constructed.

"It *does* have gears, my daughter, but the wheels are on the inside, slowly turning against each other and finally flipping over the small tiles you see through the clock's window."

Conceptually, she understood what he was describing, but she could hardly believe that so many little cogs and flaps could fit inside the confines of the clock.

"Yes, when electricity finally comes to this house, you will see these pieces move. Until then, you can have fun pretending that time is standing still at ..." he paused to look down at the white digits printed on black metal flaps. "Eleven minutes after eleven."

Ixchel stared down at the timepiece, and the graphic symmetry of the four lines divided by two dots caught her attention. "Where was it made?" she asked, never looking away from the clock.

"The United States of America," he answered. "Many days' travel from here."

"And in the United States, they keep time with Mayan numerals?" she wondered, noticing that the digits on the clock were represented by an arrangement of the same straight lines and stacked dots that her culture had used to express numerical values for centuries.

Her father hadn't noticed the startling similarity. "What?" he laughed and looked down at the clock. "No, my child, they do not use Mayan numerals there. Only at 1:11 and 11:11 would this clock ever look Mayan. But now that you mention it, it *is* quite a coincidence that it would come to us displaying those numbers, isn't it?" He lowered his voice and playfully shifted his eyes back and forth. "Maybe the Goddess Ixchel herself turned the wheels so that it would look like a Mayan clock to you," he teased.

But his daughter, who believed that coincidences were what the gods used to make themselves known to humans, found no humor in the joke.

◆   ◆   ◆

There were rumors that she had grown up in the area, but no one was quite sure about this, just as they were not certain of her real name or age. Most guesses placed her at about seventy years old, but that was only because the sun had ravaged her leathery skin fifteen years beyond her real age of fifty-four. And nobody believed that her real name was Ixchel.

Standing beside a small pushcart outside the entrance of Tulum's temple complex, she greeted the steady stream of tourists with a nearly toothless grin, extolling the virtues of her fresh mangoes in a language few people in the world could understand. Many visitors to the site would stop and drop a coin into her wrinkled hand without taking any of the fruit from the Crazy Goddess, or *La Diosa Loca*, which was the name the locals had bestowed upon her. But most just slipped nervously past the babbling old woman.

Ixchel had begun establishing herself as a fixture at the temple about two years after she received the clock from her father, and nearly a full generation of security guards had grown familiar with her. No threat to the temple, she had become part of the folklore: in a closing-time ritual that had gone on for nearly thirty-six years, the night guard protecting the grounds of Tulum would shoo her away from the temple's entrance each evening. Then, without fail, he would watch her turn and sneak back into the complex via an overgrown trail. Usually she would find her way to one of the more modest buildings, curl up inside it, go to sleep, and be gone before the next day's dawn.

Surrounded by dense tropical forestation, the temple ruins were situated at the edge of a massive cliff overlooking the Caribbean Sea's translucent waters—a view that rivaled the site's archaeological fascination for tourists. But for Ixchel, Tulum had never lost its significance as a sacred place of Mayan worship.

On this particular night, after creeping back into the complex and eating the mangoes that had not been sold that day, she lay her aching body down upon a carpet of fresh-picked banana leaves. But just as she was dozing off, a warm October wind picked up and rustled the large fronds overhead—a sure sign that the Goddess was near and that there would be no time this night for sleep. With hurried determination, she arose and grabbed a tattered satchel from her cart, nearly sprinting to the base of the Temple of the Descending God. Then, confident that no one was watching, she clambered up the stairs of the small structure and dashed into the temple's enclosed ceremonial room. She parked herself under the room's open doorway and looked out over the edge of the cliff at the ocean shimmering in the moonlight.

After catching her breath and taking a moment to give thanks to the Goddess for such a beautiful display, she reached into her satchel and carefully pulled out its contents—the birthday gift her father had given her so long ago. Never having been plugged in, the digital clock displayed the exact same time of 11:11.

Repeating a ritual that she had performed hundreds of times for more than three decades, she placed the clock on top of the folded satchel in the sand outside the doorway, sat cross-legged under the threshold to face both the clock and the incandescent sea, and began to chant to her namesake Goddess of the Moon, Ixchel. "Ixchel, Most Beautiful Ixchel, I thank you for this glorious evening, but now I must speak directly to the Creator above you, above me, above everything."

The words to the chant rose up quietly at first then increased in speed, pitch, and intensity with each repeating stanza. "Great Spirit, Heavenly Father-Mother, I have willingly traded a comfortable life here on earth to carry forward your message to your children all over the world. I have never doubted your instruction, never wavered in my duties. May my efforts bring light upon the true meaning of the end of the Great Cycle of Time!"

Toward the end of the chant—which lasted nearly an hour—she was screaming the words, a high-pitched wail of delirium and endorphin-stimulated ecstasy. Sweat poured down her brow and back while she kept her eyes locked on the clock's digits. Then, imagining herself as a human beacon, she focused all her energy on broadcasting not only the vision of the 11:11, but also her entire awareness of ancient Mayan heritage, knowledge, and prophecy about the end of time to the population of planet Earth.

She had no way of knowing if even a single person had ever received one of her transmissions. She hoped her efforts were not in vain, for she knew she was getting old and that no one would carry on this mission after her.

Chapter 12

Rebecca's small apartment—filled with rattan furniture upholstered in bright Hawaiian fabrics—was an eclectic shrine devoted to the ocean. Every nook and cranny contained either a seashell, a piece of driftwood sculpture, or a marine life figurine.

While she showered and changed into warm clothes, Ryan made himself comfortable on a sofa beside a solid teak bookcase. Scanning some of the titles crowded onto the shelves, he felt as if he were getting a crash course in a broad spectrum of scientific and metaphysical studies: *Understanding the Mind of the Dolphin, The Alchemist,* and *The Aquarian Gospel of Jesus* were just a few that caught his eye.

The apartment's walls were adorned mostly with inexpensive poster art, but there was also an original painting that caught and held Ryan's attention. In the painting, a feather-cloaked man stood on a cliff and gazed out over a moonlit ocean, where dolphins leaped from the water toward a strange, linear pattern of lights in the sky. A caption in the artwork's frame read, *"This is the Dawning of the Age of Aquarius."*

"I remember that song," he said loud enough for Rebecca to hear from the adjacent bedroom.

"What song?" she asked, her voice floating out of the room's open doorway.

Ryan launched into the decades-old tune, crooning the words just slightly off-key. "When the moon is in the seventh house ..."

As he sang, he wondered what she was doing in there. Probably slithering into a pair of jeans while trying to reconcile the actions of a man who'd been flaunting his celebrity all day and making offending advances at her. Despite his bad behavior, though, he had also taken the initiative to learn about dolphins, not to mention volunteering his boat for Dr. Wallace's research. What might she be thinking about him now? Had he managed to redeem himself yet?

Surprised that he could remember the lyrics to a tune that had been famous in the sixties, he set his thoughts about her aside and continued singing. "… and Jupiter aligns with Mars, when peace will guide the planets—"

Rebecca startled him by bounding out of the room. Holding a hairbrush up to her mouth like a microphone, she belted out the rest of the stanza. "And love will steer the stars!"

Together they warbled through the chorus. "This is the dawning of the Age of Aquarius, Age of Aquarius, A-quar-i-us!"

"Yikes," Ryan laughed at the end of their duet. "Good thing neither of us pursued a singing career," he added as she disappeared into her room again. "And what was that whole Age of Aquarius thing anyway?" he called after her, his attention drawn again to the painting. He was baffled why anyone would own such an obscure piece of artwork.

She reentered the room zipping up a burnt orange velour sweatshirt. The hesitation in her voice made it clear that she would rather avoid the conversation. "You know, it's kind of complicated. Besides, I doubt that you'd find it very interesting."

"Excuse me, but that's the second time tonight you've assumed I wouldn't find something interesting. Maybe *I* should be the judge of that."

His candor appeared to catch her by surprise. "Okay, but don't say I didn't warn you," she began and turned towards a mirror. Stroking her hair with the former microphone, she continued. "I'm an Aquarius, which is the main reason I wanted to learn the meaning of the song's words. I must have been about sixteen or so at the time, because I remember riding my bike to the library and checking out this big book, *The Aquarian Age*. Anyway, the first thing I learned was that an age is an astronomical measure of time. Here, it's almost easier if I draw it."

She set down her brush and located a tablet and pen in a bureau beneath the mirror. Kneeling beside him, she began to sketch a circle surrounded by a scattering of dots. "Imagine that this circle is the earth, and all these little dots are the stars that make up the twelve constellations of the Zodiac, okay?"

The smell of her damp, cascading hair was distracting. "Constellations," Ryan repeated with forced concentration. "You mean like Scorpio and Capricorn and all that."

"Exactly. Well, on the first day of spring for the past two thousand years, the sun has risen in an area of the sky occupied by the constellation Pisces. But, due to a wobble in the earth's rotation, in 2012 the sun will begin to pass through the space framing the constellation of Aquarius, which will start the clock of a whole new age. Modern astronomers call this the precession of the equinox."

"Whoa, slow down," he interrupted. "What are you, some kind of closet astronomer?"

"I said it was complicated," she retorted. "Which makes what I'm about to tell you all the more amazing. Believe it or not, the precession of the equinox was first discovered over a thousand years ago!"

Ryan turned back toward the painting. "Yeah? By who?"

"You're looking at him."

"Huh? This Aztec guy?" he asked, motioning toward the image of the brown-skinned native in the picture.

"Not Aztec—Mayan. And though I can't begin to tell you how they did it, the Mayans created a calendar nearly one thousand years ago that was so accurate it could predict the exact date of every eclipse, equinox, and solstice all the way to the end of this age."

With her explanation beginning to sink in, her last statement confounded him. "What do you mean, *this* age? Are you saying their calendar quits working after that?"

That precise question had gnawed at her for the last sixteen years. Standing up, she stepped toward the painting and tilted her head sideways to study it. "Well, here's the deal. According to the Mayans, the precession of the equinox is like a loop of time contained within an even larger loop. There's a five-thousand-year cycle that starts and stops at the appearance of a rare planetary alignment they named the *Tree of Life*. To put it as simply as I can, this happens when all of the planets in our solar system line up perfectly with each other and intersect the hazy band of the Milky Way Galaxy to form a giant *X* in the sky. See?" she asked, pointing out how the row of planets crossed the galaxy's elongated cloud of stars—a formation that suggested a single-branched tree. "Anyway, the Mayans called this interval of time between each Tree of Life formation a *Long-Count*, and, as it happens, both time-cycles— the modern Age of Pisces and the ancient Long Count calendar—will both end on the same date, December 21st, 2012."

There was a weighted urgency to her words that Ryan could not grasp. "Okay, so these two different cycles converge, and the calendar ends in 2012. Is that such a big deal? I mean, I've got a calendar in my office that ends on December 31st, and all that means to me is that it's time to buy a new calendar."

Rebecca took a deep breath. "I'm talking about something bigger than that, Ryan. Mayan prophecy says that at the end of this long count, time as we know it will cease to exist."

Ryan's eyebrows twitched upward in response to her explanation. "I see ..." he intoned with open skepticism. "So, are you saying that you believe time's just going to stop in a few years?" He glanced around the room. The concept made him look at her collections in a different light.

"I'm not sure. What I *want* to believe is that the Mayans weren't saying time would stop at the end of this age, but that a whole new type of human experience would *begin* in the age after it. Which, of course, happens to be the Age of Aquarius." Her explanation concluded, she took one last look at herself in the mirror.

Ryan didn't know what she might be looking for—she hadn't applied any makeup, and she'd apparently brushed her hair only to remove tangles—but watching her reflection, he found himself struck once again by Rebecca's natural, radiant beauty. "So, are you going to enlighten me with what this quote-unquote *new experience* will be like?" he asked.

She glanced back at him through the mirror and smiled warily. "Not so fast, Young Grasshopper," she said, imitating a martial-arts instructor. Holding her hands together, she swung around and bowed slightly in his direction. "There is always a price to be paid for enlightenment."

Ryan had seen enough kung-fu movies to participate in her impromptu skit. "And what is this price, oh Wise Master?"

"One large pepperoni pizza and a pitcher of beer," she giggled before grabbing her purse and heading out the door. "And, as Confucius say, 'Last one to car shall stink like rotting egg!'"

◆   ◆   ◆

A multi-block promenade in the heart of San Diego, the Gaslamp District offered a vast array of fine restaurants and trendy nightclubs. So, Ryan was surprised by her choice of a cheap pizza joint tucked in an alleyway between the main thoroughfares of 5th and 6th Streets.

As they entered the bustling eatery, an electrified hush stilled the room. The crowd's reaction to his presence barely registered with Ryan. But Rebecca seemed unduly self-conscious by the intensity of stares and whispers. Clutching his arm, she asked, "Is it okay with you if we eat out on the back patio?"

Ryan gave her a sidewise glance. "The patio? Isn't it kind of cold to be eating outside?"

She took his hand and tugged him through the restaurant, making clear to him that there was no room for discussion. As soon as they exited the rear door of the building, she let out a deep, gasping breath. "Oh my God! Is that what it's like everywhere you go?"

"I'm not sure I know what you're talking about," he replied, ushering her over to one of the many empty tables on the vacant patio. Had it been a warm summer evening, the white-trellised alcove, decorated with plastic grapes, twinkling lights, and Italian travel posters, would have been the perfect place for a casual dinner.

"I'm talking about a restaurant full of people all stopping in mid-chew to gawk at you," she almost panted.

"Oh, that. Yeah, I guess it can get a little weird at times. But to be honest, unless someone comes right up and asks for an autograph or corners me for a picture, I hardly notice it anymore. Tell you what. Why don't you make yourself comfortable out here? I'll go order, and maybe I can get the manager to close down the patio so we won't have to worry about anybody bothering us."

"You can do that? You can just say the word and have people locked out of a public place?"

"Well, shutting down a patio that's already empty is a little different than an A-list movie star closing a whole department store to go shopping. But, yeah, it can be a perk sometimes."

Her quick shrug suggested she was not going to fight the prospect of being alone with him on the patio, although the idea of special treatment bothered her a little. "Okay, then. If you say it's no big deal, I'll just have to trust you. And hey, don't waste any time coming back with that beer. I can just see you schmoozing your way through that crowd and handing out autographs to all the girls in there."

"Yes, dear," he called back over his shoulder, amused to admit that she had him pegged.

◆   ◆   ◆

They did not take long to finish the first pitcher, which was followed by two complimentary glasses of *grappa*, and Rebecca could feel the awkwardness of the evening beginning to wane. Ryan was good at small talk, and by the time he resumed the discussion they'd started in her apartment, she was in a better state of mind to respond.

He circled the topic with casual wariness. "Hey, back at your place you promised me enlightenment. And I hate to tell you this, but I don't think I'm feeling any more enlightened than when we first walked in here."

"I promised nothing of the sort," she corrected. "I said enlightenment comes with a price."

"Which, if I'm not mistaken, has been paid in full. One pepperoni pizza and a pitcher of beer, remember?"

She smiled at his persistence. "I guess you got me there. So, where were we?"

"Well, the whole Mayan calendar thing was starting to sound a little apocalyptic."

"Hold on," she interrupted with a waving finger. "I mean, sure, there are people who believe the calendar is some kind of doomsday prophecy, and it *is* interesting to note the way things are changing so drastically all over the world, but were the Mayans really predicting that time would just stop in 2012? I don't think so."

"But you *did* say it could mean the end of humanity's existence *as we know it.*"

Rebecca slowed the conversation down with a thoughtful gulp of *grappa*. "Can you picture that painting in my apartment, the one with the Mayan and the dolphins?"

"I can."

"Well, I'm not sure if I'll be able to say this exactly right, but when people talk about the Age of Aquarius, the buzzword that keeps popping up is *transparency*. And it is this idea of transparency that will open us up to what the song says: 'harmony and understanding, sympathy and trust abounding.' Which, to me, means that we'll start phasing out of our historical pattern of false-pretense and fear, and slowly begin to adapt to *their* way of living."

"*Whose* way?"

"The dolphins' way. Don't you see? It's like they're the original Aquarians: social, intelligent, cooperative, compassionate. Frankly, the entire direction of my life—and my priorities—began to change after I first witnessed those remarkable behavior patterns."

Ryan did not want to be disrespectful or offend her again, but he let out a sarcastic groan before he could stop himself. "Sorry, but I ..."

"That's okay. Honestly. I know this all sounds weird, so let's back up a little." Clearing her throat, she took a deep breath and continued. "You obviously did some dolphin research on your own before coming back down here tonight, right?"

"I did. I had the studio e-mail me an old documentary."

"And did it happen to mention that dolphins use ultra-sound to see *into* each other?"

"Yes. That was pretty amazing."

"So, don't you see how truly different that makes them from us? Don't you get it that by utilizing their ultrasonic ability, they are literally living a *transparent* existence with each other?"

His expression revealed that he was not fully grasping the point she was trying to make.

"All right, here's another way to look at it. Suppose you and every person on earth were hooked up to a lie detector every single minute of your lives. Can you imagine what that would be like?"

Ryan could. "Sure. It would be terrible."

She paused, thoughtfully tracing the rim of her glass with her index finger. "It would only be terrible if you were in the habit of lying. What I'm saying is that if you knew that everyone could see into you—read your heart rate, or sense how tense your muscles were, or determine how much adrenaline you were producing—would you ever bother even trying to deceive them? And vice-versa: Would they ever try to deceive you? Can't you see what a radical shift that would be from how we currently live?"

"I guess so," he said half-heartedly. "But I wouldn't say I make a habit of trying to deceive people."

"Is that right?" she challenged. "Then let's do a little experiment of our own. Let's pretend we're both dolphins, completely transparent to one another, and that you've just asked me to reveal what I know about you. I'll tell you what I'm sensing, and if I get something wrong, or you don't want me to continue, you can raise your hand and stop me at any time. Ready?"

He swallowed. "Sure, why not?"

"Well, to start off, I'm sensing that you're a little nervous about how this might go. Am I right so far?"

His hand did not go up, but the corners of his mouth did rise in an uneasy smile when she continued.

A long silence followed where she just sat and stared into his eyes. Then, after taking another sip of the grappa, she proceeded. "You take advantage of your good looks to help you get your way," she told him and waited for his reaction.

He did not move.

"You believe that the material things you own make a statement about your success.

"You like being noticed and getting special treatment.

"You're confident and capable, usually achieving the goals you set for yourself.

"But you're also … confused," she continued, letting her intuition take her deeper as she probed the person hiding behind those darting blue eyes. "Confused by the fact that, even though you have everything you thought you ever wanted, you still feel there's something more out there waiting for you."

Wonder and amazement began to soften the rugged features of Ryan's face.

"You are genuinely interested in what you learned about dolphins today, but the real reason you came back here tonight was not to talk more about them—it was to use that information to seduce me. Even volunteering your boat was a part of this agenda.

"And you're intrigued, even puzzled, by the fact that a single, available woman like me would not jump at the opportunity to be seduced by you."

Still his hand did not go up.

"Shall I continue?"

Ryan thought not. It felt like she had X-ray vision and had used it on every part of him. "Actually, that's enough. And please explain to me again why this would be such a great thing, because I've got to tell you, being scrutinized like that really didn't feel all that wonderful."

"Only because you don't believe that you can see into me the same way." She reached over, took his hands, and placed her palms gently on top of his. "But what if you could? What if I gave you permission?"

Ryan wilted in his chair. "I—I still don't think I could do it."

"I do," she said, and her tone made him weak. "Give it a try."

As uncomfortable as he had been before, he was even more so now. But emboldened possibly by his slight inebriation, he took a couple of deep breaths and decided to let a few observations fall out.

"Okay, here goes," he said with a long exhale. "You—you like dolphins.

"You don't fall for crude pick-up lines.

"You love the ocean." But he could not reach anywhere near the depth she had achieved with him. "Aw, come on. These are all too obvious," he said, looking away.

"No, you're doing good! Keep going—just peel away one layer at a time, like an onion, and let it reveal the next."

With focused concentration, he turned back toward her and stared for a long while into those gold-speckled eyes.

"You love your job at SeaWorld.

"It doesn't seem right or fair to you that your looks helped you get that job, but you've made your peace with it.

"Even though I acted like a jerk earlier today, there is something about me that you find intriguing."

Looking away for a moment, he felt some kind of clog, a blockage deep in his chest, beginning to dissolve. With his eyes darting from one object to another on the patio—anywhere other than fixed on hers—he carried on. "You think that trust and honesty are the most important things two people can share with each other. In fact, this seems so obvious to you that you can't understand why people would choose to hide behind some kind of false exterior."

Barely able to believe the words coming out of his mouth, he was beginning to understand what she meant by letting each layer reveal the next. And she had not yet raised her hand.

He rode the current of his intuition, "And you're hopeful about the future. You believe we can change. You believe with all your heart that, someday, peace really will guide the planets, and love will steer the stars."

The moisture building in her eyes magnified those fiery golden sparks. "And why not?" she replied with soft conviction. After all, this *is* the dawning of the Age of Aquarius."

Chapter 13

Saturday morning broke with a bright flood of light streaming through the gaps between the plantation shutters on Ryan's bedroom windows. Responding to the loud knock at his front door, he opened one eye to look at his watch. Six o'clock—exactly two hours before Dr. Wallace and Rebecca were scheduled to arrive.

"I'm coming," he grumbled, making his way down the half-spiral staircase leading to the home's large foyer. He opened the door, squinting into the blinding white rays of an October sunrise.

Troy's upraised hand was still clenched, ready to knock again. "Good morning, Ryan," he said with breathless anxiety and a nervous handshake. "And please pardon us for being so early, but last night Rebecca reminded me that your boat is thirty-eight feet long."

"What are you talking about?" Ryan said, trying to process Troy's odd statement. Obviously confused, he ran his fingers through his bed hair and waved them in.

"Well," Troy replied, noting that an explanation was apparently in order, "I'm guessing a boat that size has a cruising speed of what—eighteen or twenty knots at the most, right?"

"Maybe a little faster than that," Ryan responded, the slightest smile turning up the corners of his mouth.

"A little faster doesn't help, because where I think we stand a good chance of seeing some dolphins is over sixty miles away."

"And your point is?"

"Don't you see?" Troy begged. "If it takes us three hours to get out there and three hours to return, not to mention the time I'll need to set up, we'll hardly have any time to test the equipment before having to turn back!"

Ryan frowned thoughtfully. "Hmm, that does pose a problem, doesn't it?" he replied, giving Rebecca a mischievous wink. "Tell you what. Why don't you two make yourselves comfortable, maybe grab something to eat from the fridge. It'll just take me a few minutes to shave and throw some clothes on." With that, he headed back upstairs and disappeared into his bedroom.

"One *could* get comfortable here, indeed," Troy said, moving through the foyer, with its marble floor and high ceiling, and into the home's beach-view living room.

Rebecca followed him, surveying the large open space tastefully decorated with expensive Indonesian furniture, African art, and colorful Moroccan rugs. "I have a hard time believing that he put all of this together by himself," she mused out loud. "Probably has an interior designer on the payroll."

Not bothering to respond to her, Troy disappeared through the formal dining room and into the kitchen for a moment. "Hey, Ryan's got some peaches in here. He said we could help ourselves. Want one?"

"No thanks," she replied. "I'm not hungry."

"Suit yourself," he said as he reentered the living room, rubbing the peach against his shirt. "Let's step outside while I eat this." He opened the French doors leading from the living room onto a patio deck and ushered her through them. After walking to the far side, they stood against the railing and stared out over the waves breaking on the shore. "Must be nice having the Pacific Ocean as your backyard," he reflected.

"I suppose, but you wouldn't catch *me* spending millions of dollars just for a nice view. Frankly, the whole thing is a little over the top for my taste."

"How do you mean?" he asked, biting into the peach and sending juice dripping down his chin and hand.

"Well, for starters, if I had this much money for a house, I wouldn't want to be sitting right on top of my neighbors. Look how close these places are to each other."

"Oh, I imagine you'd eventually get used to it."

"Maybe, but I honestly don't think I would."

The two of them just stood there in silence for the next several minutes, mesmerized by the rhythmic pulse of the sea. Then, as if released from a trance, Rebecca turned and headed back for the French doors where she reentered the home.

"And all this nice, expensive furniture in a beach house?" she continued her critique. "Can you imagine how quickly it would get ruined by sand and suntan lotion?"

Though she spoke softly, her words traveled upstairs where Ryan had finished dressing, and he decided to play with her a bit.

"That's why there's an outdoor shower," he shouted down while stuffing a nylon jacket and an extra pair of jeans into a small duffel bag.

"Uh-oh. You weren't supposed to hear that," she replied sheepishly. "And I *did* say it was nice."

"Nice?" he challenged. "I spend a fortune on this place, and all I get is nice?"

"Okay, how about *really nice?*"

"Still not good enough. *Coast Magazine* called it 'a celebration of world culture, where rustic elegance and casual sophistication blend to create a stylish retreat by the sea.'"

"Oh, brother. Sounds to me like somebody wrote his own review."

"Hey, you can't prove that!" he challenged, bounding down the stairs with the duffel bag slung over his shoulder. "Oh, all right, maybe you could. But can I help it if I'm such a clever wordsmith?"

"Not to mention humble," she quipped.

"I can be humble. In fact, you know what? I am now completely done talking about me and all my stuff." He paused a beat for comedic timing. "Troy, let's talk about you. What do *you* think about me and my all my stuff?"

Troy was slow to catch on to the joke. "Well, I ..."

"I'm kidding!" Ryan patted Troy on the shoulder as he led them both out the front door. "Now, how 'bout we go round us up some dolphins? I'll get my car, and you two can follow me over to the boat."

"Sounds like a plan," Troy replied, surreptitiously tossing his peach pit into one of the potted plants along the walkway and then wiping his hands on his pants.

◆   ◆   ◆

Situated on a small channel that used to be the home of a bustling fish cannery, the Lido Dry Slip Marina was less than four blocks away.

Troy pulled his cargo van into the parking lot and peered up at the boats—nearly two hundred according to his quick estimate—stacked three-high in the storage facility's open steel racks.

"Would you look at that?" Rebecca gazed up through the windshield at the highest row of boats, towering more than fifty feet above them. "I've never seen anything like it."

"Actually, this kind of facility is common on the East Coast, but there's usually a big metal shed built over the whole thing to keep the boats dry in the winter."

She opened her door and rested a foot on the van's step. "They're like a huge version of the back-stock racks at discount club stores. So how do they get the boats down from there—a giant forklift?"

Ryan slammed his door shut and walked over to join them. "The biggest friggin' forklift you've ever seen in your life," he told them. "Listen, I'm going to run down and have the guys put the boat in the water. If you want, you can grab a couple of those dock carts over there and start bringing Troy's stuff down to the launch area."

"Sounds like a plan," Troy answered, wasting no time unloading the equipment as Rebecca scurried off to retrieve the dock carts.

They converged at the marina's seawall, where the enormous forklift cradling Ryan's boat was waiting. Suspended between the fork's gigantic metal tines, the boat, a thirty-eight foot Cigarette offshore racer, was a sight to behold: a sleek and garish craft looking more like a guided missile than an oceangoing vessel.

"You have got to be kidding me," Troy stammered. "*This* is your boat?"

With a smirk and a slight shake of her head, Rebecca absorbed the vessel's sleek, fluid lines and zebra-striped paint job. When she got to the giant, graphic bamboo letters spelling out *Huntin' Fun* toward the stern, she could not help but laugh out loud. "Oh my God! Could this thing be any more obnoxious?"

"You have no idea," Ryan answered while signaling the fork's operator to lower the boat into the water. They made their way down the gangway to the dry-slip's dock, and *Huntin' Fun* settled into the bay with a loud, controlled splash.

"So, I'm guessing she'll make the run in less than three hours," Troy stated the obvious.

"Try three quarters of *one* hour," Ryan bragged. He hopped over the starboard gunwale into the boat's cockpit, which was as streamlined as a jet fighter plane.

"Wait a minute!" Troy interjected, his brow deeply furrowed. "With the dolphins sixty miles away, if we get there in only forty-five minutes, that means we'll have to be going at least eighty miles per hour!"

But Ryan didn't seem to be paying any attention.

Looking over at Rebecca, Troy's eyes widened in disbelief as he finished his thought out loud. "In a *boat?*"

At the helm, an intimidating cluster of gauges and marine electronics beeped and buzzed when Ryan inserted the ignition keys and cranked the first of the boat's twin nine-hundred horsepower motors to life. With a deafening roar, the port, then the starboard engine's exhaust thundered across the sleeping harbor.

"I told you it got more obnoxious!" he shouted above the snarling motors, taking hold of Rebecca's hand and helping her down into the boat.

Troy grimaced at the din as he passed down the boxes and cases holding his equipment. After handing the last crate to Rebecca, which she stowed carefully inside the Cigarette's long, plush cabin below decks, he clumsily hoisted himself into the cockpit and nodded that he was ready to go.

Ryan eased the shift handles forward, and *Huntin' Fun* lurched forward, its two high-performance propellers churning a frothy wake behind them while the boat idled through Newport's calm waters. Forced to keep the boat's speed to less than five miles per hour in the bay, Ryan quickly calculated that the three-mile-long harbor cruise was going to take nearly as long as the sixty-mile open-ocean trip. With Troy and Rebecca occupying the stand-up racing bolsters directly beside and behind him, he called out, "So, where are we going, anyway?"

Troy pulled a portable GPS receiver from a small valise and, after punching a few buttons, held it up so Ryan could see the coordinates on its screen. "Osborne Bank. About twenty miles past the west end of Catalina," he responded, straining to raise his voice above the clamor.

He then watched Ryan log the same coordinates into the Cigarette's dash-mounted GPS unit.

When they cleared the parallel rock jetties forming the mouth of the harbor, Ryan grabbed three sets of racing goggles from a compartment just forward of the helm seat. "Here," he shouted and handed them each a pair. "These'll help keep your eyes from being blown out of your heads!" Noting Rebecca's trepidation, he added, "Life jackets are inside that seat bench over there, if you want one."

"Oh, thank God," she replied. After taking one of the personal floatation devices for herself, she offered one to Troy as well.

"I'm okay," he shrugged at the offer. He also declined the goggles at first, but when the boat lumbered up on plane and continued to accelerate, he had difficulty keeping his eyes open against the wind produced by the boat's increasing velocity. "I see what you mean!" he yelled and grabbed both the goggles and the life jacket, putting them on with one hand while holding onto a grab-rail with the other.

Ryan glanced down at the speedometer, which was hovering around the fifty-mile-per-hour mark. "You ain't seen nothin' yet!" he shouted and jammed the throttles as far forward as they would go.

When the boat streaked past the ninety-mile-per-hour threshold, Troy's ashen face froze in wide-eyed horror.

"Next stop, Osborne Bank!" Ryan hooted, although he knew neither of them could hear him over the hurricane-force wind blasting past their ears.

Fourteen minutes later, *Huntin' Fun* was skating west along the leeward coast of Catalina Island, a fact that Rebecca could barely comprehend. After Ryan pulled the throttles back to ease the boat down to a comfortable cruise of just under seventy knots, she leaned toward him and announced, "The last time I made the run from Newport to Catalina, it took six *hours* in a sailboat!"

"I know. I grew up thinking a two-hour motor yacht trip was fast. Now if it takes me more than twenty minutes, I feel like I'm going slow!"

Chapter 14

The Cigarette's GPS unit showed they were nearing the bank, and Ryan eased the throttles back to let the boat fall gently off plane. Roughly three miles off their starboard bow, the jagged profile of Santa Barbara Island provided a visual bearing on their location.

"Forty-five minutes to Osborne Bank?" Troy stammered and peeled off his goggles. "That's impossible!"

"Bet you never thought we'd be out here by nine o'clock in the morning," Ryan ribbed him. "Just goes to show you what eighteen hundred horsepower and a hundred gallons of gas can do."

"A hundred gallons of gas in forty-five minutes?" Rebecca nearly choked. "That's not even a half-mile to the gallon! How can you afford to go anywhere in this thing?"

"Hey, time is money. And I know it sounds arrogant, but my time has become way too valuable to waste going anywhere slowly."

"The GPS says we're less than a quarter mile away from the bank," Troy interjected, his voice radiating excitement. "Have you got a depth finder?"

Ryan nodded and switched on another piece of electronics: a full-color, high-resolution depth and fish finder. The unit's five-inch monitor glowed a brilliant blue, with a line of orange traveling across the bottom of the screen to indicate the sea floor passing beneath them. On the left side of the screen, a large numerical readout told them that the depth was exactly nine hundred and seventy-six feet.

"When that orange layer starts moving upward, we'll know we're there," Troy said, and no sooner had the words left his mouth than the bottom line began to climb gradually on the monitor.

Ryan watched the depth finder with rapt attention. "Now, explain to me why we needed to come this far out. I mean, I see dolphins cruising up and down the coast all the time from my bedroom window."

"I'm sure you do," Troy responded. "But those were lucky random sightings of nomadic pods on the move, and I wasn't going to bank a one-day trip on luck."

"So, what's different here?"

"Keep watching and you'll find out."

On the depth-sounder, the bottom line was ascending rapidly; and in the gap between it and the top of the screen, a flurry of small, yellow crescent shapes appeared.

Ryan recognized the graphic depiction of fish. "Whoa, there's a whole lot of something swimming down there."

"Exactly," Troy said. "Feeding time, twenty-four hours a day."

"Upwelling," Rebecca added. "As the bottom current runs into the bank, it rises and brings all the deepwater fish with it."

"Where they congregate at a comfortable dolphin-diving depth of a hundred feet or less," Troy concluded.

Ryan was starting to understand. "I get it. This place is like an all-you-can-eat buffet that dolphins visit whenever they're hungry."

"And that's why *we're* here. Hopefully, we'll be able to keep ourselves in the midst of a feeding pod for a while." Troy watched the line on the depth sounder rise ever higher until it finally leveled off at 120 feet. In a voice loaded with cautious optimism, he announced that they were square over the highest ridge of the bank.

Ryan shut off the growling motors, and the quiet that ensued was, in its own way, nearly as intense.

"Well, I guess this is it," Troy clucked his tongue and took off his jacket. "If you'll excuse me, I've got some work to do." After ducking down into the cabin, he turned around in the narrow hatchway to add, "Let me know if you see anything, okay?"

"Roger that," Ryan winked.

Following Troy's lead, Rebecca wriggled out of her sweats, letting the warm, low sun caress her skin as she adjusted the shoulder straps of her one-piece bathing suit. Fully aware of Ryan's eyes on her body, she pulled a bottle of sunscreen from one of her bags and asked a favor he was unlikely to decline. "Will you do my back?" she asked, sweeping aside the golden cascade of her hair.

"Sure," Ryan replied. Taking the bottle from her hand, he squirted a dollop of lotion onto his palm, and then realized what she was doing.

She was testing him, giving him every opportunity to prove that he could behave himself. While warming the lotion between his hands, he imagined the proverbial angel perched on one of his shoulders and a devil on the other, and as he began to rub in the sunscreen, he had to look away from her body in order to deny the devil a voice. "So, you think Troy'll have any luck today?" He knew his words sounded as flat as if he had just made some banal comment about the weather, but at least they weren't lewd.

"I hope so. He deserves it. Oh, and don't forget my neck."

His hands slowly traveled up the supple curves of her shoulders and the nape of her neck. "How am I doing?"

She'd closed her eyes like a drowsy cat and did not look as if she found his touch unpleasant. "Good. You'd make a great cabana boy."

"I'll keep that in mind," he said, applying a little more pressure with each stroke. "It's nice to know I've got something to fall back on in case this whole Funhunter thing fizzles out."

He stopped rubbing before his sun block application became a full-fledged massage. "Okay, there you go," he said, then gave her shoulders a gentle pat. "Now I'd better get things stowed away around here to make room for Doc's equipment."

Rebecca opened her eyes and dreamily snapped herself back into the moment. "Right. Good idea. I'll give Troy a hand down below."

"No need," Troy announced, making his way out of the narrow companionway with the first piece of equipment. "I'm just bringing things up one piece at a time as I unpack them. But what I *will* need, Ryan, is help getting twelve volts from the boat's batteries to this inverter so I can plug everything in."

"Come on, Doc. Do you think I wouldn't already have an inverter system on board? How else would I run the blender to make margaritas?" Ryan stepped away from the helm and flipped open a hidden panel to reveal a standard three-pronged outlet.

"Then we're almost in business," Troy smiled. "I'll just need a little time here in the cockpit to get things set up." The invitation for them to clear the area was obvious.

Ryan assumed a thick British accent. "Rebecca, I think we have been temporarily relieved of duty. Care to join me for a sunbath on the aft deck?" He motioned toward the cushions covering the engine compartment as if he were inviting her to lounge on the rear deck of a luxury yacht.

"A sunbath sounds divine, darling. And do tell the captain to have the motor-launch ready to ferry us to lunch, will you?"

"You two are crazy," Troy laughed. Darting back and forth between the cabin and cockpit, he began setting up the millions of dollars worth of electronics that so far had proven completely ineffectual.

◆   ◆   ◆

Under a brilliant and crisp blue sky, Ryan and Rebecca dozed in momentary spells for nearly an hour while Troy finished hooking up the last pieces of equipment.

"How's it goin', Doc?" Ryan asked, rolling onto his side and seeing for the first time what had become of his beautiful boat.

In the cockpit, wires and cables were duct-taped in swags to handrails and seat posts, while electronic devices of all sizes—the biggest being a nineteen-inch computer monitor—were scattered across virtually every horizontal surface of *Huntin' Fun's* seats, floor, and helm.

When Rebecca saw the mess, at first all she could do was put a hand over her open mouth. "Gee, Dr. Wallace, I didn't know you'd have to bring this much equipment."

Troy stood amidst the jumble like a dog caught shredding a pair of slippers. "I guess it does seem like a lot of stuff when it's spread all over the floor like this. But I couldn't stack anything for fear that something might fall over while underway."

"Don't worry about it," Ryan said with an open-handed gesture. "I've done a lot more damage than this on some epic harbor cruises. I remember one time during Newport's Christmas Boat Parade…" But he stopped himself when something caught the corner of his eye. Turning to get a better look, he reached into a storage pocket and pulled out a pair of binoculars. A few seconds ticked away as he focused on the image filling his view. "Holy Christ, you're not going to believe this," he said, still scanning the distant horizon.

Though he had turned and was squinting into the same general direction, Troy could not see what Ryan was referring to. "What? What is it?"

Ryan passed over the binoculars. "There must be *hundreds* of them."

Troy peered through the lenses. "It's a mega-pod," he said, his face as animated as if he were seeing the spectacle for the first time. "And you're right, there are *many* hundreds of them." His demeanor became serious. "Rebecca, have a look while I finish hooking everything up."

Grabbing the binoculars, Rebecca raised them just in time to see a member of the pod leap in a soaring arc out of the water. That second was all she needed to recognize the species. "They're commons," she stated.

Troy darted about in frantic bursts. "Of course. Too big of a pod to be bottlenose. Rebecca, I'm going to need a hand getting the transducer in the water. Ryan, it's time to fire the boat back up."

The roar of the engines filled the air with heightened excitement.

Shifting *Huntin' Fun* into gear, Ryan could not help but imagine the unfolding adventure as a segment for his television show. In fact, it was all so perfect—the sleek Cigarette slicing through an indigo sea, the beautiful young woman, and the enormous pod of dolphins—that the scene instantly outgrew the tight confines of television. In his mind, the production exploded into *South Coast Safari: The Movie!* Soon a dramatic musical score backed by thundering drums drifted in, and when a squadron of dolphins rushed up to surf the bow wave, a fanfare of trumpets accompanied the shot.

"I said slow down!" Troy shouted for the third time. He fanned the air downward with one hand while holding onto the transducer's long black cable with the other. "We're going too fast to keep them up at the bow!"

Ryan snapped to attention. Unaware that the first group had given up trying to keep pace with him, he eased the throttles back slowly until Troy gave the okay sign. A quick glance down at the speed log, combined with the appearance of a new congregation of shadows gliding under the boat, informed him that twelve knots seemed to be the perfect speed for bow-surfing dolphins.

With Rebecca's help, the transducer was lowered over the port side, and Troy nervously watched the device tugging at the cord while slicing its way just a foot or two below the surface. Confident that the transducer's cable was securely fastened to the mid-ship cleat, he plugged the other end into the back of the main CPU sitting on the floor. Not wasting a second, he flipped a series of switches on the various devices scattered throughout the cockpit.

The monitor powered up and was soon filled with its familiar solid green glow.

"Here we go," Dr. Wallace said, just loudly enough to be heard over the engines. With fingers crossed, he toggled the last switch needed to complete the circuit from the transducer, through the main CPU, past nearly a dozen noise filters, and finally into the back of the monitor.

But the luminous green square did not respond.

Anxiously tapping his chin, Troy twisted a few dials, flipped a series of filter switches, and stood back once again to stare at the screen.

Nothing changed.

Ryan and Rebecca gave each other quick glances of pained disappointment then lurched in unison as Dr. Wallace let out a sharp, loud cry of self-criticism.

"Of course!" Troy yelped and pounded a closed fist on top of one of the bolsters. "How could I be so stupid?"

"What are you talking about?" Rebecca asked.

"The transducer—it's got to be placed *ahead* of them to receive their transmissions! Come on. Help me untie it so I can move it forward."

An experienced boater and holder of a Coast Guard captain's license, Ryan did not like what he was hearing. "You'd better let me do that. I'll stop the boat for a sec, and—"

"No!" Troy barked. "You don't stop and start up again in the midst of a traveling pod. Sometimes it spooks them and they never come back." With the cable wrapped tightly around his left hand, Troy heaved himself slowly over the windshield and began slithering across the Cigarette's long, flat deck. "All I need to do is tie this off at the bow and we'll be in business," he shouted back.

Against his better judgment, Ryan maintained the boat's slow momentum as Troy belly-crawled forward and lashed the transducer cable to the bow cleat.

"He did it!" Rebecca squealed, pumping a fist into the air.

Ryan was about to breathe a sigh of relief when, as if watching a scene from his movie go horribly wrong, he watched Troy rise to his knees in triumph, slip on the smooth fiberglass deck, lose his balance, and topple overboard backwards into the path of the oncoming boat. Despite the slow-motion feel, the accident happened in seconds.

"Oh my God! Stop!" Rebecca screamed in terror.

But Ryan had already done everything he could do. Although his first impulse told him to slam the drives into reverse, he knew the boat might have already traveled far enough ahead that any reverse motion would mean running over Troy *twice*. Instead he had thrown the shift levers into neutral and hoped that the five-bladed cleaver props would not be spinning by the time the stern of the boat reached Troy.

◆   ◆   ◆

Disoriented but fully aware of what had happened, Troy opened his eyes underwater and watched the Cigarette's slender hull glide over his head. At the last possible second, he spun around and screamed a stream of bubbles as the propellers bore down on him like a pair of gleaming circular saws.

Chapter 15

Ever since his return from Mexico a week ago, Mick Fletcher had become obsessed with the discovery of the subterranean chamber in Tulum. He had plenty of other projects that needed his attention—an astronomy lecture for the Smithsonian Air and Space Museum, a report on the role astrology played in mid-eastern religions—but as he sat in front of his computer, the haunting imagery inside the chamber siphoned the urgency away from every other task crowding his schedule.

His phone, a hulking antique of heavy beige plastic, had been ringing for over a minute before its muffled buzz caught his attention. "United States Naval Observatory, Mick Fletcher here," he announced after pushing the speakerphone button.

"Good morning, Mick. Got yourself acclimated to the weather back in Washington yet?"

It was good to hear George Baylor's voice again. "Just barely, George," Mick smiled toward the phone. "Definitely a lot colder here than in the Yucatan, that's for sure. Got anything new to report from Tulum?"

"I was going to ask you the same question. Any ideas about what we found in the chamber?"

"Are you kidding? I've got a million ideas. It's just that none of them are making much sense yet."

"I know what you mean," Baylor replied. "I keep thinking that we've stumbled onto something quite profound, but I can't put my finger on why I think so."

"Well, we know the ceiling mural depicts the winter solstice of 2012. To the Mayans, there was no date more significant."

"Yes, but there's something else going on in that room that has really got me stumped."

"Me, too." Mick eased back into his sturdy, government-issue chair and rolled his computer's infrared mouse along his thigh. He clicked on the file containing the photos he had taken inside the chamber. "Here we've got all these polarized images—life and death, feast and famine—filling the room," he said, studying the photos on the screen. "I wonder," he said, then paused. "Could it be some kind of *commentary* regarding the end date?"

"I've been thinking about that," Baylor answered. "And if there *is* a statement being made, then what is that statement? The duality of the imagery seems to suggest that you could come up with any meaning you wanted."

Baylor's mention of duality triggered something in Mick's mind. Scrolling through the photographs, he asked, "Do you remember the mural framing the door?"

"Of course. What about it?"

Mick enlarged the picture he'd taken of the chamber's doorway. "That's the one our shaman friend said was some kind of symbol. At the time, that sounded so odd. But now when I look at it, I kind of get what he means." He leaned in to study the two sets of columns, the cascading water, and the dolphins framing the composition. "It's so simple, but there's something really powerful about the design."

"I agree. And of course the Mayans painted it for a reason, but I'll be damned if I can make any sense of it. So far, the best I can come up with is that the water and the opposing sets of columns seem to relate to the last page of the Dresden Codex. You *are* familiar with that particular codex, aren't you?"

"I know a little bit. I know that it's one of only four pre-Columbian Mayan books that the Spanish *conquistadores* didn't burn, and that it somehow turned up in Dresden, Germany in the early 1700s. It's a book dedicated to prophetic visions, right?"

"That's correct, and the last page is a commentary regarding the final day of their calendar."

Mick was drawing a blank. "I'm afraid you'll have to refresh my memory."

"That's easy enough. Go to Google Images and search *Dresden Codex Last Page.*"

"Okay. I'm doing that right now," he said and was soon looking at a screen full of different thumbnail images. "Is there one in particular you want me to enlarge?"

"Yes. See the brightest one…the one with deep oranges and blues? Click on that and then click *See Full Sized Image* at the upper left of the screen.

Following the instructions, Mick was soon staring at the oldest recorded prophecy regarding the Mayan end date. As he studied the graphic, he was taken by the codex's representation of falling water, nearly identical to the falling-water imagery in the chamber. "And did you say there were also opposing twin columns somewhere on this page?" he asked.

"Uh-huh. Look at the square toward the upper right. It almost looks like the face of a wristwatch, doesn't it? A watch with a set of twin columns opposing each other on every side."

Mick squinted. "It does!"

Then Mick saw something else—something that only an expert in socio-astronomy would recognize as important. "What's going on in the middle of the page?" he asked, never taking his eyes off the figure of a mythological character pouring water out of a large urn.

"Ah, yes," Baylor replied. "The water-bearer. No one's sure how she figures into the end-date prophecy. Some say it's the goddess Ixchel, but that's just a guess. And the significance of the water jug? Again, no one knows."

Mick's heart began to race. "Hasn't anyone ever said that this image bears an uncanny resemblance to the zodiac's water-bearer, Aquarius?" As he said this, the skin of his arms began to tingle. "And that the Age of Aquarius just happens to begin within the very same time-frame that the Mayan calendar *ends?*"

Baylor fell silent for a moment. "Not to my knowledge. And *I* certainly never made that connection."

Mick nervously combed his fingers through his hair. "Jesus, this is really getting weird."

"That it is. Ever since Tac-Mol said the doorway mural was some kind of symbol, I've hardly been able to sleep at night. A symbol of what? And for whom?"

Mick clicked back to his own photo of the doorway. "I don't have a clue. Could the columns represent numbers?"

"That's an obvious guess," Baylor acknowledged. "Since *all* ancient Mayan numerals were comprised of parallel lines and dots. But they were usually laid horizontally, not vertically, as in the chamber."

"Right," Mick said. "So it's something else. Have you tried doing any kind of Internet search on similar graphic symbolism?"

"No. Besides, what would I search for? 'Parallel lines divided by two dots?'"

"Maybe that's thinking too far ahead of it. What if you just typed in the graphic exactly as it appears in the room?"

"And how would I do that?"

"Two ones, a colon, and then two more ones," he said, already typing the digits into Google's search box. "I'm doing it right now."

Baylor waited for a few seconds. "And?"

Mick's face tightened in disbelief as he scrolled down the first few matching sites. "George, I'm going to need to get back to you on this."

"I don't understand."

Mick sat frozen in his chair.

"Neither do I."

Chapter 16

Even though Ryan had shifted the boat into neutral, *Huntin' Fun* drifted steadily forward under its own momentum. He scrambled to the stern of the boat, and his heart constricted in terror at the sight of bloodstained water churning beneath the swim step.

"Oh my god!" Rebecca screamed. On impulse, she lunged off the boat then jackknifed her body into a dive. Excruciating seconds elapsed before she surfaced with a panicked gulp for air. "I don't see him!" she called out, choking on a mouth full of water before diving again.

With his pulse pounding in his head and a rush of adrenaline coursing through his veins, Ryan considered his best course of action. He knew that restarting the Cigarette would expose Troy to even more danger, but he also knew there was a better chance of seeing the doctor from higher up in the boat's cockpit. When Rebecca surfaced the second time, he yelled, "I'm starting up and turning around. Stay clear!"

Troy's limp body continued to sink until the remaining air in his lungs neutralized his buoyancy at a depth of twelve feet. With his arms extended outward and his head slumped down, he hung there as if crucified upon an invisible cross.

On his second pass over the area where Troy had fallen overboard, Ryan could just make out Dr. Wallace's motionless form. "There!" he shouted and pointed.

"I can't see anything!" she wailed.

Their life-saving window of time was closing quickly, and Rebecca knew that, if she didn't find Troy on the next dive, he would most likely be dead.

"Right over there—about fifteen feet to your left and ten down!"

With nothing but his instructions to guide her, Rebecca dove again, this time on a perfect intercept course.

Cutting the engines, Ryan sprang from the captain's seat and jumped feet first over the starboard gunwale into the cold water. He then kicked his legs straight up behind him and began to claw his way downward.

Seconds later, he and Rebecca were dragging Dr. Wallace to the surface by his outstretched arms and heaving him up onto the swim-step at the stern of the boat.

Troy sprawled sideways on the step, alternately gasping for air and howling with pain.

Ryan ripped open the sleeve of Troy's wet and bloodied shirt, exposing two clean lacerations in his triceps muscle.

Troy winced and coughed out a few words. "Guess I got cut by one of the props."

"No shit." Ryan lifted the loose flap of skin on each wound to see how deep the propeller had cut.

"I didn't think I was going to make it back up," Dr. Wallace said faintly, shaking with shock and cold.

"You didn't. Rebecca dove down and got you."

"Oh, I am so sorry. Please forgive my carelessness." He intentionally did not look back down at his wounds when he asked Ryan, "How bad is it?"

"Bad enough. Two lacerations—one pretty deep into the muscle. But trust me. It could have been a *lot* worse. Keep some pressure on your arm while I find the first-aid kit."

While Ryan cleaned and dressed the wounds, the three of them were able to reconstruct what had happened and how a major tragedy had been averted. Disoriented but conscious, Troy had opened his eyes underwater and had seen the Cigarette's slender hull gliding over his head. He remembered pushing away from the bottom of the boat, then turning to see and feel the spinning blades of the starboard propeller slice into his left arm. That's when physiology, they deduced, came to Troy's rescue. Cold and starved for oxygen, his brain automatically slowed his heart rate, temporarily stopped his breathing, and constricted the flow of blood to his extremities as his body began to sink.

"Ryan pulled the drives out of gear the second you hit the water," Rebecca explained, her own heart still racing. "If he hadn't, I don't think you'd still be with us."

"Those props are as sharp as razors," Ryan added. "They could've sliced your whole arm off in a second."

Troy breathed out an anguished sigh. "Thank you. I don't know how I could have been so stupid." He let out a groan as Ryan wrapped his arm with a thick gauze bandage. "Did I at least get the transducer cleated securely?"

"It's still up there," Ryan confirmed after glancing up to the bow.

"That's good. At least I didn't get chewed up for nothing. We still have a lot of work to do."

Rebecca's mouth dropped open. "What? You don't think we're actually going to stay out here! We've got to get you back home and to a hospital!"

Dr. Wallace pulled his arm out of Rebecca's grasp. "No. I'm not going anywhere until we've given that transducer a chance."

Rebecca reached out and laid a hand on Troy's shoulder. "Dr. Wallace, you've got to get those cuts looked at right away."

Troy looked up, engaging in solid eye contact with her. "Rebecca, I'm grateful for your concern, but I am not leaving until we've given the equipment a chance to work. If I have to, I'll jump out of this boat again to keep us from going back."

Ryan shook his head in disbelief while fashioning a sling out of two beach towels. "You are one ornery son of a gun," he quipped while tying the towels together.

◆   ◆   ◆

Less than an hour later, with his wounds cleaned and stabilized to the best of Ryan's ability, Dr. Wallace took command of the expedition once again. Reclining on the boat's bench seat, he directed his crew with a rallying vigor that surprised them. "Ryan, go ahead and start the boat and get it up to the speed where we had the dolphins surfing before. Rebecca, if you would, make sure the transducer lead is securely fastened to the back of the main processing unit."

His assistants sprang into action, and soon the Cigarette was gamboling amongst the enormous pod once again. When the boat hit the magic speed of twelve knots, a flank of seven large dolphins swooped in to romp and play in the bow wave.

"Everybody's fingers crossed?" Troy called out. With his lacerated arm held tight in the sling, he directed Rebecca to flip a final series of toggles on the equipment. As each piece beeped and clicked to life, the three of them stared intently down at the video monitor resting on the floor.

"So, what are we supposed to be seeing?" Ryan asked, watching the screen fill with an undulating blob of green light.

Troy's eyes were fixed on the monitor. "Something more interesting than this," he said. "What I hope we'll get is some kind of definable structure ... a recognizable shape rather than these random forms."

A curious thought came to Rebecca. "Dr. Wallace, what if these images *aren't* random?" she asked. "I mean, maybe these shapes are like little abstract art projects they send to each other to pass the time. Or maybe there's a definite meaning attached to each pattern, like with Japanese writing."

"Those are two very definite possibilities," Troy agreed. "But if that's the case, then all we've got is an indecipherable language, and that's not what we're here for. This project lives or dies not just with the interception of their transmissions, but the comprehension of them."

Ryan fixed his attention on the free-forming images floating across the screen. With mounting excitement, he began to grasp the enormity of what it would mean to be present the moment mankind not only eavesdropped on another animal's conversations, but actually understood them.

As the morning wore on, however, it seemed obvious that no new discoveries were going to be made that day.

With defeat and dejection in his eyes, Troy motioned for Ryan to stop the boat.

Ryan switched off the ignitions. "What's going on, Doc?"

Troy held his throbbing arm and turned away. "I think I need to rest a bit." Without waiting for a reply, he got up from the bench and ducked into the companionway hatch leading into the cabin. "Will one of you keep an eye on the monitor for me?"

"You bet," Rebecca said with a thumbs-up, but there was no hiding the fading optimism in her voice.

"So, are we done trying to keep up with the pod?" Ryan asked toward the open hatchway.

"For now, yes," Troy replied. "Besides, they'll probably keep feeding here at the bank for a while. Maybe we'll catch a random transmission or two as they swim by."

"Aye, aye, captain," Ryan saluted with a smile that disappeared the moment Troy closed the cabin door.

Rebecca sat down next to Ryan and lowered her voice to a whisper. "So, what should we do now?"

"I'll tell you what we should do. We *should* get him back home and to a hospital, but I don't think he's ready to give up just yet. And since we did get his arm to stop bleeding, I suppose it's safe to stay out here a little longer. Tell you what—we'll give it another hour. By then he'll probably be okay with heading back."

Rebecca nodded, then grabbed a towel from one of her bags and proceeded to make herself comfortable on the upholstered sun pads at the stern of the boat. Lying on her back and turning her head to one side, she had a clear view of the monitor on the floor. "I'll keep an eye on the screen if you want to rest a bit," she volunteered.

"Naw, I'll watch it for a while."

"I was hoping you'd say that. After all, I did get up at four o'clock this morning for this little adventure. You sure you don't mind if I take a little nap?"

"I'm sure. Besides, I'm kind of enjoying the view," he said, allowing himself a quick scan of her figure.

"Hey, you watch the screen, mister," she pretended to scold before rolling onto her side. Curling up into a relaxed fetal position as the sun warmed her body, she quickly fell asleep.

Long, quiet minutes passed. The Cigarette bobbed languidly upon the calm surface of the ocean, and though Ryan did his best to keep a vigilant watch, he too found himself beginning to nod off. With his arms crossed against his chest and his head tilting ever lower, he felt himself drifting further away from consciousness. Then, with a restless twitch, he snapped his head up and opened his eyes for a fraction of a second.

And that was when he saw it.

He was groggy enough to think he might be dreaming, but the longer he stared at the monitor, the more he realized the image being displayed on it was definitely no figment of his imagination. All he could say was, "What—what the hell is that?" as if he had just seen a ghost.

Rebecca sprang up from the sun pad. "What are you talking about?"

Ryan did not answer her. "Troy!" He opened the hatch and bellowed down into the cabin. "Troy, get out here right now!"

"What is it?" Rebecca asked, this time with alarm. It hadn't dawned on her to look down at the monitor. When she noticed where Ryan was staring, she darted toward the helm and steadied herself by hanging onto his shoulder.

Troy emerged as quickly as he could from the cabin, shielding his eyes against the blinding sun. "What's all the racket about?"

Ryan was holding his head between his hands, still in a state of shock. "I saw something on the monitor, and it was just like you said! It had a definite shape."

A quick glance down at the monitor revealed that it looked no different than it had before. "A shape? What kind of shape?"

Ryan was nearly panting. "I don't know. It kind of looked like a flower."

Troy looked at the screen once more, then back at Ryan with an injured expression. "Ryan, if this is some kind of joke ..."

"I swear to you I saw it! It had these five rounded petals!"

But Ryan didn't need to continue, for there on the monitor another distinguishable image appeared.

The hair on the back of Troy's neck sprang up.

"That's it!" Ryan yelled. "See? I told you! But wait, this time there's only *four* petals on the flower."

Dr. Wallace knelt down for a closer inspection. "Ryan, that's not a flower. Don't you see? It's a propeller. A boat propeller. Look at the detail in the pitch and shape of each blade."

Incredibly, they were looking at a perfect, three-dimensional reproduction of a four-bladed propeller. The image was breathtaking in its precise detail, the variably-shaded green surface portraying incredible depth, form, even texture. Seconds later, an exact replica of one of *Huntin' Fun's* cleaver props filled the screen, which was then followed by an underwater view of the entire bottom of the Cigarette's stepped hull.

Then, to their astonishment, the hull—complete with its twin drives, trim tabs and twirling propellers—began to *move* across the screen like a short animated video.

Hardly able to believe what they were seeing, the three of them watched in stunned silence as a perfect duplicate of Dr. Wallace fell into the scene and was slashed on the arm by one of the whirling props.

After that, the screen went blank.

Ryan held a clenched fist up to his mouth. "Okay, we did not just see that," he said flatly. "Those images could *not* have come from a dolphin."

Dr. Wallace, though ecstatic, kept his wits about him. He had to know the reason for the sudden success. "Ryan, quick! Look over the side and tell me if you can see the dolphin that transmitted the sonograms."

Leaning far over the starboard gunwale, Ryan peered into the water and was able to make out the distinct shapes of a pair of dolphins swimming directly below the Cigarette. "Yeah!" he shouted. "There are two. One's big, maybe six or seven feet. The other one's real small— probably no more than three feet long."

The revelation came to Troy and Rebecca in the same instant.

"A mother and her calf," Rebecca intoned with quiet awe.

"A mother and her calf," Troy echoed.

"Um, am I missing something here?" Ryan asked.

"No," Troy replied. "*I'm* the one who's been missing something."

Ryan was confused. "And what does *that* mean?" he begged.

"It means that we can go home now," Dr. Wallace answered with a serene smile.

"What? Are you serious? You finally get this equipment to work, and all of a sudden you're ready to go home?"

"Ryan, I know it might not seem logical to you, but trust me on this. We've accomplished more than I ever would have thought possible today. Right now, I think the best thing to do is get ourselves packed up and headed back to Newport."

Rebecca seemed to pick up on the urgency in Troy's words and movements.

"Troy, before we start packing, maybe we should take a look at your arm."

He flinched involuntarily. "My arm?"

"Yes, your arm," she said, unwinding the gauze bandage. Each layer became increasingly bloody. When the damage was laid bare, she inhaled sharply. The lacerations had begun to bleed again, and she knew she would not be able to staunch the flow with a simple dressing. "Dr. Wallace, this is serious."

"Jesus Christ, Doc," Ryan fumed. "Why didn't you tell us?"

"It doesn't matter," Rebecca said. "We have to get him to the nearest hospital as soon as possible. Is that Newport?"

After firing up the engines and making his way up to the deck to un-cleat the transducer, Ryan scrambled back into the helm seat and jammed the shifters forward.

"No, Avalon. I figure we can make it there in about fifteen minutes."

Seconds later, the Cigarette was thrusting them across the calm Pacific like a missile on a direct course to Santa Catalina Island.

Chapter 17

With a call from *Huntin' Fun's* VHF radio, Ryan alerted the staff at Catalina Island Medical Center of their arrival. Banking the Cigarette into the sheltered waters of Avalon Harbor, he could see the ambulance already making its way to the base of the city's renowned pleasure pier, which bisected the bay.

Troy noticed the small crowd of onlookers that had begun to gather upon the bright turquoise pier. "This is embarrassing. Don't those people have anything better to do?"

Ryan slowed the boat to idle and expertly maneuvered it through the orderly rows of yachts moored in the harbor. "Hey, not much goes on around here in the off season. You'll probably even be on the front page of the weekly newspaper."

Rebecca, obviously calmed by the fact that professional help was near, scanned Avalon's jumbled assemblage of vacation cottages, restaurants, and souvenir shops lining the bay. "This place sure hasn't changed much over the years, has it?"

"Nope," Ryan agreed. "It's like the whole town's stuck in some nineteen-forties time warp." With a wave up to the harbormaster monitoring their approach, he reminisced over the hundreds of crossings he had made in his life to the island. "I suppose that's why I keep coming back—it reminds me that Southern California wasn't always freeways and shopping malls."

After laying the Cigarette up to a section of dock usually reserved for a sight-seeing boat, Ryan helped two paramedics escort Troy and Rebecca onto the gangway leading up to the pier. Then, after getting the nod that his assistance was no longer needed, he climbed back into *Huntin' Fun*, re-started the motors and headed for the nearest white spherical mooring can dotting the bay's placid waters. "I'll find you after I get moored up," he shouted over his shoulder.

Once the boat was secured to a permanently anchored mooring line, Ryan hailed Avalon's water taxi on the VHF radio. Less than twenty minutes after their arrival, he was on shore and making his way on foot to the hospital, a half-mile away on the inland side of the tiny town.

He could feel the anxiety beginning to build inside him as he entered the hospital's lobby. "Hi, I'm Ryan Ericson, and I need to know how Dr. Troy Wallace is doing."

Just as the nurse was beginning to explain that he would have to wait to speak to a doctor, Rebecca appeared from a nearby office, smiling and shaking hands with the physician who had apprised her of Dr. Wallace's condition. Taking Ryan's arm, she led him back outside.

"It's all right. Troy's going to be fine," she began. "It'll take a couple of hours to stitch up his arm, and they want to hold him overnight to make sure there's no infection."

Ryan nodded solemnly.

"They said he was lucky," she explained, tracing a finger down the back of Ryan's arm to demonstrate. "The prop missed his subclavian artery, which is right here, by less than a quarter of an inch. If that artery had been severed, Troy probably would have bled to death no matter how soon we got him here."

Ryan sat down on a tiled bench outside the hospital, breathing deeply while he collected his thoughts. "Well, this certainly has been an eventful day, hasn't it?"

Rebecca eased onto the bench beside him and stared out over the tranquil expanse of ocean in the distance. "You can say that again. I'm having trouble believing any of it—Troy's accident, of course, but especially what we saw on the monitor. I mean, did we really see the images dolphins transmit to each other?"

Ryan slowly rubbed his hand over his face. "I can't get them out of my head. And I think I finally caught on to why you and Troy were excited about them being sent from a mother to her baby. It's like we were watching a safety education video—"

"On the things dolphins should stay away from, right?" she interrupted. "It's like you instantly understood what she was saying with each image! 'Now, Junior, these are all different kinds of propellers, and you don't want to get too close to them. Why, look at what happened just a few minutes ago to that poor human who fell off this very boat.'"

"Right!" Ryan blurted. "Jesus, can you imagine how much Troy could learn if he got his own mother-and-baby pair like that to do his tests on?"

"I'm sure he's already working on a plan to make that happen."

"And I'm curious," Ryan wondered aloud. "Since his equipment never worked before, does that mean dolphins only use this kind of picture language when they're teaching their young?"

The same thought had crossed her mind. "I don't know. But a three-dimensional sonogram sure would be a valuable teaching tool, wouldn't it?"

"Kind of like a virtual show-and-tell," he surmised. Then, as if it had taken this long for less important details to catch up with the more dramatic events of the day, he replayed in his head something she said just a few minutes before. "Um, did you say Troy had to spend the night in the hospital?"

"Uh-huh, but they're pretty sure he'll be up to making the trip home by tomorrow morning. Why?"

Ryan fidgeted on the bench. "No reason. It's just that we're going to have to figure out some kind of sleeping arrangements."

"Sleeping arrangements? I just assumed we'd be staying on your boat. I mean, we can't leave Troy's equipment unattended, right?"

Ryan hadn't given a thought to the equipment. "Oh, right," he agreed. "But you *do* know there's just the one V-berth in the cabin."

"Yeah, so. It's big enough for two people, isn't it?"

Her candor caught him off guard. "Well, yes. But those two people just so happen to be you and me."

"What are you saying? That I wouldn't be safe spending the night with you?"

"Of course not. It's just that, after our conversation at the pizza place, you obviously know where I'm coming from."

"And you know the same about me. But just in case there's any confusion on your part, let me state it as clearly as possible. Nothing's going to happen on your boat tonight. Do I need to make it any clearer than that?"

He searched her eyes for a mixed signal, maybe a hint of weakness or vulnerability, but saw only conviction. "Okay," he said with surprisingly little damage to his ego. Even so, he had to ask the question. "Is—is it because there's still something you don't like about me?"

With her amber eyes glimmering into the soft afternoon light, she placed one hand delicately on his knee.

"No, Ryan," she said. "It's because there's something I *do*."

◆　　　◆　　　◆

After strolling through the seaside town for a few hours and absorbing the quaint, nostalgic aura of the community, Ryan and Rebecca headed back to the hospital to check on Dr. Wallace. They were relieved to find him alert in his bed, already sitting up.

"Hey, you two!" Troy beamed and waved with his good arm.

"Hey, Doc," Ryan smiled back. "They get you sewn up okay?"

"Ninety-three stitches later, they sure did. And it looks like there's no threat of infection, either."

"That's wonderful," Rebecca chimed in. "And they're going to let you out of here tomorrow?"

"Uh-huh," Troy nodded, rubbing the front side of his bandaged arm.

They all waited to see who was going to continue the conversation from there.

Troy finally broke the pregnant silence. "So, I guess we know that the new transducer works." His grin was infectious.

Rebecca rolled her eyes. "Now *there's* an understatement. I'm still kind of in shock at what we saw out there today."

"Me, too," Ryan added. "It's like a dream, or something out of a science fiction movie."

Troy lay back in the bed. "It *was* incredible, wasn't it? In a million years, I never would have imagined that we'd get that kind of resolution! And of course, the real breakthrough was discovering that dolphins use ultrasonic holograms almost like instructional videos." His voice grew hushed with wonderment. "Do you have any idea of the implications? Can you even begin to imagine what we might learn by eavesdropping on a dolphin history lesson?"

Ryan pondered the absurdity of being a part of such a monumental discovery, which in turn made him wonder how dolphin sonograms could have evaded marine scientists for so long. He broached the subject as tactfully as possible. "Doc, how is it that no one figured this out before? I mean, you can't be the only scientist in the world working on this stuff."

Troy pursed his lips. "You're quite right," he replied, his tone sobered by Ryan's observation. "I'm sure that there *are* others out there who are conducting similar experiments. And for all I know, they might even be farther along with this research than I am."

Rebecca recoiled at Troy's supposition. "But if that were true, wouldn't you have heard about it?"

"Not if they've had results similar to what we saw out there today. The scientific community is very possessive when it comes to significant discoveries like this." Suddenly, Troy's expression shifted to brooding anxiety.

"What's wrong?" Rebecca asked.

With his eyes taking on a distant look, Dr. Wallace explained his concerns in one brief sentence. "It just dawned on me how careful we need to be from here on out." It sounded like a statement that would be followed by a long explanation, but he did not elaborate any further during the rest of their visit.

◆   ◆   ◆

Following a late-night dinner of cheeseburgers and margaritas at a tiki-themed bar called *Luau Larry's*, Ryan and Rebecca caught the water taxi to his boat moored in the harbor. A marine layer of condensation had arrived with the darkness, leaving the Cigarette's open cockpit and decks as wet as if it had just rained.

Stepping off the bobbing taxi, Rebecca slipped on *Huntin' Fun's* swim step and fell back into Ryan's waiting arms.

"Okay, let's not go through *that* again," he said, helping her over the lounge pads and down into the forward cabin. With the flip of a few switches, the long, narrow cabin—finished in brushed stainless steel and ultra suede upholstery—lit up like a nightclub built for two.

"Gee, how cozy," Rebecca groaned sarcastically. "Who decorated this thing? Hugh Hefner?"

"Hey, they don't call these *stabbin' cabins* for nothing."

"Eww, that's disgusting," she said, fumbling in her bag for a scrunchie to hold her hair back. "And let me guess. You've probably entertained your fair share of groupies down here."

"Actually, I've only had this boat a couple of months. Believe it or not, you're my first overnight guest."

Gathering her hair into a ponytail, she took one last look around the plush cabin. "Well, I guess that maybe makes it a little less creepy. Can you at least tone down the lounge-lizard lights?"

"Your wish is my command," he answered and turned off every fixture except two low-voltage dome lights directly over the V-berth. "How's that?"

"Much better. Now, do you have any sheets and pillows?"

"Sort of." He pulled out a fuzzy leopard-print blanket and two zebra-striped throw-pillows from a small hanging locker. "It's not like I do a lot of camping in this thing, you know."

With playful exasperation, she snatched the blanket and pillows, crawled into the forward berth, and stretched out with a yawn. "Wow. This certainly has been an incredible day, hasn't it?" she proclaimed while peeling off her jeans and jacket. Her swimsuit stayed on, shimmering in the faint light and accentuating the shapeliness of her body.

Pouring himself a shot of the Patron Silver Tequila that he kept in the cabin's wet bar, Ryan sat down on the settee aft of the bunk. "*Incredible* doesn't even come close."

"I'll never forget it," she mused, then added, "for many reasons."

He took a swig and let the tequila linger on his tongue before swallowing it. There was so much he wanted to say. But as he stared into his glass, all he could come up with was, "Same here."

Rebecca picked up on his hesitation. "Oh? Care to elaborate?"

Ryan settled back into the short sofa and kicked off his shoes. He could feel his pulse beginning to throb in his temples. "I was afraid you were going to ask me that," he said with a nervous laugh.

He poured himself another shot.

"I guess," he began. "I guess I'm just having trouble getting myself synched up with everything that's happened lately: meeting Vern, you and Doc, and then seeing what we saw today. It almost feels like too much to handle."

"Even the part about meeting me?"

Ryan let out an involuntary sniff of a laugh. "Are you kidding?"

"I see."

"No, I don't think you do. And I know this is going to sound like some totally rehearsed line, but I have to say that I've never met a girl like you before. And it's not just because you're this beautiful dolphin trainer." He took a moment to organize his thoughts. "It's more than that. There's something about you that I never would've thought I'd find appealing, but somehow you *make* it appealing."

She could tell he was having trouble expressing himself, but she could also feel the genuineness in his words. "And what is that?"

"I don't know. It's like you always seem to have an answer for everything, which is usually a real turnoff for me, but..."

He stopped, as if he'd lost his place reading a cue card.

She waited.

"But with you, it doesn't sound all opinionated or preachy—it just feels like the right answer. Do you get what I'm trying to say?"

She took a moment to digest his assessment. "I think so. And what you're talking about started for me back in back in high school. That's when it dawned on me that there really *might be* some kind of always-right answer that I could apply to any situation in my life. I chased it for a while, thinking I might find it in religion, then psychology, but it never really hit me until I stumbled into a dolphin healing session in Florida more than ten years ago. That's when I got my first real taste of *it*."

He shifted to make himself more comfortable on the couch. "Okay, now that you've got my undivided attention, are you going to tell me what *it* is?"

Her words flowed out in a gentle stream. "It's love. *Love* is always the right answer."

Ryan waited to hear the rest of her explanation, but nothing followed. "I'm not sure I know exactly what that means."

"I didn't either until I saw it happen between a boy and a dolphin. It was at one of those swim-along places in Florida. I was driving a group of girls down for spring break, when, all of a sudden, they made me turn off. Next thing I knew, I was watching this incredible encounter—this unconditional act of healing and love—that challenged me to always try and do the same, no matter the circumstance."

Ryan had touched the surface of this with her during dinner at the Italian restaurant, but he could not have guessed how strongly she felt about it. "Go on," he coaxed.

"Well, everyone from Buddha to Gandhi to Martin Luther King has talked about it, but I think Jesus said it best. One day, so the story goes, he was out walking with his disciples when one of them asked: *Teacher, how many times should I forgive someone who has wronged me? Seven?* And Jesus said something like, *Seven? Are you kidding? Try seventy times seven!* Which, to me, means: *Do you hear the absurdity of what you're even asking? Once you learn the right answer, it never stops being the right answer!*"

"And that's what you truly believe? That there's never a time for anything but love?"

"In its various forms—forgiveness, kindness, compassion—yes. It's really as simple as that."

Ryan was willing to acknowledge the nobility of her beliefs, but he could hardly imagine the practicality of them. "Impossibly simple, if you ask me. I mean, of course we all know those things are the right things, but everyone has their limits."

"Then they should be honest with themselves, own up to those limits, and admit that they are still trying to work things out. They shouldn't brag about how patient they are if what they really mean is that they're only patient until something pisses them off."

He fidgeted on the couch, recalling specific incidences in his life that seemed to prove her point. "You know, I remember as a kid, if I got into trouble my dad would always say something like, 'Ryan, I'm a very tolerant man, but what you just did …' And then he would let me have it—yell, cuss, spank."

"Ah, there it is," Rebecca interjected. "The infamous *but*. 'Of course I believe in forgiveness, *but*. I'm all for peace, *but*. I'm not one to judge, *but*.' Don't you get it? If you can only stand by your convictions just so long as they're not being challenged, then they're not really convictions, are they? In the end, all you're doing is proving that you don't really believe the things you say about yourself."

Ryan finished the tequila with a loud gulp. "I suppose I get what you're saying. But in this day and age, I don't think there are very many people who are willing to stick to their principles like that." As he spoke, the word *age* reminded him of the conversation they'd had where she explained the workings of the Mayan calendar.

She rolled over and looked at him in the dim light.

"Maybe not," she agreed. "But don't forget, according to the Mayans, *this* age is almost over."

Chapter 18

Outwardly, Newport's familiar landmarks—the stately Pavilion restaurant, the Balboa Island Ferry shuttling its first load of cars onto the peninsula—looked just like they did the day before. But as Ryan eased the Cigarette through the Bay following a smooth crossing from Catalina, he knew that something was different.

He was different, forever changed by the fact that, as far as he knew, he was the first human in history to view the picture-language of dolphins.

Idling through the harbor and watching people take their Sunday morning strolls along its perimeter, he could not help thinking that, in some way, each one of them would be affected by what had happened yesterday on his boat.

Upon their arrival at the Lido Dry Slip, Ryan switched the engines off for the last time. "Mission accomplished?" he asked while thoughtfully rubbing the morning stubble on his face.

Troy shook his head at Ryan's understated question. "Mission accomplished," he confirmed. Cradling his bandaged arm, he looked up and gazed deeply into Ryan's eyes. "And, Ryan, I want you to know that I will never forget everything you've done for me. Thank you."

Ryan felt the blood rushing to his face. He turned away and watched the first rays of sunlight stream across the water. "It—it was an honor to take part in your discovery."

"I'll second that," Rebecca chimed in while giving them both a tender pat on the back. "And, Troy, if you don't mind me asking, what happens now?"

Her question brought a troubled look to his face.

"Well, there are a few different options I need to consider." His halting speech conveyed that he was still unsure of how to proceed. "But the minute I figure something out, you two will be the first to know. Until then, I hope it's understood that what we saw yesterday must not be discussed with anyone. Am I making myself clear about this?"

Ryan mimed zipping his lips. "You've got my word on it."

"Me too," Rebecca concurred.

Troy took a deep breath, exhaled slowly, and relaxed a little. "That's good to hear. Now, let's get this stuff packed up. I've got a lot of work ahead of me."

It did not take them long to get the equipment off the boat and transferred back to Troy's van in the Dry Slip parking lot. When the last piece of gear had been loaded, they gathered together beside Ryan's Mercedes to say their final good-byes.

"So, I guess this is it, huh?" Ryan asked while unlocking the car's door. "The end of our adventure."

Troy smiled and held out his uninjured arm, beckoning them into a group hug. As they stood there holding each other, their heads nearly touching, he whispered the thought that had been swirling around in his mind since seeing that first image on the monitor. "Trust me, Ryan, this adventure is just beginning."

Rebecca looked at Ryan and gave him a secret smile that set his heart racing. "And I love beginnings," she said softly. "Especially when it's the beginning of something you just know is going to be wonderful."

Though none of them seemed in a hurry to end the embrace, eventually Troy gave them both a fatherly rub on the head and turned toward his van.

"Shall we go?" he asked Rebecca, and lifted himself up slowly into the cab.

"You sure you're okay to drive?"

He looked down at his arm. "You mean this? Heck, it would take a lot more than a couple of scratches to keep me down."

With a lingering look at Ryan, Rebecca climbed into the van's passenger seat and kept waving good-bye until she could no longer see him in her rearview mirror.

Ryan slid into the Mercedes and started it with the intent of heading straight for home.

But while driving down the peninsula, a startling new realization came to him—a realization that forced him to take an unexpected detour.

◆   ◆   ◆

Toiling in the early morning shadow of Newport's Municipal Pier, the men of the dory fleet were settling into the predictable rhythm of the day.

Nestled inside his locker on the beach, Vern took a sip of coffee and leafed through the morning newspaper scattered across an old oak desk. He did not react one way or another to the knock upon the shed's open door.

"Anybody home?" Ryan asked, poking his head into the small room.

The old fisherman seemed momentarily oblivious. "Nobody important," he replied, and greeted Ryan with a casual nod into the tight confines of the locker. "You're welcome to come in if you like."

Ryan took a halting step forward and squeezed himself in amongst stacks of yellowing newspapers and retired fishing equipment. "I suppose you're wondering why I'm here." His voice broke slightly as he hoisted himself up onto a rusting stool.

Vern wrinkled his nose and turned a page. "No more than I wonder why I'm still here after nearly sixty years."

Vern's ready response threw off Ryan's timing. "Well, just in case you *were* curious, it's because we—I don't know—it seems like maybe we didn't finish our conversation the other night."

"We didn't?" Vern eyes remained focused on the newspaper.

Ryan cleared his throat. "Or maybe we did. All I know for sure is that this has been one hell of a week, and it started with something you said."

"Guess you'll have to refresh my memory."

"Well, you said you wondered why some people are drawn to the ocean when there's no logical reason for a land animal to feel such a thing."

Vern nodded slowly and smiled. "Ah, yes, I remember that."

"You know what, though? I don't think you wonder about that at all. You can't live around dolphins your whole life and not know that *they* were the first land-dwellers to feel the lure of the sea."

"No, I suppose you can't," Vern admitted.

"So why didn't you say that the other night?"

The old fisherman took off his hat and rubbed his balding head. "Because I still haven't figured it all out myself, that's why," he finally answered. "Listen, when you've spent as much time around dolphins as I have, you can't help but notice …" His voice trailed off before he finished the sentence.

"Can't help but notice what?" Ryan prodded.

Vern hesitated. "How smart they are."

Not grasping the point the old fisherman was trying to make, Ryan leaned against the locker's plywood wall and crossed his arms. "Listen, I hate to be the one to break it to you, but lots of people are aware of how smart they are."

"You see. That's just what I'm talking about. People think they know everything there is to know about dolphins, but they don't."

Ryan fidgeted on the stool. "Yeah? How do you mean?"

Vern folded the newspaper, then reached into a drawer of the desk and pulled out an old *National Geographic* magazine with a dolphin on the cover. "Best as I can tell you, it seems to me like they know something—something important—that we haven't figured out yet."

"And why do you believe this?"

"Because I've spent so much time out there with 'em, that's why. And it might sound crazy to you, but I swear I have watched them *think*. I'll sit in my boat studyin' what they do, and I'll be damned if I don't feel like *I'm* the one being studied. I can't count how many times one of 'em has come right up to my boat and just stared at me for the longest time."

Vern's voice became distant.

Ryan tried to bring him back. "Okay, so they're observant, or curious, or whatever you want to call it. So what?"

"So what? Don't you get it? They're not just curious. It's like they're *learning*—studying us, taking notes, keeping records, just like we do with them."

With Vern's suppositions beginning to overlap what happened yesterday on his boat, Ryan pensively stroked his chin and asked, "Keeping records? And just how do you suppose a dolphin would go about keeping and sharing these records?"

"I don't know," he shrugged. "Maybe it's just something they remember and pass on to one another," Vern surmised before replacing his cap and stuffing the magazine back into the desk.

Ryan closed his eyes tightly and rubbed them hard with his fingertips. "That's quite a theory. And just for kicks, let's say you're right—that they have been keeping records of some kind. Do you suppose—?"

Vern leaned in. "Suppose what?"

"Do you suppose we'll ever be able to access those records?"

Vern looked out through the shed's open door toward the surging ocean. "Well, if you're asking me if I think we'll ever have a conversation with a dolphin, my answer would be no. But maybe..." he said, pushing himself up out of his chair.

Ryan waited nervously to hear the rest of it.

Vern shuffled toward the door. Stopping at the threshold, he turned and let his tired blue eyes meet Ryan's.

"Maybe, someday, we'll figure out a way to eavesdrop on the conversations they have with each other."

Chapter 19

For Jerry Spears, it was a morning like any other. The sun was too bright, the air too hot and sticky. The birds swarming in the trees were nearly as loud and obnoxious as the dark-skinned children playing in the dirt street outside his window.

He rolled his large body over in bed to face the tight confines of his rented room. Propping himself up on one elbow, he reached for the joint on the nightstand. Had the phone not rung, it would have been impossible to differentiate this day from the thousands that had gone by since Troy left.

But the phone did ring. He had forgotten how loud it was, and as he sat there listening to the rotary-dialed relic, he wondered how he should answer. "Yes?" he finally said, putting the receiver to his ear while fumbling around for his glasses.

"Hello," an unfamiliar voice replied. "Is this Jerry Spears?"

Jerry scanned his memory, but he could not come up with a face to match the voice on the other end of the line. "Who wants to know?"

"My name is Calvin Brooks, and if you *are* Jerry Spears, I met you a long time ago at the dolphin research facility there on Tortola."

The scene came back to him in an instant. "Of course, Mr. Brooks!" He heaved himself up and swiped his matted red hair away from his sweating face. "It's a pleasure to hear from you again. How long has it been?" Jerry asked, strictly to make conversation. He knew to the day how long it had been.

"Nearly fifteen years," Calvin answered. "Can you believe it?"

Unable to come up with anything other than a sarcastically bitter reply, Jerry held his peace and let Calvin tell him the reason for his call.

"Listen, I'm trying to track down Dr. Wallace. Have you heard from him lately?"

Again Jerry remained silent.

"Hello? Are you still there?"

"I'm here," Jerry replied at length, "but I haven't heard from Troy in ages. Last I knew, he was doing some work in San Diego. Aren't you still funding his research?"

"We *were*. Just a few days ago, Chad and I went down to see the newest version of his transducer, which, I'm sorry to say, didn't work any better than all the others. At that point, we let Troy know we were finally finished underwriting his experiments."

Jerry hung onto every word. "What happened after that?"

"Well, we gave him a week to wrap things up, but when I stopped by a few days later to check on how things were going, I discovered that he and about half of the equipment were gone."

Jerry held the receiver away from his face while his mind raced ahead of the conversation. "What do you mean, gone?"

"His phone numbers are disconnected. His apartment's vacant. He just disappeared with roughly three million dollars worth of my gear."

"And you're wondering if he might have shown up back here with it."

"I thought it was at least worth a phone call. Is that little research facility of yours even still there?"

There was no reason to lie, but Jerry did anyway. "Barely. Place's all falling apart. Completely unusable."

"I figured as much. Okay then, if you do happen to see or hear from Troy, can I give you my number? Any information would be greatly appreciated."

"Sure thing," Jerry said, then he repeated the telephone number as if he were actually writing it down.

◆   ◆   ◆

Twilight had fallen on the island, and amidst the sounds of the tiny village coming to life—people venturing out of their homes to stroll the neighborhood, a reggae band practicing in the front yard across the street, animals of all sorts bleating and barking and cackling in the cool evening—the phone rang for the second time that day.

Jerry let it ring a few times while he practiced his greeting. "Good evening," he announced over the phone's repeated clang.

"Good *evening!*"

Brrrring.

"This is Jerry."

Brrrring.

"Good evening, Jerry Spears here."

Brrrring.

A smart-mouthed child stuck his head into the open window and said, "First you pick up de phone, *den* you answer it."

"Shut up, you little brat!"

After the next ring, he cleared his throat and announced, "Good evening, this is Jerry."

Troy was glad and more than a little surprised to hear Jerry sounding so alert. "Hi, Jerry. It's me," was all he said.

Jerry had rehearsed his reaction all day. "Troy? Wow, what a pleasant surprise! How have you been?"

"Not bad. And you? Have you been doing much research lately?" Troy asked as casually as if they had just chatted last week.

So this is how it was going to be.

"Well, I made some progress with my tonal experiments," Jerry replied, trying to keep contempt out of his voice. "Even had some decent repetition and mimicry going on for a while. And what about you? How's your sonographic work going?"

"Oh, you know, still pluggin' away."

It was time to tighten the noose a little. "Any luck?"

"Nothing significant, but that hasn't stopped me yet."

Using the information he'd received earlier that day, Jerry knew he would be able to maneuver around Dr. Wallace's deception. "I know what you mean. You still being funded by those guys at the salvage company?"

"Yes, but they're finally starting to lose interest. They've given me a few more weeks to test a new 'ducer design, but after that I'll be on my own."

"I see. So, what can I do for you?" He didn't need to ask, but he wanted to hear Troy's fabrication just the same.

Troy cleared his throat. "I was wondering—how's the facility holding up these days. Is it still standing?"

"Are you kidding? That place will probably outlast us both, and I'm pretty sure the floodgate to the lagoon still works. Why?"

"I was just thinking that, you know, it would be kind of fun to finish up my work down where it all began. Do you think you could spruce things up to where I could run a few tests? I'd pay you for your time, of course."

"Sure, I don't see why not. And, of course, I'm assuming you'll be needing a dolphin."

There was a telling lapse in the conversation.

"Actually, a pair of dolphins."

Jerry snapped to attention. "A pair? As in two?"

"As in a mother and her calf," Troy said as casually as possible. He knew he was tipping his hand, but it had to be done.

The unusual request provided Jerry with the last piece of information he needed to complete the puzzle. Troy wouldn't risk smuggling three million dollars worth of property out of the country if he hadn't already achieved some level of success with such a pair, and now he needed his own dolphins to complete his experiments in private before publishing any kind of official findings.

"Um, I suppose I could make that happen. When do you need them?"

Troy was forced to lay a few more cards out on the table. "The sooner the better. I'm not doing much out here otherwise."

"I'll see what I can do," Jerry said without a trace of suspicion in his voice, which he instantly regretted. The request for a mother and calf, he rationalized, should have been met with at least some degree of intrigue.

Prepared for a barrage of questions, Troy was indeed perplexed by Jerry's rapid acceptance of his specifications. "Thank you. I'll call back in a couple of days to see how things are going, okay?"

"You got it."

"I knew I could count on you, Jerry. Good night."

"Good night, Troy," Jerry said into the receiver then set it back in its cradle. The mystery had been solved. "So, you actually figured it out," he seethed aloud, taking off his glasses and polishing the lenses with the hem of his shirt. "After all these years, you somehow stumbled onto the right combination, didn't you?"

With great effort he got up, shuffled over to a cupboard, and pulled out a bottle of local rum. He took a giant swig, wiped his chin with his sleeve, and projected the events that were about to take place.

"And now you think you can just trot back here to rub my nose in your success."

With his face getting redder by the minute, he continued his one-sided conversation. "You think there's nothing I can do now but sit back and watch you get all the glory. Isn't that right?"

He took another gulp of the warm liquor and let his rising anger guide a new thought.

"Well, let me tell you something, Dr. Wallace. You'd better think again."

◆   ◆   ◆

Making the decision to return to Tortola had not been an easy one for Troy. He knew his departure from the island more than fifteen years earlier had left Jerry bitter and hurt, but he'd hoped that the passage of time would have tamed those hostilities. *Apparently not,* he thought after hanging up the phone, noting that Jerry's falsely-sweet voice could not mask his lingering disdain.

Nonetheless, Troy had weighed his options and priorities carefully, and what he needed now more than anything else was to isolate himself from outside scrutiny. He realized he was on the verge of one of the most significant scientific discoveries in history. No one—not SeaWorld, not Calvin and Chad, no one in the scientific community—must find out what he was doing until he'd taken his research one more step, fully verifying, documenting, and recording his findings. Tortola was the only place he could think of that would afford him such privacy. *They'll track me down eventually,* he thought. *But perhaps not before I've finished the next crucial tests.*

He was sorry he'd had to pull a disappearing act on Calvin and Chad, since he never would have reached this point without their backing. But the move was only temporary, and he prayed that the magnitude of his breakthrough would eventually eclipse any ill will between them. Besides, he wasn't taking *all* of their equipment—just the key components needed to finish his work.

Wincing from the pain in his injured arm, he pushed through the discomfort as he finished packing up the lab equipment. Feeling a bit like a spy on the run, he'd shut off his residential phone, put his small accumulation of furniture and belongings in a public storage unit, and left a note for his landlord on the kitchen counter. He wrote that he would no longer need his apartment and attached a check for the next month's rent. A small bag of clothing and personal items was already set to go, and he was both happy and relieved that Rebecca had agreed to accompany him without asking any questions. The fact that her life had intersected his just a few weeks ago was as fortuitous as the fact that he had maintained ownership of the Tortola property all these years. Everything was coming together for a cause greater than he dared let himself imagine. The objective now was to maintain secrecy at all costs.

Chapter 20

Watching the lights of Los Angeles recede into a twinkle of stardust below, Rebecca leaned against the plane's window and started to cry. With Troy seated next to her aboard a red-eye flight to San Juan, Puerto Rico, she revisited the questionable decisions she had made over the last few days and hoped that, this time, they would seem right.

But how would she ever explain to Ryan her refusal to take his calls since that day out on his boat? How could she justify the fabricated story she had told her superiors at SeaWorld about needing to visit her gravely ill mother? And how had she let herself be persuaded to leave the country without even knowing their final destination?

Troy looked over at her and wished she and Ryan had not been caught up in the web of deceit he had spun in order to disappear. Placing a steady hand on top of hers as she nervously tapped the armrest between them, he could only say, "I'm sorry."

At first she did not respond. Then, without turning away from the window, she asked, "Do I at least get to know where we're going now? I'm pretty sure it's not Puerto Rico."

"No. We're headed for Tortola. Which I'm sure comes as no surprise, but I did not want you to have to protect that information in case someone came asking."

"You mean Calvin and Chad," she surmised. "But they already know about your research facility on the island. Why wouldn't they look there first?"

"I can't guarantee that they won't. But I don't think they'd just show up without doing some investigation first, and the only person who knows we're coming is not an easy fellow to reach, even for me."

"Is that Jerry?" she asked.

Troy froze. "Yes. So you caught on to Calvin's question about him the other night."

"How could I not? Just the mention of his name made you nervous. Kind of like right now, actually."

Troy blinked at her astute observance. "Rebecca, I think I need to tell you a little bit more about what happened on Tortola."

Drawn by the mystery in his voice, she shifted around to face him and leaned a shoulder into her seat. "Consider me a captive audience."

With a distant look in his eyes, Troy spun out his tale. "Back in 1987, when I was just beginning to form my theories about sonographic communication, I realized I needed to find an assistant who was proficient with computers. A phone call to MIT led me to a talented young man named Jerry Spears, who was not only doing some of the first computer-aided imaging in the world, but also happened to have a degree in marine biology. As you can imagine, Jerry was intrigued that dolphins might use dimensional imagery as a form of communication, and before I could even think of looking for someone else, he was down in Tortola assisting me with my research."

"That must have been an exciting time," Rebecca interjected.

"You have no idea. Every morning we would wake up thinking, *this could be the day!* Not realizing the limitations of the technology we were working with, we truly believed a breakthrough was always just around the corner."

"When, in reality, that corner was many years away."

"Exactly. And, at first—about the time that Calvin and Chad came into the picture—we weren't discouraged that we hadn't had any success. But as time wore on, it got harder and harder to keep our spirits up."

"What happened then?"

"In the simplest terms, our ideologies just drifted apart. Jerry got tired of my imaging theories and suggested we focus on using computers to digitally recreate their vocalizations, while I saw no point in duplicating dolphin sounds just because it was technically possible to do so. What good is mimicking a squeak or a click when you have no idea what it means? Anyway, we struggled for a while to keep a good working relationship, but it became apparent that this wasn't going to happen. In December of 1989 I left Tortola—and Jerry—to carry on with my research back in the States."

"And he's been there ever since?"

Troy nodded silently. "For a while he kept up his sonic research and wrangled enough grant money to keep the facility open, but eventually he just quit. That was back in '93 or '94."

"What's he been up to since then?"

"I don't know. Except for two short conversations we had a few days ago, I haven't spoken to him in nearly ten years."

"What?"

Troy squirmed uneasily in his seat. "When I left, Jerry made it clear that he felt I was abandoning him."

"But you weren't keeping him there. Couldn't he have just moved back to the States?"

"Of course he could have. But I think he always felt I would return some day and that we would pick up where we left off."

"And here you are, fifteen years later, headed back to Tortola. Obviously this guy's no dummy."

"Far from it," Troy acknowledged, his stomach a nervous knot.

◆   ◆   ◆

The commuter plane from San Juan to Tortola's Beef Island airport bounced on impact with the jungle-fringed runway. As Rebecca watched the hulks of dead and abandoned airplanes streak by her window, the realization hit hard: she was a very long way from home.

"See that plane right there?" Troy asked, pointing to an antique McDonnell Douglas DC-3 lying on its belly alongside the runway. "They call it the ghost plane."

"Is that because nobody lived through that landing?" she wondered at the sight of the wrinkled fuselage and slightly bent starboard wing.

"No. Back in the eighties, some cocaine smugglers stole her from Colombia, used her to make a drop over the ocean then bailed out with parachutes. Believe it or not, that plane ran out of fuel and literally landed itself in a field not more than a mile from here."

"Lovely," she deadpanned. "I hope you're going to tell me that Tortola's drug trade died out back in the days of *Miami Vice*."

"For the most part," Troy confirmed nonchalantly. "But a lot of these little Caribbean islands still serve as smuggling outposts for

South and Central America. It's the economy-behind-the-economy that people here fall back on if they need to."

"I see."

Their plane coasted to a stop outside a small tin building. When the pilot, who had also been their ticket-taker and baggage handler, jerked open the door to the cabin, a blast of hot, humid air rushed in with smothering force

"Welcome to the Banana Republic," Troy smiled, feeling a wave of nostalgia washing over him as he took in a deep breath of the thick, floral-scent.

After passing through a lackadaisical customs inspection, Troy and Rebecca lugged the equipment out onto the gravel road fronting the airport, he using his one good arm to lift what he could, and she hefting the rest with surprising strength. They hailed the only taxi in sight, an old, dust-covered Ford van parked in the shade of one of the palm trees surrounding the airport's lone terminal.

The taxi's driver, a young and lean black man—eyes hidden behind enormous mirrored sunglasses—loaded the heavy bags and cases in silence. He slammed the van's doors, got himself situated behind the wheel, and drove off along a rutted road.

"Where you folks want to go?" he asked.

"I've got a little place not far from Smuggler's Cove," Troy answered. "I'll give you the directions once we get to the other side of the island."

"Sure ting. You want some music?"

"That would be fine," Troy replied while watching the landscape go by his window. With each familiar sight, he felt himself being drawn back into the memories he had created there so many years ago.

A cassette tape was pushed into the van's player, and soon the young man was swaying languidly to a slow reggae tune. He looked back into the rear-view mirror to make sure his guests were enjoying the music as well.

Rebecca smiled warmly at him. But when the driver kept diverting his attention from the road to the mirror, she became uneasy. Finally she had to say something. "Shouldn't you be paying more attention to where you're going?" she asked.

Seconds later, the van skidded to a stop in the dirt. Spinning around, the man thrust his face to less than a foot away from hers and Troy's. Then, with an enormous grin full of perfect white teeth and bright pink gums, he peeled up his glasses and let out a cry of recognition. Rebecca was not the one he'd been scrutinizing.

"Is dat you, Dolphin Man?"

The question instantly transported Troy back in time. He studied the driver's face and voice until a name popped into his head. "Randi? Oh my god, it *is* you—only now you're a grown man!"

"Dat's what happens in fifteen years," Randi beamed.

Still in shock, Troy turned and introduced Rebecca to the boy who had named the dolphin that he had worked with for nearly three years. "Rebecca, this is Randi. His father, Haden, supplied us with all the fish that we fed our dolphin at the compound."

As the two of them shook hands, Troy could hardly contain his exuberance. "And how is Haden these days?"

Randi's toothy smile disappeared, and he turned his attention back to the road. "Daddy died nearly t'ree years ago. Jes' up an' died of a heart attack. Warn't even fifty years old, neither."

Troy hung his head in sadness for Randi's loss and remorse for not knowing. "I'm sorry. I would have thought that Jerry'd call me with the news."

"*Jerry?*" Randi hissed. "What'd Jerry ever care about my daddy? What's Jerry care about anyt'ing 'cept eatin' and drinkin' and tokin' all day long?"

While Rebecca gave him a look of nervous concern, Troy closed his eyes for a moment. "Surely he's been doing *something*," he replied, feeling more than a little anxious.

"Are you kiddin'? 'Cept for goin' out to de complex dese last few days, he hasn't done nuttin' wid hisself." It was at this instant that Randi seemed to make the connection between Jerry's recent and incongruous spurt of industry and Troy's arrival. "Say, you're not here to work wid 'im again, are you?"

Troy's sheepish expression said it all.

"Aww, Jeez, mon!" Randi fumed and slapped the steering wheel with his open palms. "Den you watch out! Dat Jerry is not de same man you left here. Do you understand what I'm tellin' you?"

"I'm afraid I do," Troy acknowledged, slumping under the burden of Randi's disturbing yet highly valuable information.

Chapter 21

Every bend in the road, every lush feature of Tortola's tropical landscape, was familiar to Troy. Passing the island's protected harbor in Road Town—a natural lagoon with water so clear that the boats in it appeared to hover in midair—he pointed to a bustling marina and harbor-side restaurant.

"Are you a Jimmy Buffet fan?" he asked Rebecca while keeping his eyes on the boats bobbing in the neon turquoise bay.

"From way back," she nodded. "I've always liked his music, but it was a quote from one of his books that really hooked me. He said something like, 'I grew up Catholic, but over the years I've decided that water is my real religion.' I'd never heard something like that before, but it made perfect sense to me the second I read it."

Troy smiled, recalling the time he had he heard the same quote—in person. "So, being a Jimmy Buffet fan, you must know the song 'Cheeseburger in Paradise.'"

"Of course."

"Well, do you see that marina right there—the Village Cay? That's the restaurant where *that* particular cheeseburger came from."

"Yeah, sure it is. I've heard that on just about every vacation I've ever been on. Hawaii, Tahiti, Key West, Barbados—they've all got some little burger joint claiming the same thing."

"Okay, then let me put it another way. One day as I was having lunch there with Jimmy—I'm guessing it must have been in either '88 or '89—he told me himself it was the Village Cay that had inspired the song. If I remember right, that burger was actually made out of horsemeat!"

Rebecca's eyes opened wide. "Are you serious? First I find out you were one of John Lilly's assistants, and now you're telling me you used to hang out in the Caribbean with Jimmy Buffet?"

"It really wasn't that big of a deal. Back then, he used to vacation here quite a bit, and whenever he was in town, he'd always look me up and ask me how my work with the dolphins was going."

Rebecca leaned her incredulous head against the window. "You *are* full of surprises, aren't you, Troy Wallace?"

"I guess maybe I am," he replied with a smile, his gaze still fixed on the Village Cay. "And you know what? When we come back to Road Town for supplies, we'll go there for lunch. By the looks of it, it hasn't changed all that much over the years. In fact, it's amazing how little *any* of Tortola has changed."

Threading their way past the harbor and through jumbled neighborhoods of brightly painted cinderblock houses, where dark-skinned men and women socialized in the shade of banana palms and children played among wandering goats, dogs and chickens, Rebecca drifted easily into the relaxed pace of the island.

When the van finally found its way onto the dirt road leading to the compound, Troy's heart began to beat a little faster. "We're close," he said with hushed excitement. "It's just around the next bend."

And there, straight ahead in the clearing, stood the research center Rebecca had imagined a hundred different ways, none of which had been correct. "*That's* your research center?" she asked, surveying the lonely rock shack with obvious disillusionment.

"I told you it wasn't much to look at."

"So you did. I just never imagined it would actually be so... rustic."

"I tink it's beautiful," Randi said. His tone was nostalgic, as if he were remembering the days when he and his father delivered fish to the complex. "Besides, what more do you need? De important part's what's swimmin' over dere in de lagoon."

Rebecca's attention was attracted to a small inlet connected by a flood-gated channel to the ocean, and even though they were still a hundred yards or so away from the little lagoon, she could see the two dorsal fins—one noticeably larger than the other—slicing cleanly through the water. "They're already here?" she squealed with delight, her impression of the place instantly changing.

Troy's pulse began to race. "By golly, Jerry said he could get me a mother and calf, and that's just what he did! Randi, stop the van. We'll walk in from here."

"Fine wid me. Sand's so soft we'd be sinkin' in it soon anyway."

Walking down the path, Rebecca was the first to notice Jerry emerging from the tiny shack. She could not help imagining him as an oversized, red-headed troll exiting an elfin house of stone. "Is that your assistant?" she asked quietly, giving a nod in Jerry's direction.

Troy was taken aback at the sight, guessing that Jerry must have gained at least a hundred pounds since they last worked together. "No, *you* are my assistant," he answered her under his breath, "and I don't want there to be any confusion about that while we're here. Understood?"

"Understood," Rebecca whispered, apprehensive about how Troy would introduce her.

"Welcome home, Troy!" Jerry said in greeting, holding out a thick, sweaty hand. "And Randi? My, this *is* quite the reunion, isn't it?"

Other than tilting his chin up slightly, Randi made no attempt to return Jerry's cordiality.

"And who do we have here?" Jerry asked with a leer so slight that it was almost imperceptible. Almost.

"I'm Rebecca Larson." Despite his moist and lingering grip on her hand, she managed a smile.

"Rebecca is a dolphin behaviorist at SeaWorld in San Diego," Troy announced. "I brought her along to help get the dolphins acclimated to their new environment as quickly as possible."

"Good idea." Jerry nodded thoughtfully.

"How long have they been here?" Rebecca queried, looking toward the lagoon.

"Two days."

"Have they eaten anything yet?"

"I tried tossing in a couple of mackerel, but neither of them went for it."

"That's common enough—I'm sure they're feeling a bit disoriented. Is there anything I need to know about their capture and relocation?"

"Nope," Jerry assured her. "Everything went pretty smoothly. They were netted with a school of tuna and handled with as much care as possible." He was quite sure she didn't want to hear the real story about how black market dolphins are handled by their captors.

"That's good. Maybe I'll work with them a little this afternoon and see how they're adapting to their new surroundings. Any fish still around?"

Jerry seized the opportunity for self-promotion. "Uh huh, in an ice chest right behind the shack. I also loaded in a couple of cots and a few provisions to get you by for a day or two."

"Cots?" Rebecca asked with some trepidation. "We're sleeping on cots? Next thing you're going to tell me is the place doesn't even have a bathroom."

Troy realized he should have done more to prepare her for life at the compound. "That depends. Does a plastic Porta-Potti count as a bathroom?"

"Oh boy," she replied with a rueful twitch.

"You'll get used to it," Jerry said. "The most important thing is that you've got four walls, a roof over your head, and a generator to run the equipment. Which reminds me, I need to get us some extra fuel from town."

Jerry's use of the word *us* was not lost on Troy. "Well, it certainly looks like you've thought of everything. And I hope it's okay to call you back out here if we end up needing a helping hand."

Encouraged by Troy's proposition, Jerry lumbered forward and eagerly gave Dr. Wallace a smothering hug. "Just say the word, and I'll be here."

Troy looked past his one-time partner and gave a nervous, knowing wink toward Rebecca.

◆   ◆   ◆

Beneath a sky of pink twilight, Rebecca sat on a log at the edge of the lagoon and finished her meal of campfire-roasted hot dogs and canned beans. Watching the first twinkling stars appear, she contemplated the best plan of action for getting the dolphins to eat. Though she did not want to dwell on a worst-case scenario, she still had to acknowledge the fact that if they did not eat within the next day or two, the pair would have to be released back into the ocean.

"Now, what's the best way to introduce myself to the two of you?" she asked the mother and calf as they swam past her on their endless, counter-clockwise loop around the lagoon. Closing her eyes, she breathed deeply and recalled every book, research paper and article she had ever read regarding human-dolphin interactions. She had never worked with first-contact animals before, yet while poring over the information in her head, a clear statement began to emerge regarding such encounters: *Dolphins are wary of people wearing artificial devices.* Encumbrances such as scuba tanks and regulators nearly always drove wild dolphins away, but so could snorkels and dive masks, swim fins, cameras, plastic toys, even jewelry.

The next strategic element of her approach concerned dolphin behavior in the wild, specifically in the care of young and newborn members of a pod. As had been documented many times over, mother dolphins were often assisted with child-care duties by another female in the group, allowing the birth-mother to hunt for food or simply escape from her offspring for a while to socialize.

When these two ideas merged, a definitive plan began to form, and though it initially seemed strange to her, she knew it offered the best hope for success. "I'll be right back," she called out to the dolphins, then hopped up from the log and sprinted toward the shack.

In the glow of a kerosene lamp, Dr. Wallace was busy unpacking and arranging his equipment.

"How's it goin'?" she called into the shack's only window.

"Not bad. Just getting things set up. How about with you?"

"Good. The dolphins appear to be healthy and calm. I'm going to grab a couple of fish from the cooler and see if I can get Junior to eat."

"Great," Troy replied. "But why only the calf? Doesn't the mother have to eat as well?"

"I think she will, once she's sure the baby's okay. And, if you don't mind, can I have the next hour or so alone with them?" She knew it was a strange request, but she also knew that Troy would honor it.

"Be my guest. I've got plenty to do in here," he said with a wave and watched her speed off toward the back of the shack.

Darkness enveloped the compound quickly. With a full, bright moon creeping over the horizon, Rebecca sat down at the edge of the lagoon, her feet barely touching the warm water. "Okay, you two, I hope you're in the mood for some company."

She took the mother's loud and properly timed exhalation as a response of welcome, though she knew it could have just as easily been a signal of agitation or distress.

"I understand how confusing all this is to you, and I want to do everything I can to let you know you're safe here." As she spoke, she wiggled out of her shorts and T-shirt and for an enchanting moonlit moment just stood there in her SeaWorld swimsuit, letting the soft trade winds tickle her skin. Then, silently, she removed the band holding her hair in a pony tail, the dolphin-shaped ring on her right pinkie, the small gold studs from her pierced ears, and finally—after one last glance toward the shack—the clinging bathing suit itself. The determination to enter the water nude had not required much thought, for she knew that an artificial second skin may be just as alarming to a wild dolphin as a gurgling scuba tank. Closing her eyes and breathing deeply, she stood ankle-deep in the water and acknowledged how good the moist night air felt against her body, how right it felt to be her most natural self in this primitively beautiful place.

With deliberate confidence, she waded deeper into the lagoon until the water was up to her shoulders, then ducked her head under and pushed off from the sandy bottom into a slow glide toward the middle of the pool. With her arms and hands held close to the sides of her body, hopefully conveying to the dolphins that she had no intention of touching either of them, she kicked her legs in unison as if they had been fused together into a mermaid's tail.

Long minutes passed in complete silence under the water, but then came the familiar buzz of a sonic scan—the high-frequency pulses reverberating through her entire body.

Nice to meet you, too, she thought to the dolphins swimming outside the scope of her blurry underwater vision. *Are you okay with me being here?*

There was no way of knowing how well the dolphins were adapting to her presence—they kept their distance for nearly half an hour while she rhythmically dove and surfaced for air—but finally Rebecca sensed that she was being followed. A quick look back revealed the ghostly appearance of the mother swimming not more than three feet behind her. And even with her vast experience as a behaviorist telling her she should not be afraid, the sight of the large dolphin shadowing her every move made her nervous.

Well, hello there.

It was encouraging that the dolphin did not retreat when Rebecca slowly turned to face her.

I'll bet this has been a scary couple of days, huh? And I know you must be hungry.

Making her way to the side of the lagoon, Rebecca waded out for a moment to grab one of the two dead mackerel then retreated beneath the surface once again. Holding the fish close to her face, she made no effort to give it to the mother; rather, she turned and swam away, pushing the fish around the perimeter of the lagoon as if it were some kind of pool toy.

I've got a little something for Junior here—will you let him eat it? Mimicking a behavior she had seen dolphins execute in the wild, she nudged the fish forward then stopped to let its silvery body hang suspended in the water.

When the fish began to sink, she repeated the action again.

On the fifth push and release, she watched with glee as the infant charged up from the darkness, snatched the fish into its open beak, and swallowed it whole.

In that instant, Rebecca realized the most important hurdle regarding the dolphins' captivity had been cleared.

"Yes!" she exclaimed after surfacing. "That was amazing!"

She strode confidently out of the lagoon to retrieve the other mackerel, exuberant that this night could not be going any better.

Crouched amid the dense foliage surrounding the lagoon and watching her every move, Jerry Spears was thinking the exact same thing.

Chapter 22

Shuffling through the warm, white sand, Ryan felt more at peace and uniquely connected with himself than he ever had before. As he walked along the shore, he basked in a newfound self-awareness and purpose—thankful for every event in his life that had led him to this place and moment.

"What are you thinking about?" Her voice—tranquil, soft, sweet—was a perfect match for his mood.

"Everything," he replied with wonder. "I'm thinking about who I used to be and what I used to consider important. I'm thinking about how good it feels to have such a clear vision of who I really am and why I'm here."

"It *is* liberating, isn't it?"

He stared out over the glistening ocean and watched the sun rise over the horizon. "Liberating doesn't even come close. It's like waking up in someone else's body, or seeing the world through different eyes, and then realizing that this is who I was supposed to be all along."

"That's a good way to put it."

He felt that there was more she wanted to say, but by the way she left the statement dangling between them, he knew he would have to wait until she was ready.

For a long time they walked in silence, the balmy morning air caressing their skin, until a new thought came to him.

"I have to ask you—does everybody get this opportunity?"

Understanding exactly what he meant, she smiled and said, "Of course they do, but ..."

"But what?"

"But first they have to wake up."

With one knee on the edge of Ryan's bed, Jen bounced on the mattress with increasing intensity. "I said *wake up!*" She marched over to the window of his bedroom and yanked the shutters open. "What the hell is wrong with you? You look terrible, you've been moping around all week, and now you're … you're *hung over* on an interview day?" She scowled, picking up an empty bottle of Patron Silver Tequila from the nightstand.

Covering his closed eyes with both hands, he could barely bring himself to face another day. "How'd you get in here?" he groaned, awakening to the unwelcome fact that she was definitely not the woman from his dream.

"Through the front door, which was wide open. And Jesus, you really do look like shit."

"Thanks. I feel even worse. What time is it, anyway?"

"Time to get your sorry ass out of bed. The interview at the Long Beach Boat Show is in less than two hours."

"The boat show? Oh, come on, we've done the same old thing there for the last two years. Can't you just shoot this one without me and let me do a voiceover later?"

"Are you serious? The crew's been setting up since six o'clock this morning. There's no way you're getting out of this."

Still tequila-poisoned, he unsteadily propped himself up against the headboard. "You know what? I'm sorry, but I honestly don't think I can do this." He did manage to stop himself from adding *any more,* but that's what he was feeling about the whole FunHunter business.

"Oh, you'll do it all right. If I have to drag you out of bed and dress you myself, you *will* make that interview." Flinging open his closet and picking out a few things for him to throw on, she seemed to think this was as good a time as any to get to the bottom of his mounting despondency. "Seriously, what is going on with you lately? You've been moping around like a whipped dog for nearly a week. It's like I don't even know who you are anymore."

Her words penetrated his alcohol haze. "I can't explain everything to you, but in some ways it's like *I* don't even know who I am."

Jen momentarily shifted out of executive-producer mode and into the more unfamiliar role of concerned friend and confidante. From this perspective, it did not take her long to realize what was going on. "Oh my god! You're … you're in *love,* aren't you?"

His involuntary flinch let her know she was right.

"Oh, but it's even worse than that. You're actually love-*sick!* Ryan Ericson, the player of all players, has gotten himself all twisted up over a woman!"

"You don't know what you're talking about," he snarled, holding his queasy stomach.

"The hell I don't. But the real question is: Who's the girl?" Tapping her chin while looking up at the ceiling, Jen finally put it all together—the time frame, the behavior, the woman. "Oh, it's the dolphin trainer at SeaWorld—of course! Who else would you fall for other than the one woman who wasn't instantly smitten by you?"

There was no use trying to hide the truth, or at least this one, any longer. "Crazy, isn't it?"

"It is if you're so screwed up that you can't do your job. You know what I mean?"

"I know." He turned away before he could let slip any further life-changing events—the incredible discovery, the wonderful night in Catalina, the cruel abandonment—that had taken place during the past week.

◆   ◆   ◆

The Boat Show shoot was every bit the circus he knew it would be. Wearing a cruise-ship captain's uniform, he dutifully interviewed the event's promoter aboard one of the yachts featured in the show. He drove the Jeep around Shoreline Village Marina for a few establishing shots. He silently acquiesced to countless pleas for autographs while walking the docks and shaking hands with yacht brokers and accessory vendors. Except for the nautical theme, it was a *South Coast Safari* segment like any other.

At sunset the call to wrap was finally given, and while the various crews dismantled their lighting rigs and sound equipment, Ryan crept away without even bothering to change out of the ridiculous captain's outfit.

Less than an hour later, back home in Newport, he was pouring himself the first of many shots of Chivas Regal. Another day, another round of drug therapy.

He went upstairs to change clothes. Entering his dark and silent bedroom, he noticed the phone on his night-stand blinking to announce that he had received eight messages. He didn't feel like listening to eight calls, but to fill the silence while undressing, he pushed the machine's playback button. He could have predicted the first seven voicemails: Fox wanted to take some new promotional shots. His agent was trying to set up some kind of shopping mall appearance. Jen berated him for leaving without returning the rented uniform.

The eighth call, however, made him freeze. Over clamoring voices and loud party music, Rebecca cleared her throat and spoke hurriedly.

"Hi, Ryan, it's me. I had to call you to tell you how sorry I am for not letting you know what's going on. Please don't be mad. Troy just didn't want to drag you into something bigger and messier than you'd want to deal with. I promise I'll tell you everything when I get back. And Ryan? I want you to know that I…"

With his heart racing, Ryan knelt down to get closer to the answering machine.

"I miss you very much." The line went dead.

Every cell in his body was energized by the sound of Rebecca's voice. Staring wide-eyed at the silent machine, he pumped his fists in thanks that hers had been the last incoming call. He snatched up the receiver and pushed the asterisk, which automatically redialed the last number to appear on the phone's caller-identification screen. After a series of long delays, a few echoing clicks, and an unrecognizable ring tone, someone finally picked up the phone at the other end of the line.

"Hallo! You got de *Virgin Queen*." The lilting accent was thick, possibly Jamaican.

Ryan blinked and shook his head at what he was hearing. "What is the Virgin Queen?" he asked.

"What you mean? It's de same ting it's always been, mon."

From the name and the ambient noise in the background, Ryan surmised that he was calling a nightclub of some kind. "Is this a bar?"

"Come on. Why you be jokin' at dis hour?"

Ryan thought quickly. "I'm sorry. Somebody said you mixed the best drinks in town, and I don't know exactly how to find you."

"If you can't find us, den God's sayin' you don't need any mo to drink! Now I gotta go. Bar's closin', anyway." *Click.*

Ryan tried the redial feature again, but obviously the person at the other end had had quite enough of what he must have thought was a prank call.

In euphoric inspiration, Ryan bolted downstairs to the computer in his office and did a quick Internet search typing: "Virgin Queen Bar." In seconds, a number of sites popped up, all mentioning a drinking establishment of that name on Tortola, British Virgin Islands. And no wonder the person had seemed perplexed at his question about the location of the bar. A map search verified that Road Town was small enough that a person could get lost and still find the place by accident.

"Tortola?" Ryan asked out loud, his voice reverberating through the silent house. "What are you doing in Tortola?"

It didn't matter. It could have been the middle of the Sahara Desert. He would still find her before the next day was over.

Chapter 23

Mick Fletcher kicked his way through a carpet of autumn leaves during his lunch break and considered his brief career at the United States Naval Observatory—a career he was quite sure would be over in less than an hour. Bracing against a cold October wind that had been blowing through the nation's capital for days, he pulled the Post-it note from his jacket pocket and read the terse message aloud once again: "My office. After lunch. Lieutenant Hightower."

Wadding up the pale yellow note and throwing it to the ground, Mick spat the words out as if someone with a sympathetic ear was listening. "Hightower—how appropriate. Why doesn't he come down from that tower of his and give me a little more respect than a goddamn Post-it?"

He crept in by one of the back doors of telescope-domed Building One, the most recognizable and hallowed on the campus. The long walk to the security checkpoint gave him time to reflect that he had actually held a job at one of the oldest and most prestigious scientific research facilities in the country. Whether it was tracking the satellites that form the Global Positioning System network or keeping tabs on the famous Atomic Clock, the USNO was the primary source of relevant cosmological information disbursed from Washington to the world, and Mick had been thrilled to be a part of its legacy.

As he hung up his coat and waved his personnel badge in front of the automated security checkpoint, Mick stewed over his impending dismissal. After a year heading an experimental research program in socio-astronomy, he was well aware that most of his colleagues considered him nothing more than a thinly-veiled astrologer, the scourge of true astronomical science. During meetings, it was almost impossible to avoid their dismissive glances.

"But I was just doing what I had been hired to do!" he fumed under his breath while passing through the checkpoint.

"Hey, Cosmick!" Earl, the uniformed Naval security officer, called out. Earl was the one person Mick had to engage, as he could not get to the lieutenant's office otherwise. "What's the good word, son?" A career Navy man, Earl was one of the first men of color to wear a captain's bars. Now he was just an elderly sentry, thrilled to still be employed by the government.

"You know, I can't think of a single good word right now," Mick replied without a trace of emotion. "And do you have to call me Cosmick?"

"Everbody else does. Why can't I?"

It wasn't worth wasting his breath to explain why he had never found Cosmick funny. "I'm here to see Lieutenant Hightower. Is he in?" Mick flashed his clearance badge.

"That he is," Earl smiled, gesturing down the wide corridor that led to every high-ranking official's office at the observatory.

Moments later, Mick was tapping lightly on a solid mahogany door marked with a plaque bearing Hightower's name.

"It's not locked," a graveled voice announced.

Mick stepped into the office and was instantly inundated with the sights and smells of naval history. Sextants, astrolabes, and chronometers crowded the room. The antique instruments were designed to track the movement of heavenly bodies and the passage of time, and they were all treasured heirlooms of maritime navigation.

"Sit down." Hightower motioned to one of the two leather-clad armchairs in front of his desk. Portly and balding, the scowling lieutenant paced around the room. "Cigar?" he asked, and opened a wooden box of hand-rolled Robustos.

"No thanks," was all Mick said at first. Then, summoning unexpected confidence, he forged ahead. "Sir, may I ask the nature of this meeting?"

Peering over the top of his wire-framed glasses and sliding an ancient, hand-printed document across the top of his desk, Hightower gave Mick a withering stare. "Read this. But don't pick it up."

Mick delicately swiveled the paper, which he guessed to be over two hundred years old, and began to silently read the document.

"Out loud," Hightower commanded.

As if he were taking an elementary school reading exam, he cleared his throat and read, *"The U.S. Naval Observatory performs an essential role for the United States, the Navy, and the Department of Defense. Its mission includes determining the positions and motions of the earth, sun, moon, planets, stars and other celestial objects; providing astronomical data; determining precise time; measuring the earth's rotation; and maintaining the Master Clock for the United States."* When he finished, he looked up with a confused expression.

"Tell me, Mr. Fletcher, how does your job fit in with the stated purpose of this observatory?"

So this really was the end. While he had responded to such scrutiny before, never had the tone of the interrogations been so hostile. Surprisingly, along with the certainty of his position being terminated, a newfound resolve took hold of him. He reclined into the chair's rich leather and spoke with quiet determination. "My position fits into the scope of that document perfectly because, whether or not you want to believe it, socio-astronomy *matters.* Mankind has always attached meaning to the movement of stars and planets, which in turn reveals valuable information about the nature of mankind."

Hightower, appearing only mildly interested in Fletcher's reply, silently beckoned for more information.

"Imagine," Mick continued, "if this document had come from the Treasury Department and said something like: *'The U. S. Treasury exists to print and distribute money.'* Well, what good would it do to print money if there was not a shared cultural perception that it had value? Those printed pieces of paper would be worthless."

"So, in your mind, this theory validates the study of such things as astrology and mysticism?"

The question sounded like a trap to Mick, and in a way it was. "Let me make something clear to you: While I do not personally believe that the movement of celestial bodies has any quantifiable influence on human events, I cannot deny that billions of people throughout history have assigned significant meaning to cosmological observations. After all, the detail of three wise astrologers following a star in the east is crucial to the Christmas story, is it not?"

"Good answer," Hightower nodded, his tone more amiable. "Now, let's take a slightly different tack. I'd like you to tell me about the significance of a *particular* cosmological event."

"Okay, what event is that?"

Hightower paused, took a deep breath, and let the weight of his words build in a moment of tactical silence. "The winter solstice of 2012."

Beginning to suspect some ruse, Mick squinted warily into Hightower's probing eyes. Since returning from the ruins of Tulum two weeks ago, not once had he discussed his findings with anyone from the observatory. "What did you say?"

"I said, tell me about the meaning of 21 December, 2012." There was not a trace of anything but focused intensity in Hightower's demand.

"Well, according to ancient Mayans, it represents the last day of their 5,000 year-old-calendar. But what I think you're really getting at is that some people are relating this event to an apocalyptic moment in human history."

Hightower disengaged himself from Mick's stare and strolled over to a large window overlooking the observatory's campus. "But there have always been crackpots who believed the world was coming to an end... look at what we went through with the whole Y-2-K fiasco a few years ago."

"That's true, but Y-2-K and 2012 are totally different. The incredible accuracy of the Mayan calendar, combined with the fact that it has always been a device dedicated to both tracking time *and* predicting the future, gives it a certain credibility that other doomsday prophecies do not have."

"Hightower did not divert his gaze from the window. "And you're sure that doomsday is what the Mayans had in mind when they came up with the end-date? Could it not have been something more like an end to an era... or possibly a moment of *transition* into a new one?"

Mick was flabbergasted. "Well now, someone *has* been doing his homework, hasn't he? Actually, George Baylor, the archeologist in Tulum, is intrigued that the Mayans assigned the symbol of a water-bearer to the end-date."

"And what's so intriguing about that?" Hightower asked.

"Well, according to more modern astronomical data, the Age of Aquarius—which also happens to be symbolized by a water-bearer—is set to *begin* within the same time-frame that the Mayan calendar ends. It's almost like the Mayans foresaw the symbol of a person pouring water from a jug announcing this momentous occasion."

Hightower was still listening, but he seemed to be following another thought. With a finger laid delicately on his chin, he asked his next question in a voice so soft it did not seem to come out of the same man. "Speaking of symbols, what do you make of the 11:11 phenomenon?"

Absolute silence filled the air as Mick's mind raced for a reply. "I'm—I'm not sure I understand what you're talking about."

"The report you wrote after returning from Tulum says otherwise."

"You actually read that report?" Mick coughed with astonishment.

"Of course I read it. The only reason we never discussed it is that I thought your comments were ridiculous. I mean, come on," he said and looked toward the ceiling to recall Fletcher's handwritten notes. "The artwork surrounding the chamber's doorway looks like the numerals 11:11 on a digital clock? The shaman Tac-Mol says it is a symbol that many people will recognize?"

A strained pause in the conversation allowed each man a moment to decide how deep into this odd conversation he would venture.

"I'm sorry, but that's what it looked like to me, and that's what Tac-Mol said."

"I see. And that's what prompted you to search 11:11 on the Internet?"

"What?" Mick gasped. "You monitor my Internet activity?"

Hightower was unfazed. "Mr. Fletcher, we monitor everyone's Internet activity here at the USNO."

Breathing heavily and taking a moment to regain his composure, Fletcher realized he had to tell everything he knew. "The search started as a whim. And, as you can imagine, there were hundreds of unrelated 11:11 matches—times of news reports, dates of events, game scores— but among the top ten suggestions was a web site called '*The 11:11 Phenomenon.*' And while there was no specific connection to the Mayan calendar on the site, there *was* a compelling mystery waiting for me there. I remember the first page of the site saying something like, 'Have you been noticing 11:11 on digital clocks recently? Does this trigger a strange sense within you that an important event is about to take place? Do you feel as if you are being awakened to a new beginning?'"

"And you were you intrigued," Hightower stated.

"How could I not be? Here I am searching an image that's possibly related to the Mayan calendar's end date, and I learn that this very image happens to refer to a moment of some kind of new beginning! What are the odds of that?" Mick challenged.

Hightower did not respond.

"Anyway, so after seeing that site, I wanted to know just how many people were noticing 11:11 in the way described, and I was stunned to find that there are thousands, maybe *millions* of them! What's more, many of them have been attaching similar meaning to 11:11 without hearing about it from anyone else, making it a true phenomenon of shared cultural perception."

Hightower studied Mick in silence for a moment, then walked over and picked up a manila folder sitting on the top of his desk. Opening it, he said, "I wanted you to see this before we posted it on our website." He handed over a single sheet of paper from the file.

Mick took the paper. "I've seen this before," he said. "It's the Observatory's forecast for future season changes."

"You haven't seen this one. I just got a hard copy of it yesterday."

Mick studied the document more closely. "You're right. This one goes all the way to 2020. Am I supposed to notice something in particular?"

"I'll let you decide."

Mick's eyes scanned the military-time postings for every coming eclipse, equinox and solstice for the next sixteen years. When the information regarding the winter solstice of 2012 came to his attention, his face drained of color.

"Something wrong?" Hightower asked.

"Is this … *for real?*" Mick stammered.

"It is."

Mick's eyes stayed locked upon the numbers on the page. "You're telling me that 2012's winter solstice—the very event the Mayans said time would end and the Age of Aquarius is said to begin—will happen at exactly 11:11 in the morning?"

"How's that for a phenomenon of shared cultural awareness?" Hightower asked. "I must admit, I'm having a hard time explaining this to myself, or anyone else for that matter. Could these people who see 11:11 really be tuned into the same vision that the Mayans saw all those years ago?"

Mick slumped back into the chair, hardly able to process the barrage of information. "I don't know," he said with a slow shake of his head, "but it sure seems worth investigating." At that moment, a trivial realization came to him. "Oh, so, I guess I'm not being fired after all."

Hightower looked down at the paper. "At this moment, I'd say you're the only one around here with any kind of job security. Now scram, and start figuring out how the Navy's going to handle this situation once we post these times on the Internet."

Chapter 24

Hardly able to believe how well this part of his plan was going, Jerry ambled around the perimeter of the compound and whistled a lively tune. After watching Randi leave with Troy and Rebecca in the van for a supply run into Road Town, he knew he had the place to himself for at least a couple of hours.

He pushed the research facility's sturdy wooden door open and was immediately stricken by the sight of Troy's newest equipment lined up in neat stacks around the room. "My, my, we *have* come a long way, haven't we, Dr. Wallace?" Jerry studied each device and quickly determined its function. The four new transducers lying next to each other on a bench were especially intriguing. Though many times smaller than the original transducers they had used years ago, he knew they must be thousands of times more powerful. "So, these are the new 'ducers, huh? Small, elegant … not bad," he mused. He picked one of them up. "But how well do they work? That's the question."

He began to pace the floor. With beads of sweat rolling down his face, and with his lips pursed in contemplation, he allowed a risky idea to turn into an even riskier plan of action. "The way I see it, you wouldn't have these transducers if it weren't for the prototypes I developed for you. No reason I shouldn't be entitled to check them out."

On an impulse, Jerry began flipping the equipment's numerous switches, and soon the larger monitor came on in luminous green. He pushed his hair out of his face and pondered what he was seeing on the screen. "Hmm, now, *that's* different. Why did you switch from a wire frame construct to this solid field?" Answering his own question, he brought his face to within a few inches of the monitor and noticed that the green square was actually comprised of thousands of tiny, free-floating pixels.

While never taking his eyes off the monitor, he raised the transducer up like a microphone to his mouth and said, "Testing, testing." In a fraction of a second, the pixels assembled themselves into a three-dimensional form, looking somewhat like a bowling pin lying on its side.

Jerry's stomach lurched, and with the transducer still near his mouth, he spoke once again into the device to see his voice onscreen. "Holy Christ! The resolution is incredible!" He said *incredible* numerous times because the word created a mesmerizing pattern. "So, you finally came up with the right transducer, didn't you, Dr. Wallace? And now you've come back here to rub my nose in your success?" His jaw tightened in an outrage that quickly became painful.

Thrusting his hand deep into the front pocket of his baggy shorts, he withdrew an electronic device of his own. Holding the tiny transmitter close to his face for a final inspection, he continued his one-sided conversation. "But did you really think I'd just stand back and let you take all the credit?"

He didn't need much time to hide the bugging device. After removing a side panel from the largest monitor's aluminum case, he simply laid the transmitter amidst a jumble of wires near the bottom, then quickly closed the unit back up again. "That should do the trick."

After flipping every switch to its original position and taking one last look around the room, he slipped out of the shack and into the jungle.

◆   ◆   ◆

Though she had only been on Tortola for two days, Rebecca adapted easily to the relaxed rhythm and pace of life on the island. And although the accommodations at the compound would require some continuing adjustment, such things as bottled-water showers and plastic-bucket toilets were a small price to pay for the experience of living in an unspoiled tropical paradise.

She loaded the provisions she and Troy had bought at a market in Road Town, then took a seat on the rear bench of Randi's van and breathed in deeply. The air had just been purified by a brief and sudden rainstorm, and now it smelled of damp earth and flowers. Watching the sun's afternoon rays break dramatically through the squall's scattering clouds, she reached over and placed her hand on Troy's arm.

"What's this about?" Troy asked.

"I just want you to know how grateful I am that you brought me here. I've been to lots of different tropical islands, but Tortola has a certain magic to it that's hard to describe."

"It does, doesn't it?" he replied with a wistful longing in his voice. "Sometimes I wonder why I ever left."

"And last night was a lot of fun, too. We'll definitely have to visit the Virgin Queen again before we leave."

"Well, I figured we had to celebrate you getting our two guests to eat. I still don't know how you did that so quickly."

Rebecca shrugged her shoulders. "Just lucky, I guess. Which reminds me, we need to have Randi deliver us a fresh batch of mackerel every day from here on out."

"Hear that, Randi? Think you can take over your dad's old delivery schedule?"

"Wouldn't let nobody else do it, dat's for sure. And by de way, are you two in a hurry to get back to de compound? Dispatch called while you were in de store. I got a pickup at de airport."

"That's fine with me. Rebecca?"

"Sure. The only thing we have left to do is put the transducers in the water, and it's too late to do that today anyway."

Randi drummed his fingers on the steering wheel. "Den it's off to de airport we go."

With the van bouncing its way to the airfield, Randi sang to the rhythmic squeaking of the shocks bottoming out on the rough road. "Do you know de Dolphin Man, de Dolphin Man, de Dolphin Man? Do you know de Dolphin Man, who lives down de lane …"

The song instantly transported Troy back in time. "I'd almost forgotten," he whispered just loudly enough for Rebecca to hear.

"Forgotten what?" she asked, curious about how this variation on 'Do You Know the Muffin Man?' had evolved.

"I used to invite schoolchildren to the compound, and somehow they came up with that song to sing to me."

"I was one of dem children," Randi chimed in. "Comin' to yo' place and seein' dat dolphin was a treat I'll never forget. Remember how you'd ... Hold on a minute, I tink dat's my fare," he said while turning the van onto the gravel road in front of the terminal.

To Rebecca, the sight of Ryan standing there could not have been more disorienting.

Troy's look of stunned betrayal said it all. "Oh, Rebecca," he gasped, holding a hand over his open mouth. "I ... I thought I could trust you. I thought we had an understanding."

"We did. I mean, we still *do* have an understanding! I swear that I did not tell him where we were. You have to believe that I wouldn't do that to you!"

As the van approached, Ryan was just as surprised to see Troy and Rebecca inside it. And while he was relieved to have found them so effortlessly, he could tell that Troy was less than thrilled by his arrival. Sliding open the van's side door the instant it stopped, he hurried into his practiced explanation. "Listen, Dr. Wallace, I understand why you don't think I should be here, and I want you to know that Rebecca did not tell me where you were. She called last night and left a message saying she missed me, but that's all. I rebounded the call and got connected to The Virgin Queen. I swear, the blame is all mine."

Troy's expression softened quickly. "Ryan, I never wanted to exclude you from coming here. It's just that I didn't want you to be burdened with a secret that would be too hard for you to keep."

"I know that. And I promise, I have not breathed a word about what happened on my boat that day to anyone."

"And no one knows you're here?"

"Nope. Everybody thinks I'm in Florida attending a funeral."

"And the station just let you go?" Rebecca asked, still hardly able to believe he was standing right there in front of her.

"Well, by the time my producer finds out, she won't have much choice, will she? Besides, we have a light load ahead of us for the next few days. I don't think I'll be in too much trouble when I get back. Now, explain to me why you two are in this taxi when you obviously didn't even know I was coming."

Troy offered his hand to help Ryan up into the van. "We were just picking up a few groceries in town when Randi here got the dispatch."

Ryan sat down next to Rebecca in the back seat and gave Randi a quick nod of greeting. "Did you count on a third mouth to feed?"

Rebecca made no attempt to hide how happy she was that Ryan had found his way to the island.

"We didn't count on it, but we have enough food to entertain any unexpected guests. Isn't that right, Troy?"

"That's right," Troy smiled.

She then leaned in close to Ryan and whispered directly into his ear. "By the way, you weren't *completely* unexpected. Caller ID wasn't invented yesterday, you know."

Chapter 25

In the dim light of predawn, Ryan peeled off the flannel blanket and rose stiffly from the shack's wooden floor. Peering out the building's open window, he scratched his bare stomach and tugged at the waistband of his boxer briefs, which accentuated the trim, muscular proportions of his body.

Ryan sensed that she was watching him from her cot just a few feet away. After slipping into a pair of baggy nylon trunks, he was nearly out the door when he turned toward her and quietly asked, "You awake?"

Rebecca gave an exaggerated stretch and yawn. "Almost. And why are you up so early?"

Ryan motioned toward the window. "Troy's already out there. He's got a fire and a pot of coffee started, and it looks like he's getting the transducers ready to put in the water. I thought I'd go see if I could make myself useful."

"He'd appreciate that. Just make sure neither of you go in with the dolphins. I want to take it really slow today so we don't spook them."

"Gotcha." He nodded.

"And, Ryan?"

He paused in mid-exit and turned to look at her. "Yes?"

"I'm really glad you're here."

Smiling, he came back into the room, knelt down beside the cot, and gave her a quick peck on the forehead. "So am I. Even if there isn't a bed for me to sleep on," he said while heading out the door. "Or a bathroom. Or running water. Or a TV."

Shaking her head and letting out a muffled laugh, she rolled over and closed her eyes to get a few more minutes of sleep.

Ryan scooted barefoot through the powdery white sand and stopped by the fire to warm his hands. Crouched beside the flames, he watched Troy unwind the four long transducer cables. "Looks like you've got everything ready to go," he said while pouring himself a cup of coffee.

"Just about. I'll let Rebecca decide when we can put the transducers in." He fed the trailing end of each cable through the shed's lone window. "The last thing I want to do is upset our guests over there."

With the cables laid out neatly in the sand between the shed and the lagoon, Troy ambled over and sat down next to the fire. "Of course, I'd be lying if I said I wasn't anxious to get things rolling. I mean, who knows? The mother may have started sending images to the baby the very moment it was born."

"You think?" Ryan asked, pouring Troy an aluminum cup full of the strong, thick brew.

"It's possible. That's the beauty of communicating with pictures. You don't have to learn a language to be able to exchange ideas."

"I guess that's true, huh?" Handing the coffee to Dr. Wallace, Ryan raised his own cup. "Then let's make a toast. Here's to success beyond your wildest dreams."

Troy clinked his cup against Ryan's and smiled. "To success!"

◆   ◆   ◆

With the intense midday sun bearing down on the complex, Rebecca made her final preparations before going into the lagoon.

Ryan sat fidgeting in the shade of a palm tree near the water's edge. "Are you sure there isn't something I can do to help?"

"If the dolphins are ready to eat, I'll need you to keep tossing me mackerel from the ice chest over there. And later on I'll need a hand placing the transducers in the water. But right now there's not really much for you to do," she said while slipping out of her shorts and tank top, down to a jade-green bikini.

Accustomed to seeing her in her turquoise one-piece, Ryan relished the way the bikini exposed her curvaceous figure. "Whoa. I was beginning to think you lived in that SeaWorld suit."

"Sometimes I feel like I do," she laughed. Turning to catch a glimpse of the dolphins as they swam by, she hoped that wearing the suit would not impede the progress she had made with them the other night.

With his eyes following her golden mane downward, Ryan's attention was drawn to a tattoo barely peeking over the bottom of her bikini. "And would you look at that—I wouldn't have pegged you as the tattoo type." Opening his eyes a little wider, he asked, "Can I see the rest of it?"

She rarely wore a two-piece, so it had been quite some time since anyone had seen the design inked into the small of her back. "I guess so. You're not going to make fun of it, are you?"

"I can't promise that until I see it," he snickered.

Slightly embarrassed and sure he wouldn't let the issue drop, she turned down the waistband of her suit just far enough to reveal the whole tattoo. "I had it done about five years ago. I'll bet you've never seen anything like it before, have you?"

Ryan felt his throat tighten slightly as he studied the image: 11:11, flanked by a pair of angel wings. "Why do you have *that?*"

Rebecca could feel herself blushing. "I wish I had a good answer." Her voice then took a distant tone. "The truth is, I started noticing eleven-eleven on digital clocks back when I was in high school. And every time I did, I got the strangest feeling that it meant something important. I know it sounds crazy, but it felt like I was receiving some kind of message."

He gave her a skewed look. "What do you mean, message? From who?"

"Well, that's the really weird part. It was almost as if there was some kind of ..." she paused and struggled for the right words. "Some kind of *presence* trying to attract my attention. And it got to the point where I was seeing eleven-eleven so often that I would literally shout out things like, 'What are you trying to tell me? What does it mean?'"

Ryan's expression turned to troubled intrigue. "Who were you talking to?"

"I didn't know, but eventually I came to believe that it was something like my guardian angel."

"And did you ever get an answer?"

"No. But I *did* get the feeling that my spirit was receiving some kind of important information, even if my mind couldn't figure it out. I'll tell you, there were times when I thought I was going insane—that I was the only one having this bizarre experience."

Ryan did a double-take. "You mean you *weren't?*"

"Hardly. Believe it or not, there are a *lot* of people who notice 11:11."

"How do you know that?"

"The Internet. That's where we found each other, because that's where we all went to look for an explanation."

"And is there an explanation?"

Though Rebecca had discussed this a few times before, she had never seen someone so intensely curious her story. "Some people think it's a kind of genetic alarm clock embedded in our DNA. Others think it symbolizes a gateway to higher spiritual awareness." She noticed the glazed and distant look in his eyes. "Hey, are you okay?"

"Yeah, I'm all right," he stammered. "But there's something I need to show you." He slowly unclasped and peeled off his wristwatch—a heavy, stainless-steel Rolex—and handed it to her.

"What's this?" she asked, her confusion apparent as she studied the watch.

"Turn it over," was all he said.

Inscribed on back of the watch were the words, *For my 11:11 angel. Love, Mom.*

She could not have looked more perplexed. "I don't understand. Why do you have this?"

"November eleventh is my birthday, and, get this, I was born at exactly eleven minutes past eleven in the morning."

Rebecca just stared at the inscription.

"Anyway, the doctors and nurses at the hospital all made a big deal out of it, and pretty soon even my mom got caught up in the whole thing. She figured out that she had gotten pregnant on February eleventh—two-eleven, get it? Since the day I was born, I've always been my mom's little 'eleven-eleven angel.'"

Rebecca took a moment to process what she'd heard. "So, do you notice it on a clock?"

"Oh, I'll see it every once in a while. But the only significance I ever attached to it was that it's my birthday."

"And you've never known anyone else that it means something special to?"

"Other than my mom and dad, you're the first."

She ran her fingers thoughtfully over the back of the watch. "I'm sorry, but I just don't know what to say. Do you realize how strange all this is?"

"Are you kidding? Of course I do. But after everything that's happened to me these last couple of weeks, I'm beginning to believe that strange is the new normal."

◆　　　◆　　　◆

Following an early dinner of flame-grilled chicken, Dr. Wallace wiped the sticky residue of a roasted marshmallow off his mouth and smiled at the progress they had made that day: Rebecca had coaxed both dolphins to eat their fill of mackerel, while Ryan had been a big help getting the transducers placed evenly in the water around the perimeter of the lagoon. The equipment, including a new DVD recorder, appeared to be functioning flawlessly.

Ryan rose from the log bench near the campfire and stretched his arms high above his head. "Well, Doc, looks to me like you're just about ready for business."

Troy stirred the fire's glowing coals with a long stick. "Thanks to the two of you, we're much further along than I would have ever imagined. And Ryan, I want to take this opportunity to tell you how good it feels to have you here. It was wrong of me to not invite you in the first place."

Ryan waved off Troy's apology. "Listen, I know you thought it was the safest thing for everyone concerned. I probably would have done the same thing if I'd been in your shoes."

Rebecca stood up and wiped the sand off the back of her jeans, then laid a hand on each of their shoulders and nudged them toward the shack. "Okay, now that we've gotten all the apologies out of the way, what do you say we go in there and see if this stuff's really going to work?"

"That sounds like a great idea," Troy replied and led the way into the building.

With darkness enveloping the compound, they filed into the room and gathered around the workbench full of equipment. Watching intently while Troy flipped a series of switches, Ryan and Rebecca held each other's hand as the large video monitor began to glow its familiar monochromatic green. When it came time to throw the final toggle, Dr. Wallace, his face bathed in the emerald light, took a deep breath. "Everybody ready?" he asked and flipped the switch.

To their amazement, success was instantaneous.

On the screen, a perfect digital representation of Rebecca swam back and forth. Closer inspection revealed that she was pushing a small fish ahead of her. Every so often she would stop and allow the fish to hover motionless at her side.

"Oh my gosh, that's *me!*" Rebecca blurted. "That's what I was doing when I was trying to get the baby to eat for the first time."

Ryan craned forward and squinted at the highly-detailed sonographic image on the monitor. "Are … are you *naked?*" he asked with a gulp.

After watching herself swim through a repeating loop of the same animated clip, Rebecca noticed what he was noticing and turned away in embarrassment. "Listen, I can explain what I was doing."

"Hey, you don't have to explain anything. Just be sure to tell me the next time you decide to go skinny-dipping!"

"All right, now, Ryan," Troy interjected. "That's enough. We all need to maintain some scientific objectivity here. The real news is that the equipment seems to be working perfectly." With an exuberant smile, he reached over and turned on the DVD recorder.

"Sorry, Doc. I almost forgot that this is science." Hanging his head in feigned shame, Ryan prepared his punch line. "And just so I can make a few more observations of my own, would you make sure I get a copy of that disc?" He winked and gave Troy a playful nudge with his elbow.

"Jeez, give it up already, would you?" Rebecca groaned, her face still turned away from the screen. "Just let me know when the mother starts projecting something else."

But as minutes passed and the identical scene played over and over again on the monitor, Troy's ebullience began to wane.

"This is so similar to what we saw on Ryan's boat that I'm beginning to wonder if the primary function of their ultrasonic imaging is nothing more than an instant-replay machine."

"Would that be so bad?" Ryan asked. "I mean, we're still talking about a major scientific breakthrough."

Troy barely acknowledged the comment. "Ryan, if that's all I was after, I would have stayed at SeaWorld. The whole reason for coming back here was because I thought we might actually learn what dolphins *teach* each other."

Ryan nodded and kept his eyes fixed on the screen. "I get your point."

Fifteen uneventful minutes later, Rebecca stood up and began to putter around the shack. Unrolling her sleeping bag onto one of the cots, she allowed herself to imagine a worst-case scenario. "You're not thinking this is all we're going to see, are you, Troy?"

"No, but I have to admit that I'm a little disheartened. I had imagined a much more significant use of their abilities than this."

"Well, I wouldn't get too bummed out yet," Ryan said, his eyes beginning to glaze as he stared at the screen. "I'll bet something new comes up any minute."

But contrary to their hopes, the imagery never changed. In the darkened room, lit only by the green glow of the monitor, the same patterns of light cast the same shadows on the walls for hours on end. And even though no one said anything more about it, each one of them dealt with the disappointing situation in their own way. Troy fidgeted with the equipment. Rebecca kept herself busy straightening up the room.

Ryan lay down on a pile of blankets he'd assembled on the floor and fell asleep.

Chapter 26

The dream, more vivid than any he'd ever experienced, resumed at the exact place where it had been interrupted days before. He was walking barefoot in the sand, squinting into a blazing yellow sun as it rose over the ocean. The tranquility of the moment permeated his entire being.

"Does everyone get this opportunity?" he asked while walking beside her along the shore.

"Of course they do," she replied. "But …"

"But what?"

"But first they have to wake up. Do you understand the meaning of what I'm telling you?"

In a strange new way, he *was* beginning to understand. "I do. And I also now know that 11:11 is somehow connected to this process of waking up."

She smiled. "For some people, yes. For others it represents a profound moment of growth. Still others receive it as an affirmation of what they already know." Her stride and speech were full of purpose, and when she stopped and turned to look in his eyes, the intensity of her gaze was almost unbearable. "The difference depends on the person receiving it."

The word *receiving* struck a chord of awareness that was growing stronger within him. "Are you saying this wake-up call has been *sent* by someone?"

"I am saying exactly that." Her reply seemed intentionally vague.

Ryan stared out over the sparkling ocean and chose his next words carefully. "Is it important to know the sender?" he asked.

She lowered herself down to sit and seemed to be looking for a way to explain the unexplainable. "It's only as important as a drop of seawater is to the sea."

Ryan pondered her analogy, realizing that—as a unit of measure—a drop was insignificant. But taking the meaning of her statement another way, he realized that a single drop of water could also reveal the very nature of the entire ocean.

She could see the reflection of the rising sun in his eyes. "You *are* beginning to understand, aren't you?"

Ryan nodded. "I think I am."

"Then you should also understand who sent this wake-up call."

The analogy of the drop and the ocean helped him focus his thoughts. "It was humanity sending a message to itself," he answered. "From one moment in time to another."

A tear formed and streamed down her face as she stood. Shaking the sand off her flowing dress, she said, "Come with me, there's something I want to show you."

◆   ◆   ◆

He woke slowly, disoriented by his surroundings. With Troy and Rebecca perched on stools barely three feet away, he shifted uncomfortably while regaining his bearings.

"Good morning, Sunshine," Rebecca said, and reached over to tousle his already tangled hair.

"Man, where was I?" he asked, rubbing the crust from his eyes.

"Out, that's for sure," Troy chuckled. "One minute you were here with us, the next thing we knew you were curled up and sleeping like a baby."

Ryan sat up and scratched his stomach. "Did anything change on the monitor?"

"Unfortunately, no," Troy answered. "It's like a scratched record that keeps playing the same thing over and over."

"And you're sure it's not a problem with the equipment?"

"I'm sure. For some reason, she just keeps transmitting this image. My guess is she's been sending it ever since Rebecca got in the water with them two days ago."

Rising stiffly from the floor, Ryan put a hand on a corner of the monitor and leaned into the screen.

"You know," Rebecca observed out loud. "You stare at this thing long enough, and you start to forget what you're looking at."

"Speak for yourself," Ryan leered with a playful smirk.

"No, seriously. After a while, the repetition gets to you and kind of puts you in this meditative state. I'm actually beginning to think it's why you got so sleepy: it's like a visual alpha-wave generator."

Ryan latched his hands behind his head. "You know, you're right—it *is* just like an alpha-wave generator! Now, what the hell are alpha waves again?"

"They're brain waves," Troy volunteered. "They're the ones your brain produces while you're either dreaming or in a deep state of meditation."

At that, Ryan recalled every detail of his own recurring dream. He stared at Rebecca with alarming, wide-awake intensity.

"What is it?" she asked.

"I just remembered something—something important that I need to tell you."

She could sense the difficulty he was having at expressing himself. "Okay. What is it?"

"Well, I…" he stammered. "I mean, it's kind of personal."

"Oh."

Troy cleared his throat. "You know, there's no reason for all three of us to be watching the monitor the whole time. Why don't the two of you take some time off and go explore the island a little bit? There's a beautiful beach at Smuggler's Cove, and it's not more than a twenty-minute walk from here."

Rebecca snapped to giddy attention. "Really? Are you sure?"

"Of course. After all, who knows how long she may keep retransmitting this same image? We certainly don't need more than one person at a time to keep watch. Besides, there's still plenty for me to do around here."

Rebecca turned to Ryan. "What do you say?"

"Are you kidding? I say we get the hell out of here before Troy changes his mind! You grab us a couple of beach towels, and I'll pack us a picnic lunch." He bounded out the door and headed straight for the ice chest. "Oh, and thanks, Doc!" he called back as the door slammed shut behind him.

"Yes," Rebecca added. "Thank you so much, Troy. I owe you one."

Dr. Wallace stopped her with a wave of his hand. "Rebecca, *I'm* the one who owes both of you. Don't you see that I wouldn't even be here if not for you and Ryan? Now hurry up and get going. I can't wait to see what becomes of this little chemistry experiment going on between the two of you."

A bashful grin spread across her face. "It shows?"

"Only from the minute I first saw you two together," he laughed, shooing her out the door.

Chapter 27

Ryan and Rebecca pushed their way through the thick foliage surrounding Smuggler's Cove. Sweating and breathing heavily from their hike, they stopped at the first clearing in the shoreline and absorbed the panorama unfolding before them.

"It's like a postcard," Ryan marveled. In the distance, towering thunderhead clouds mushroomed over a calm sea, while tiny waves lapped against one of the most beautiful beaches he'd ever seen.

"It *is* amazing," Rebecca concurred, shielding her eyes against the sun. "Until you see it in person, you can't believe the ocean could be such a bright turquoise."

"Bimini has water like this," he said, leading her onto the white, powdery sand. After staking a spot on the vacant beach, he opened the canvas tote they'd brought along, pulled out two towels, and spread them neatly just a few feet away from the water's edge. "That's one of my favorite places to dive."

"You're a diver?" She planted her hands on her hips and shook her head. "You know, how is it that I have so many things in common with a guy I could barely stand the first time I met him? Am I really that poor a judge of character?"

He slipped off his tennis shoes and sat down on one of the towels. He knew better than to try to hide anything from her. "No, you were a perfect judge of character—at least of the character I was being that day."

"So, what are we talking here? Multiple Personality Disorder?"

"No, more like a television personality who was a bit too taken with himself and became the Funhunter off screen as well as on. And I know it's not a very good excuse, but in the back of every actor's mind is this fear that he'll be out of a job tomorrow. That fear tells you that you might as well take advantage of whatever your celebrity can get you today."

"And your particular level must get you plenty of girls without even trying," she deduced while stripping down to a vermilion one-piece suit and making herself comfortable on her own towel. "Because you stink at making a good first impression."

Ryan turned away and spoke toward the open expanse of beach. "Yeah, I know. But, believe it or not, I really wasn't like that before I started doing the *South Coast Safari* thing." He lay down and rolled onto his side to face her. "To be honest, over the past couple of years, I've spent more time and effort getting *away* from women than I did trying to get hooked up."

"Oh, poor baby!"

"Hey, I know it sounds conceited, but it's the truth. And you know what? I'll bet it isn't that different for you. You're a beautiful woman with an incredible figure who makes her living in a Spandex uniform. Care to tell me how many propositions you have to decline in a week?"

The way she arched her brows and shifted her eyes was answer enough.

"I thought so." He propped his head up. "I guess what I'm trying to say is that once you get in the habit of turning people away, you kind of forget how to invite them in." A sudden shift in his voice—a soft and distant longing—tinged his words. "Maybe that's what we really have most in common."

His insight and candor caught her off guard. Staring into his eyes, she searched for a sign of false pretense. Finding none, she finally asked, "So, is this the real Ryan Ericson, or are you just that good of an actor?"

"Well, faking sincerity *is* one of my gifts," he smirked while unconsciously drawing four lines—all equal in length and parallel to each other—in the sand. "But I didn't come all this way to impress you with my acting."

Noticing the lines, she reached over and poked two small dots between them. "No, I don't suppose you did. Besides, there's no denying that we really *do* have something special in common."

He looked down at the digits in the sand. "Yeah. I'm still trying to wrap my mind around that one. Which reminds me," he began, sounding slightly lost as he put his thoughts together. "Is there something more to this whole 11:11 thing than what you've told me? I know you said that there are others like you out there who see it and think it symbolizes a moment of ..."

"Spiritual awakening?"

"Yes, but why would anyone associate that kind of meaning—*any* kind of meaning—with seeing numbers on a clock? It just doesn't make sense."

"No, it doesn't. That's why it's called the 11:11 *phenomenon*. No one can explain why it's happening."

"It's just so weird. And there's something else: Has it occurred to you that this phenomenon happens to be taking place around the same time as the end of the Mayan calendar and the beginning of Aquarius, which both seem to refer to the same message of awakening?"

Her eyes locked onto his. "Ryan Ericson, you *are* full of surprises, aren't you? I've never told anyone this, but, to me, the synchronicity between these three things is almost impossible to ignore."

Falling quiet for a long time, Ryan retraced the digits in the sand over and over again. Then, almost in a whisper, he asked, "What does it feel like when you see it?"

"Oh, that's right—Mr. 11:11 himself has never had the experience," she answered with an incredulous laugh. "Tell you what—let's try something. Lie down flat on your stomach and let me see if I can do this." As she spoke, she propped herself up onto her knees.

Turning over and making himself comfortable on the towel, he could hear her breath becoming slow and deep. He closed his eyes, and he sensed that his own breathing was beginning to synchronize with hers.

Rebecca's voice, quiet and steady, floated into his head like soft music. "The most memorable times for me are when I'm really busy—running around doing errands or whatever, and then it'll just hit me: this impulse to look over at my watch or a clock exactly at 11:11."

She gently laid her right hand on the lower part of his back.

"Whenever this happens, I get this feeling that I'm not alone—that something, or someone, is trying to get my attention."

She then placed her left hand just below his shoulder blades.

"And as I get more fully drawn into the moment, I find myself immersed in a certain kind of knowingness that goes way beyond my everyday life."

With her hands resting flat on his skin, she slowed the tempo of her speech. "It's the hardest thing to describe, but for a split second I feel like I truly understand my place in the grand scheme of things." She paused and waited for the words to come. "I understand the way that I am connected to everyone and everything in the universe."

She became quiet. Closing her eyes and recalling the physical tingling that often accompanied her 11:11 sightings, she imagined herself being able to transfer this sensation out through her hands and into his body. The process took only minutes, but they were long, silent minutes that seemed to defy the usual measurement of time.

He knew it might be his imagination running away from him, but Ryan began to feel a cycling sensation, a movement of energy, flowing between her hands. Soon his whole body absorbed the slow and rhythmic pulse.

"Then, when it's all over, I'm usually left with this overpowering sense of gratitude, wondering if other people get the opportunity to experience such a deep level of peace within themselves."

Hearing her words echo the dialogue of his recent dreams, he felt like he was losing his grip on reality. "Rebecca," he spoke softly, never opening his eyes, "I don't know if I'm ready for what's happening."

She breathed deeply and slowly for a prolonged moment, then moved one of her hands to the back of his head and tenderly stroked his hair. "Yes you are, Ryan. In fact, the only reason any of this is happening to you is because you *are* ready."

◆　　　◆　　　◆

Sheltered under a cluster of rustling palm trees, they lay there on the beach and talked for hours. The sun's low position in the sky let them know how much time had passed since their arrival.

"Well, it's official," Ryan announced. "I now know more about you than any woman I've ever met in my life."

Lying on the towel, Rebecca rolled over and rested her head upon his outstretched arm. "I don't believe that. What you really mean is that you've learned certain things about me that you've never cared to know about any other woman before."

He considered her observation. "I guess that may be true."

She nuzzled her head next to his. "So, aren't you wondering how I *do* compare to what you know about other women?"

With his face only a few inches away from hers, he feigned coyness. "Umm, I'm not exactly sure what you mean."

"I mean, for instance, aren't you wondering how good of a kisser I am?"

He had never felt such expectation. "The thought may have crossed my mind."

Before he could finish, she drew slowly closer to him until there was just a fraction of an inch between them. "Then let the comparison begin."

It was as if they were being drawn together by a gentle, magnetic force, and when their lips touched, Ryan let her take the lead. Impulse told him otherwise—to take charge as always—but intuition won the moment. With his mouth relaxed and barely open, he let himself enjoy the sensation of the softness of her lips, the slow and tantalizing intrusion of her tongue. A quiet moan of pleasure deep in her throat sent his pulse racing.

"And I'm curious," she whispered seductively. "How do curves like mine compare to all those skinny Hollywood girls?" Saying this, she reached over and guided his hand on a trajectory that started at her waist and moved upward.

Ryan savored the feel of her toned yet supple body. Then, with delicate yet confident force, he kissed her neck just below her earlobe and whispered, "I wouldn't have thought it possible, but every inch of you is as beautiful on the outside as you are on the inside."

She closed her eyes while his hands glided over her skin. "I'd like to believe I'm the first person you've ever said that to."

He kissed his way down her neck to the top of her shoulder. "Would you settle for being the first person I've said it to and meant it?"

She tilted her head back and let out a surrendering sigh of pleasure. "You know, if settling feels this good, I suppose I could lower my standards a bit and still live with myself."

Chapter 28

Late afternoon had arrived by the time Ryan and Rebecca returned to the compound. Holding hands as they bounded into the dimly lit shack, they found Troy sitting precisely where they had left him.

"Hey, Doc. Any luck?" Ryan asked and plopped himself down on one of the cots. A quick glance at the screen revealed that nothing had changed.

Taking note of Ryan's cheery tone and Rebecca's relaxed, replete posture, Dr. Wallace could see that their chemistry had proven compatible indeed. He himself had made less progress. "I'm afraid not," he said, the dejection apparent in his voice.

"Hey, it's only been a day," Ryan interjected. "You're not giving up on seeing any more images, are you?"

"Of course not, but by the same token, I don't have all the time in the world, either. Remember, this equipment isn't mine to keep—and Calvin and Chad aren't stupid. They'll figure out where I am before long, if they haven't already."

Rebecca attempted to steer the conversation away from the negative. "Well, at the very least, you've got the DVD proving that your theory on dolphin imaging was correct. And I'd say that's worth a special dinner. How about we grill the steaks we bought in town?"

Ryan rubbed his stomach. "Oh, man, a steak sure sounds good to me."

"Me, too," Troy said. "Besides, you're right, Rebecca. Just from the few images we've already recorded, I'd have no trouble raising grant money to continue my research wherever I wanted."

"Then it's settled," Rebecca declared. "Ryan, do you want to start the charcoals?"

"Aye, aye, Cap'n." Ryan saluted and headed out the door.

Rebecca watched him through the window before directing her attention to the dolphins gliding slowly though the water. "Have they eaten yet today?"

Troy walked over to the window and looked out. "No. I thought I'd keep the routine constant, with you as the provider of food. There's a fresh batch of mackerel that Randi brought out a couple of hours ago."

"That's good. I guess I'll go ahead and feed them while Ryan cooks the steaks." She took a couple of steps toward the door.

Troy followed her out. "Thanks, Rebecca. For everything. And I know I keep saying this, but I can't begin to tell you how grateful I am for all you've done for me these past few weeks."

◆　　　◆　　　◆

Miles away, in a small unkempt house on the side of a bustling dirt road, Troy's voice crackled over the speaker Jerry had placed near his bed.

"*Weeks?*" Jerry yelped at the speaker. He took another long drag on the joint he'd rolled and watched the smoke drift over his head. "These last few *weeks?* Oh, that's rich!" He scratched an itch on his shirtless belly as he lay there.

Under the influence of the drug, the volume of his voice rose steadily. "What about the *years* you got out of me, huh, Dr. Wallace? What about all those *years?*" His ranting was so loud that people passing his window heard him and, unnerved, crossed to the other side of the street.

◆　　　◆　　　◆

Standing chest-deep in the warm water of the lagoon, Rebecca was glad to see both the mother and the baby quickly devour the entire cooler's worth of mackerel.

"You two were hungry!" she said, persuading the dolphins to take the last two fish directly from her hands.

She was famished as well, and with the sun setting behind the low hills of Tortola's summit, the smell of sizzling steaks was tantalizing.

"Who's ready for a nice, juicy T-bone?" Ryan shouted, as if reading her mind. "'Cause these babies are just about ready to ..."

Suddenly, the alarming sound of falling furniture and frantic, garbled exclamations coming from inside the shack shattered the evening's quiet.

"Ryan, Rebecca! Get in here, quick!" Troy's agitated voice caused nearby birds to flee in a panic and Ryan to drop one of the steaks into the fire. "Hurry!"

Though alarmed, Rebecca exited the water slowly so as not to startle the dolphins. Then she sprinted up the beach to the shack as fast as she could run. She opened the door to find Ryan and Troy staring intently at the monitor. "What? What is it?" she asked, trying to catch her breath. "Did you see something?"

"Take a look," Troy answered and stepped away from the monitor to give her room.

Rebecca studied the image on the screen—a headless female form holding a fish in each hand. "That's me again! Or most of me, anyway." It was the dolphins' view of her body from the shoulders down. Grabbing a chair, she parked herself between Ryan and Troy and peered in wide-eyed astonishment at the screen. "And those are the last two fish I just fed them."

"How's it feel to be the star of your own television series?" Ryan asked.

Before she had a chance to answer, the imagery changed, making it immediately clear to them that this session was going to be far more eventful than the one the night before.

Troy glanced over to make sure the DVD recorder was on, and together they watched with rapt attention as the scene went from an exact duplication of a past event to that of a completely fabricated reality. In seconds, the fish she was holding simply disappeared, revealing her bare hands opening and closing as if she were doing finger-dexterity exercises. Seconds later, the image zoomed in on her left hand, which was still flexing rapidly.

"Wait a minute. I never did that," Rebecca was stumped. "Troy, what's going on?"

Dr. Wallace did not answer, but his trembling fingers drumming against the plywood shelf relayed something monumental was taking place.

A moment later, the skin on Rebecca's animated hand disappeared, just as the fish had vanished before.

"Holy shit," Ryan stammered.

In a surreal moment that challenged their ability to believe it was actually happening, they found themselves staring at a high-resolution scan of the muscles and tendons in her hand, contracting and relaxing with each clench.

"Oh my god," Rebecca whispered as the digital muscles peeled away to reveal the still-flexing skeletal fingers behind them. The clarity and detail was beyond what any X-ray could have provided.

The screen went momentarily blank.

Seconds later, a new image appeared. It was the skeleton of a five-fingered appendage once again, only this time it was not human—it belonged to a dolphin.

Rebecca's face was ashen. "Dr. Wallace, could she be doing what I think she's doing?"

Troy gave a slow and thoughtful nod.

Ryan had no idea what was going on. "What? What is she doing?"

Troy's voice was shaky yet full of conviction. "You're not going to believe this, but I think we are watching a lecture on the differences and similarities between dolphins and humans."

"Yes!" Rebecca squealed. "Don't you get it? It's as if she's saying, 'The person that's been feeding us these last couple of days is an animal with a five-fingered hand similar to ours, but which is shaped to better suit life on land instead of in the ocean.'"

"What? How the hell are you getting all that from pictures of hand bones?"

"Because she's using the same visual aids I do when I give my lectures at SeaWorld."

"I concur," Troy said, his voice still wavering. "I wonder if they compare any of our other similarities …"

He did not have to wonder long.

On the monitor, the image of a human skull appeared. Then the skull dissolved to reveal a high-resolution image of a brain with two hemispheres and a cortex. Then, just as Troy had surmised, a dolphin skull filled the screen before fading away to reveal the similar structure of a dolphin brain.

The next images depicted a human walking upright, followed by the figure of a dolphin swimming through an invisible body of water.

"This is incredible," Troy marveled with a shake of his head.

Viewing the comparisons, Ryan recalled the old *In Search Of* episode he had watched in his car, reversing in his mind the show's title from *Dolphins, Humans of the Sea* to *Humans, Dolphins of the Land.* "This can't be real," he muttered and placed a hand on the monitor to steady himself.

To their astonishment, the images that followed seemed to convey nothing less than the evolution of *Homo sapiens*. The sequences— separated by an occasional pattern of dots on a field of black—displayed various stages of human development, beginning with a bipedal creature barely walking upright and ending with a modern hominid repeatedly flexing its dexterous fingers as it strode across the screen. After a close-up of two human hands, the scene snapped to a video representation of a crudely manufactured building of stacked stones.

"Are you kidding me?" Ryan blurted. "We're watching *human* history? How is that possible?"

Troy forced a detached, professional calmness into his voice. "Ryan, dolphins have been on earth for forty million years. That's plenty long enough to witness every single stage of our development."

Another pattern of dots filled the screen, followed by a slow-motion animation of two humans fighting each other with their bare hands.

"I assume that what we're watching is a basic explanation of how dolphins perceive human beings," Troy surmised. "We're warm-blooded, air-breathing mammals similar to them in many ways, but different in that we live on land, walk, build things, and are preoccupied with conflict and violence."

The final animation, depicting humanity's more recent inventions of machines, vehicles, and weapons of all shapes and sizes, terminated with the image of a nuclear explosion's mushroom cloud. Following that was one last view of the stationary dots. When the speckled pattern disappeared, the screen went blank, as if someone had just turned off the computer.

The lesson, which had lasted no more than five minutes, was obviously over.

A long, surreal moment passed before any of them spoke.

"Okay, did that really just happen, or are we all hallucinating the same thing?" Rebecca asked nervously.

"I'll play it back and we'll find out," Troy answered and pushed a few buttons on the DVD recorder. Soon the mother's transmissions were showing again on a smaller playback monitor.

As the lesson replayed, Troy took special notice of the dark gaps between sequences. "What do you think these interruptions between scenes are?"

Ryan, squinting at the screen, volunteered an explanation. "They remind me of the timing markers that are placed between segments of a television show. They're usually solid black, and they indicate where a commercial would be inserted."

Troy considered Ryan's answer. "Timing markers," he said with deep concentration. When the next break between animation sequences appeared, he paused the recorder on the speckled image. "But what are these little dots, and why are they always in the same identical place?"

Incredibly, Rebecca recognized the pattern. At first she couldn't believe it, but the longer she stared at the screen, the more certain she became. "Those aren't dots." She swallowed hard and took another long look at the monitor.

Troy blurred his vision to see if the speckles blended into some kind of hidden connect-the-dots image. Then he asked, "Well, what are they?"

Rebecca did not speak right away, and the quiet tension built to a nearly unbearable level. "They're stars and planets."

"I'm afraid I'm not following you," Troy said. "Stars and planets?"

Ryan *was* following her, though. He recognized the image from the poster in Rebecca's apartment. "Okay, this is just getting too damned weird. Is that the *Tree of Life?*"

"Excuse me," Troy interjected. "Since I'm obviously the only one here who doesn't know what you two are talking about, would someone please fill me in?"

"It's the planets of our solar system perfectly aligned with each other and crossing the center of the Milky Way. See, these brighter dots in a row are planets, and this elongated cloud of tiny specks is the Milky Way. It's a unique conjunction that only happens about every five thousand years. Ancient Mayans named it the *Tree of Life* because the line of planets looked to them like a massive branch crossing a tree trunk."

Troy pondered her explanation. "Every five thousand years? Could that be it? Is that what these screens are—timing markers placed between five-thousand-year sequences of events?"

He restarted the video, noticing that the dot-pattern appeared far more frequently near the beginning than it did at the end. He had to acknowledge the logic of the theory. "Look at this," he said, pointing to the screen. "Here's one of the last markers, right before the bare-handed fight scene. Then we see another marker, which is followed by every invention of modern times: ships, planes, nuclear weapons. And then there's this one last marker before the screen goes blank. It's almost like she's referring to a *Tree of Life* conjunction that hasn't even happened yet."

"That's because it hasn't," Rebecca said cryptically. "It's still a few years away."

Troy spun around to stare at her. "Wait a minute. Are you telling me you know the exact *date?*"

"It's no secret. It's December 21st, 2012, the day of the winter solstice."

Ryan waited for her response to sink in. "Go on. Tell him the rest of it," he prodded.

Troy had to sit down. "The rest of it? The rest of what?"

Rebecca cleared her throat and continued. "All right, here it is. According to the Mayan calendar, December 21st, 2012, marks the last day of time as we know it."

The vision of the screen going blank converged in Troy's mind with those ominous words. Moving in fitful jerks, he opened his laptop computer, which was connected to the internet via a global cellular network. "Are you telling me that if I Google 'December 21, 2012,' the first sites that come up will be about some kind of Mayan apocalyptic prophecy?"

"See for yourself," Rebecca said, with a nod toward his computer.

Troy typed furiously and, watching the first ten matches appear on the laptop's monitor, he read the titles of each. "You're almost right. Except for one, they're all about the Mayan calendar."

"What's the other one?" Rebecca asked.

"It's the U.S. Naval Observatory's forecast for future season changes." As he said this, he clicked on the observatory's website, knowing it would contain nothing but factual information regarding the winter solstice in question. Accessing the page that gave the exact date and time of every season change for the next sixteen years, he scrolled down to the year 2012. "Here it is: the winter solstice of 2012, which will occur at exactly 11:11 in the morning, Universal Standard Time."

Ryan and Rebecca turned to give each other a similar look of slack-jawed astonishment.

"What did you just say?" In the unique urgency of the moment, Ryan sounded like a man challenging Troy to a fight.

Rebecca had gone pallid and still.

"I just read what's on the screen." Troy could not have been more confused by their reactions. "What's the matter with you two?"

Without a word, Rebecca stood up, turned and pulled the top of her jeans down just far enough to reveal her tattoo.

Dr. Wallace did not know how to react. "Why do you have *that?*" he asked, his rational mind struggling to make sense of what he was seeing.

"Maybe you should tell him, Ryan. I can't seem to think very clearly right now. Oh, and while you're at it, why don't you go ahead and show him your watch?"

"Your watch? Now, what's *that* got to do with anything?"

Ryan simply removed his wristwatch and placed it face-down in Troy's hand. Even in the dim light, the engraved 11:11 on the back was easy to see.

Alarmed, Troy backed away from them. "Ryan? Rebecca? What the hell is going on here?"

"That's a damn good question," Ryan answered before lowering his head into his trembling hands. "All I know for sure is that my life was a whole lot simpler before I met the two of you."

Chapter 29

Just before nine o'clock in the morning, Rebecca rolled out of the cot and slipped into her jeans. As quietly as possible, she made her way past Troy and Ryan, both still asleep, and slid the lock of the shack's door open. She walked out into the bright sunlight and headed down toward the lagoon, where she hoped some alone-time with the dolphins would help her sort through her disjointed thoughts.

The sense that something was wrong crept slowly into her consciousness. Then it hit her like a punch to the stomach—the black wires leading from the shack to the four transducers in the lagoon were gone, their cables clipped just below the open window's sill.

"Oh, no," she moaned, then repeated the words over and over again in a screaming crescendo. "No, no, no!"

Crouched behind the windowless back wall of the stone shack, Jerry peeked around the corner. He watched her sink to her knees in the sand. *"Oh yes, yes, yes,"* he thought. *"Jerry was a busy boy last night. Now get up. Jerry's got a few more surprises for you."*

As if responding to his menacing suggestion, she sprang to her feet and bolted to the lagoon. The sight of the open floodgate confirmed her worst fear.

"They're gone! Troy, Ryan, get down here!"

"That's it." Jerry coaxed under his breath. "Time to get up. Let's get everybody down to the lagoon."

Ryan burst out of the shack. Disoriented by the sight of the missing transducer cables, he sprinted as fast as he could to Rebecca's side. "What the hell's going on?"

Seconds behind Ryan, Troy emerged and stumbled recklessly to the water's edge. Scanning the surface with wide, disbelieving eyes, he fell to his knees. "Oh, Jerry, you didn't! You wouldn't!" he wailed, clutching his hands together as if in agonized prayer.

Relishing his view of the scene playing out in front of him, Jerry knew he still had one last job to do, and he needed to move quickly. With surprising speed and agility for his size, he slipped into the shack once the men were gone. Once inside, he turned on the main computer, entered a few commands, then ejected and snatched the DVD disc that had recorded the images the night before. "Your bad habits have made this far too easy for me, Troy," he mumbled, happy to discover that the scientist had never heeded Jerry's repeated warnings about the need to back up important data and regularly change access passwords. "You're not only an arrogant son-of-a-bitch, but you're a lot dumber than you look."

◆   ◆   ◆

Down at the lagoon, Ryan felt more confused than ever. "Troy, are you saying you know who did this?" he asked.

Troy did not—or could not—reply.

"We know," Rebecca answered. "His name's Jerry Spears. He was Troy's assistant here years ago."

"But why would someone do such a thing?"

As if on cue, Jerry emerged from the shack and lumbered down toward the lagoon. Stopping roughly thirty feet away from them, he squatted down and took a few labored breaths before speaking.

"That's a very good question," he huffed. "Dr. Wallace, do you want to tell them, or should I?"

The sight of the DVD in Jerry's hand sent a wave of panic rushing through Troy's body. Choosing his words carefully, he struggled to appear calm. "I'll tell them," he said, his voice unsteady while his eyes stayed transfixed on the disc. "Jerry must be assuming that I would not have given him credit for his involvement in our discovery—which, of course, could not be further from the truth."

Jerry sat down in the sand, Troy's speech barely seeming to register with him. He balanced the disc on one bulging thigh, and then, with unnerving control, pulled an antique gun—the black Luger that Troy had been given all those years ago—from his waistband. "Wrong answer, Dr. Wallace!" he spat. "The truth is that you *never* had any intention of sharing your research with me. And that's why I'm taking it for myself."

Troy froze at the sight of the gun. "Then take it. You've already got the transducers and the disc. What else do you need?"

Jerry fondled the gun like some little pet. "I need the three of you out of my way, that's what I need," he said flatly. "I need to be the one who brings this discovery to the world."

Troy felt his heart constrict. "Are you saying that you'd kill us for it? Jerry, you're not a murderer."

Jerry waved the gun in their direction. "And I didn't think you were a traitor," he snarled. "But after listening in on your conversations these last few days, it's obvious you never had any intention of including me."

Troy let out a sickening groan in response to Jerry's revelation. "So, you bugged the place, and now you know everything. You know what we saw last night."

"Yes," Jerry nodded. "Amazing stuff, I must admit."

Rebecca could not contain herself. "Which makes what you're doing seem all the more ironic. I mean, here you are, willing to use violence so *you* can be the one to spread the dolphin lesson that humans use violence to solve their conflicts!"

"Hey! Survival of the fittest, sweetheart. Plain and simple. And right now, I'd say this baby makes me the most likely to survive, wouldn't you?"

"You obviously missed the message," Rebecca persevered courageously. "If anything, the mother was making the point that violence *decreases* the prospect for long-term survival of a species. Look at it logically: dolphins have been around for nearly forty million years, and they're still thriving, while in a few thousand years of fighting each other, we've pushed ourselves to the brink of extinction."

Unprepared to have his logic challenged, Jerry snapped, "Shut up! I don't need SeaWorld Barbie lecturing *me* about dolphins."

Troy seemed to be trying to appeal to Jerry's innate need for order. "So, what happens from here—you take the equipment back to the States and continue the tests? Do you really believe that people—people like Calvin, or the staff at SeaWorld—won't recognize the work?"

Jerry had smoked more marijuana than usual that morning. Otherwise, he might have been prepared for this battle of wits. "I said *shut up!* All I ever wanted was for you to share your research with me—research that I have every right to claim as mine! But no, you couldn't do that, could you? You had to keep it all for yourself!"

"Jerry, you know the information on that disc is bigger than the issue of who discovered it." There was genuine compassion in Troy's voice. "Don't you realize the magnitude of what's going on here? Dolphins are teaching their young that the human species is destined for self-destruction."

"Of course I realize that! I'm not stupid."

"Then you have to know that we've been given a chance to change that destiny! Just think what it would mean if the whole world got the chance to see what's on that disk."

"It would mean that you'd be worshipped as some goddamned hero," he replied, using the tip of the gun's barrel to wipe a tangle of hair away from his forehead, "and I'd still be here, stuck on this island like the anonymous stooge I've always been. Sorry, Dr. Wallace, but that's not going to happen."

With startling agility and speed surpassed only by his rage, Jerry grabbed the DVD and slammed it flat onto the ground. Then he placed the barrel of the gun directly on top of the disk and fired. With a roar that echoed through the jungle, the explosion sent a cloud of sand and silvery fragments into the air, showering Jerry with the remnants of his revenge.

Stunned by Jerry's desperate act, Troy, Rebecca, and Ryan stood paralyzed with disbelief and fear.

"Good God, Jerry!" Troy exclaimed, feeling numb and barely able to get the words out of his mouth. "Do you know what you've just done?"

Jerry looked down at the gun, as if he were evaluating the question. For an instant, he allowed them a fleeting glimpse into his tortured, conflicted soul. Staring into Rebecca's eyes, he gave a sad, misplaced smile. "Yes, I know," he answered. "I did what I had to do to keep from killing the three of you." With that, he rose with a labored grunt and trudged up the beach. "Oh, I almost forgot," he called back and waved the gun in their direction.

"What's that?" Troy challenged.

"Format C, slash S," was all Jerry had to say.

Rebecca was perplexed by this announcement. "What does that mean?"

Troy closed his eyes. "It means he wiped out the computer's hard drive," he answered, the reality catching in his throat. "It means that all the evidence is gone. No one will ever believe what we saw."

Jerry turned back. "Oh, I don't know about that," he said with a snicker. I bet one of the tabloids back in the States would publish your incredible findings—right next to the articles about Bigfoot and Loch Ness Monster sightings!" The snicker rose to a maniacal guffaw. "Oh, and just in case you were thinking about trying to get the transducers back—since you're the one who stole them in the first place, you may not want to face the grand larceny charges that would be filed against you. The Brits down here take that kind of thing very seriously."

Ryan was ready to chase after Jerry and force him into telling them where he had hidden the transducers, but Troy grabbed Ryan's arm tightly and held onto him.

"Don't. I'm not willing to take the chance that he really might use that gun."

"Prudent decision, Dr. Wallace," Jerry said. "Since you all did so well at keeping your whereabouts a secret, it really would have been quite easy to make your disappearance permanent."

Without another word, Jerry turned away, trudging through the sand and vanishing into the dense foliage surrounding the lagoon.

Chapter 30

Shipwreck Salvage had made more money for Calvin Brooks and Chad Hanover than either of them would have ever thought possible—a single recent find off Florida had yielded more than $25,000,000 in silver coins intended to fund the Confederate Army. Even so, the recent loss of the sonographic equipment ate away at them as if they had been robbed at gunpoint.

"I always knew we were throwing our money away on his research," Chad growled as he reclined on a plush leather sofa in Calvin's office. "But I never thought Troy would actually *steal* from us. How could he do that after everything we've done for him over the years?"

Calvin leaned back in an ornate wooden captain's throne and rested his feet on his desk. He picked up one of the Confederate coins and twirled it in his fingers. "I don't have an answer to that, but I will say that it doesn't seem like something he would do. Not to us, not to anybody."

Calvin's answer did nothing to calm Chad. "What is it with you and that old coot? From day one, he's had you snowed, and now you sound like you're actually defending him. And it's not even about the money at this point. It's about the fact that he betrayed the trust of the only two people who ever gave him a fighting chance to prove his theories."

"I know," Calvin admitted.

A gentle tap on the door announced their personal assistant, a voluptuous brunette who never seemed to mind the occasional flirty advances they would throw her way. "This just came," she said, handing the FedEx overnight envelope to Chad. Leaning over the couch, she offered Chad a beautiful view past the top of her open blouse. "Need me for anything else?"

"If Calvin weren't here, I could probably think of something," he smirked.

The girl just shook her head playfully and left the room.

"What's in the envelope?" Calvin asked.

Chad flipped it over to study the sender's address. His face tightened as he read aloud the information. "No name, but it's from Tortola, British Virgin Islands."

"Didn't I tell you that's where he'd go?" Calvin sputtered, leaping up from the chair and grabbing the FedEx out of Chad's hand. He ripped open the envelope, pulled out a single piece of paper, and began scanning the letter in silence.

Chad sat up on the couch. "Well, what's it say?"

Calvin looked at the letter a long while before replying. "It says what I thought it might say."

"So, are you going to let me in on it, or am I supposed to read your mind?"

Calvin cleared his throat and began to read aloud.

Dear Calvin and Chad, the letter began. *I can only imagine your reaction to my leaving with the equipment. Please believe that it was the hardest decision I have ever made in my life. And while this is not the time or place to defend my actions, I do want you to know that what I did was in all of our best interests.*

"Yeah, right," Chad scoffed. "Probably sold everything for pennies on the dollar."

"Will you just shut up and let me finish?"

At this point, all I can tell you is that my theories were correct. Two days ago, I finally was able to prove that dolphins do indeed send ultrasonic images to each other, and the nature of those images is so profound that it will send shock waves around the world.

Which brings me to the real reason for this letter. If you are only interested in salvage operations, I will make sure that every last piece of equipment is returned to you or paid for in full. The transducers are no longer in my possession, but manufacturing replacements will not be difficult now that I know the design is functional.

However, if you have any desire to participate in what I believe is one of the most significant scientific discoveries in history, I will honor our relationship and give you the first right of refusal to underwrite my continuing research. This is not a plea for money. This is an invitation to positively impact the world on a scale never before imagined.

I will be talking to you in person within the week.

Yours truly,
Troy Wallace

Calvin placed the letter down on his desk. "Well, I'm not quite sure I know what to say to that."

Chad lay back down on the sofa. "Oh yes you do. It's the same thing you've been saying ever since the day we first met him."

Calvin smiled. "Does that mean you're in, too?"

"What... like I'd let you change the world without me?"

Chapter 31

The plane flew in low over a black expanse of Pacific Ocean on its final approach to John Wayne Airport. Bucking a strong and dry offshore wind, the jet banked high over Catalina Island, allowing Ryan a view of the familiar lights of Avalon harbor. He tapped Rebecca on the shoulder and pointed out the window. "Feels like a long time has passed since we were there, doesn't it?" he asked, still barely able to fathom all that had taken place between that day on his boat and the dramatic events at the compound two days ago.

"A lot has happened since then, that's for sure." She leaned over his lap to get a view of the lights.

"I'd call that the understatement of the century." He shifted in the seat. "So, what do you think Troy will do now?"

Rebecca hesitated. "I'm not sure. He'll either stay on the island and figure out a way to get the transducers back from Jerry, or he'll build a new set and start up his research someplace else. Either way, I'm sure he'll call from wherever he is and ask for our help."

Ryan's face was expressionless. "I suppose so. But you know what? Even if he *did* ask me, I'm not so sure I would go. Everything that's happened just feels too, well..." Gifted as he was with words, he couldn't find the right ones for this experience.

"Too big?"

"Something like that. Dolphins, Mayans, the Aquarian Age, and now the whole 11:11 thing—it all just feels like more than I can handle."

She laid her hand on top of his. "I know. It's as if what we've learned is too important to keep to ourselves, but at the same time, it sounds too weird for anyone to ever believe. It breaks my heart that we don't have any proof of what we saw."

Meditating on these words, Ryan retreated into thoughtful silence as the plane bounced and lurched against the air currents.

◆   ◆   ◆

The Santa Ana winds whistled through the palms outside Ryan's darkened home, the dry gusts giving an ominous feeling to their arrival.

It was this feeling that ultimately manifested into an urgent impulse—an impulse Ryan could not ignore. After opening the front door for her and bringing in their luggage, he turned around and stood motionless in the threshold of the gaping doorway. With his arms hanging limp at his sides, his eyes closed and his open palms facing forward, he tilted his head up toward the night sky and braced himself against the increasingly powerful gusts.

"What are you doing?" She sheltered herself behind his body for whatever wind-protection it would provide.

He did not turn around. With his hair whipping about his face, he let the thought come out exactly as he was hearing it in his head. "Rebecca, I know this doesn't make much sense, but I need to talk to Vern. I'm going to go see if he's down at the dory village."

"Vern? The fisherman?" she asked, confused. "But it's almost midnight. Why would he be there?"

"That's what I'm about to find out," he said. Then, without further explanation, he grabbed a khaki *South Coast Safari* production jacket from a closet near the front door, gave Rebecca a kiss on the forehead, and walked out into the darkness.

The boardwalk leading from his house to the dory village was as deserted as he knew it would be. Not even the drunks, who normally used the thoroughfare as a bicycle expressway from one bar to the next, were out on such a night, bitterly cold by coastal California standards. There was no logical reason to believe that Vern would be in his locker, but Ryan believed it anyway.

He entered the village, noticing that the only light on in the entire place was a bare yellow bulb dangling over the stoop of Vern's locker. Standing in front of the shed's door, he tapped a few times.

Meowing loudly, a cat approached from the shadows and rubbed up against his leg.

"Hey there," he said, squatting to pet the purring tabby. "What're you doing out on a night like this?"

Following the sound of turning locks, the plywood door creaked open.

Vern poked his head out. "I suppose someone might ask you that same question," he said, hurriedly motioning for Ryan to come inside. The flimsy walls of the wooden locker creaked at every joint as the shed shuddered in the wind. "Coffee?" he asked, slamming the door shut and gesturing toward the same stool that Ryan had sat in on his previous visit.

"Sure," Ryan replied, propping himself up on the stool. He wondered how he should start the conversation.

Vern poured two ceramic mugs to the brim and handed one to his guest. "So, what *does* bring you out on such a night?"

Ryan saw no point in being evasive. "You. And, more to the point, what you know about dolphins." He took a sip of the steaming coffee and wrapped both hands around the warm cup. "I get the feeling that there's still something more you want to tell me about them."

Vern studied Ryan with quizzical eyes, then sat down in the heavy oak chair next to his desk.

Ryan waited.

Taking a deep and labored breath, Vern turned his attention to an old high school textbook, *Cetaceans of the Pacific*, sitting on the desk. The book's fading cover depicted the silhouettes of two bottle-nosed dolphins. Opening the book and perusing some of its dog-eared pages, he smiled in surrender. "Ryan, there *is* something I want to tell you, but for some reason, the right words just aren't coming to me."

"I'm not in any hurry."

Set at ease by Ryan's patience, Vern gazed at the pages of the book as a query began to take shape. "Okay, then, I'll start with a request. I want you to describe the perfect person to me."

Ryan frowned. "Come again?"

"I want to hear your definition of the ideal human being. Can you? What traits would this person have?"

Ryan was not surprised at his first response. He thought of Rebecca. "I suppose he or she would be kind, intelligent, honest ..."

"Cooperative?" Vern prodded.

"Sure."

"Destructive?"

"Of course not."

"Violent?"

"No."

Vern stroked the stubble on his chin and studied Ryan's eyes. "I see. So, does it seem odd to you that, in defining the perfect human being—one you wouldn't meet very often, maybe never—you chose traits found abundantly in dolphins?"

Ryan's brow furrowed. "I never would have thought of it that way."

"Hardly anybody does. Yet here we are, sharing a planet with a species that has been here millions of years longer than we have, and we never stop to think that maybe the reason they've survived so long is because they possess these ideal qualities."

Ryan considered Vern's statement and let it merge with what had been revealed on Tortola. "You know, a few weeks ago, I would have said that survival of the fittest meant survival of the most aggressive. But a lot has happened in those few weeks. Now I'm beginning to think that what we've always considered acts of submission—love, forgiveness, compassion—are really what's going to determine how much longer we'll be around."

Vern smiled. "I'm impressed. Somehow you've managed to pick up in a few short weeks a lot of what I've learned by observing dolphins for fifty years. But more than that, I'm relieved," he said with a deep sigh.

"Yeah? About what?"

"I'm relieved that you're ready to hear what I have to say next."

"You mean something else about dolphins?"

"No. It's an assignment."

A weighted silence followed. "What's an assignment?" Ryan asked.

"It's the real reason you're here tonight."

Disoriented by Vern's response, Ryan knew the only thing he could do was sit back and see where this strange exchange was headed. "All right, I'm listening," he said, taking another sip of coffee.

Vern turned his attention away from his book and looked up at an old black and white photograph of himself as a young sailor.

"See me there?" he asked, a misty glaze rising up in his eyes. "I was just a kid in the Navy, serving my time on a destroyer in the Pacific. One night—just a few days after the bomb was dropped on Hiroshima—one of the ship's boilers exploded and blew me and a buddy into the drink. He was killed instantly, I was hurt pretty bad. And as I floundered there in the water, waitin' to find out what dying was going to feel like, I hear this voice tellin' me not to worry. That I'd be okay."

Two weeks ago Ryan would have made a hasty retreat from such a conversation. But in those two weeks, he had become a different person, one who could no longer discount such statements. "Go on."

Vern felt himself drifting back in time. "The voice told me that I wouldn't die that night—that I was going to be okay because I still had a job to do." Feeling the awe almost exactly the same way he had nearly sixty years ago, he asked, "And do you know what that job was?"

Ryan shook his head.

"That job was to deliver a message. And when I asked her—"

"Hold on, did you say *her?*" Ryan interrupted, though at the moment he wasn't quite sure why.

"Yes, it was a woman's voice. Anyway, when I asked her what this message was and who I was supposed to deliver it to, she told me that I would know both of these things when the time was right."

"So, was the time ever right?" Ryan asked.

Vern sat motionless. "Not until tonight."

Ryan's stomach lurched. "I—I don't understand."

"I think maybe you do," Vern replied with quiet assurance. "Ryan, you're the person she was telling me about."

Swaying on the stool, Ryan stared at Vern in astonishment. "*I'm* the person?" he asked, pointing to himself. "Why, of *course* I'm the person!" he babbled. "With only six billion other people on this planet, who else could it possibly be, right? It all makes perfect sense."

Vern waited for Ryan's ranting to subside. "Are you done?"

Ryan rocked back and forth. "You know what? At this point, I think that maybe I *am* done. I'm done trying to make sense of everything that's happened to me since I met you."

Expressionless, Vern slumped into the chair's tattered vinyl upholstery. "So, now you're saying that you don't want to hear what I have to tell you?"

Ryan realized he was being backed into a corner. And while his rational mind told him that he should get up and get out of there, his pounding heart told him he had to stay. "It feels like I don't have much choice."

An unsettling smile spread across Vern's wrinkled face. "Ryan, you have always had a choice. Stop, go. Give, take. Left, right. Don't you see that *you* are the one who has chosen every step of the path that has led you here tonight?"

Ryan recalled the events leading up to this moment—the decision to become the Funhunter; the offer of his boat for Troy's research; the phone call he made to find Rebecca—and realized that he had willingly chosen to partake in every one.

With a deep breath, he surrendered to what he was about to hear. "Okay, let's have it."

Vern reached out to cradle Ryan's hands in his own. "Ryan, over the last sixty years, I've been shown that there's more to life than what everyone thinks. We're on a path of growth and discovery that's not so different from the dolphins' path, but if we don't recognize this in ourselves, we are likely to lose our way forever. I've seen it coming. I was there when we destroyed a city with a nuclear bomb, and I've seen how we've created the means to do the same thing to an entire planet. I know first-hand the effect our ignorance and recklessness have had on the delicate balance of life in the ocean. We've reached a crossroads on our journey, and we are in grave danger of taking a wrong turn."

Ryan closed his eyes and let the weight of Vern's words settle. "I understand. I understand in a way that I never would have thought possible. But I still don't see why you picked me to tell this to."

Vern took a deep breath.

"I didn't pick you," he said with a gentle smile. "I just recognized you when you showed up."

Chapter 32

Though exhausted from the long flight home, Rebecca woke to the sound of Ryan creeping into the master bedroom. Barely mustering the energy to raise the blanket and welcome him into bed, she asked, "So, was he there?"

By the light of the moon streaming through his window, Ryan could see that she was still wearing the jeans and T-shirt that she had worn on the plane. "He was there." He slid into the bed in just his boxers and nestled up against her warm body.

"Do you want to talk about it?" The sound of her voice was a soothing comfort.

Knowing how tired she was, Ryan decided that this was not the time to discuss the conversation he'd just had with Vern. "Not tonight. I'll tell you everything tomorrow."

"Okay. Sweet dreams," she said, and then kissed him on his forehead. "And Ryan?"

"Yes?"

"I want you to go to sleep tonight," she reached to kiss his neck, "knowing that," she kissed it again, "I'm falling in love with you."

Her words eased their way deep into his heart as he lay there beside her.

"I'm glad to hear you say that, because I'm already past the falling part." With his admission, he kissed her delicately on the lips and combed his fingers once through her flaxen hair. "Good night, Rebecca."

The howling wind made dozing off difficult, but eventually he slipped into a fitful sleep.

It did not take long for the dream to come.

Once again he was beside the woman on the beach. As they ambled along the shore together, she continued their conversation.

"Come with me," she said, smiling. "There's something I want to show you." Though she spoke a language he did not recognize, he was somehow able to understand every word.

For the first time, Ryan noticed a group of crumbling white buildings jutting above the shoreline in the distance. Marveling at the way their bleached stone walls caught the day's first light, he stopped to take in the view.

"Wait," he called ahead to the woman. "Before we go any further, I need to know who you are."

The woman turned and extended a brown, weathered hand for him to hold. Her black hair glistened in the morning sunlight. "My name is Ixchel," she said. "And I have been waiting a long time for you." Offering no other information, she pivoted back around and guided him onto a footpath that led away from the beach and into a thick growth of trees. After a short hike, they arrived at a stone archway built into the side of a hill. It was a portal marking the entrance to some kind of underground tunnel.

Feeling his way through the long, narrow passageway, Ryan asked, "Where are we?"

"Under the sacred temple complex of Tulum." She stopped in front of an imposing stone door that had been built into a wider section of the tunnel. Motioning toward the upper left corner of the door with an upraised arm, she said, "Open it."

Obeying, he pushed on the corner, and the massive slab pivoted in place. Turned ninety degrees, the door created two passages of equal size into a brightly painted chamber.

"This is what I've brought you here to see," Ixchel said, stepping reverently through the opening and beckoning him to follow.

The vibrant colors—turquoise, gold, garnet—of the room's circular interior assailed his senses as he entered and let his eyes adjust to the dim light. Moving toward the middle of the chamber and looking up at the high, domed ceiling, he was struck by the sight of the now familiar Mayan calendar over his head. Studying the painting, he began to grasp its complex concentric design. "What is this place?"

"We are in a shrine commemorating the end of time."

Ryan lowered his eyes to the walls of the room, processing the information depicted in each polarized scene. In one, a prone woman was delivering a baby, while right next to her a terror-stricken woman was stabbing herself in the abdomen with a knife. In another, a man held a bounty of fruit in his hands as a gaunt figure went begging beside him. In the next panel, a spear-toting warrior stood beside an empty-handed but otherwise identical version of himself.

When Ryan finally noticed the open doorway, with its identical twin columns painted on either side, he realized he was looking at an image that had haunted humanity at least a thousand years before digital clocks were ever invented. Silently he walked up to one pair of columns and laid his hand upon the wall. "Did they know what this meant?" he asked.

Ixchel approached and traced the outline of one of the columns with her finger. "They knew it was a symbolic way to validate their predictions," she replied. "But more importantly, they hoped it would serve as a warning to humanity."

Ryan tilted his head and carefully studied the graphic mural surrounding them.

The frail, stooped woman walked the perimeter of the chamber, stopping in front of each scene before continuing on to the next. "Isn't it obvious?" There was a pleading tone in her voice now. "They were telling us that *we*—we who have had our souls activated by the symbol—are the generation that will decide the very meaning of time's end."

Deciphering the murals, Ryan began to grasp the duality of their imagery: life and death, feast and famine, war and peace. "I think I understand," he said. "It's up to us to choose whether or not the calendar's last day represents an end or the moment of a new beginning."

She nodded. "That is correct. By the time the winter solstice of 2012 arrives, mankind will have already decided what its future will be."

Ryan found a place deep inside himself for her message to reside, and in that place a feeling of heightened understanding began to grow. "I'm not the only person having this experience, am I?"

Ixchel smiled. "No. This prophecy is reaching more and more people every day. Triggered by the symbolism of the columns, they are receiving the same urgent message—they are becoming aware that the future is in their hands."

Ryan was relieved to know that he was just a small part of a much larger event taking place around the world, that there were others who had awakened to the message of the Mayans.

"However," Ixchel told him, "you *are* unique in all that you have witnessed. Do you understand?"

"I do," he admitted, recalling the incredible events of the past two weeks.

"Then you must also know that you are to share this information."

Ryan knelt on the chamber's sandy floor. "I do know that," he said. "But how? How am I supposed to get someone to believe what I can barely believe myself?"

Ixchel walked over and laid a comforting hand on his shoulder. "Look around you. The people who painted these walls knew they had an important message to convey, and they did it to the best of their ability." She stooped down so that her round, leathery face was just inches away from his. "Now you must do the same."

Ryan searched the depths of her midnight eyes, then felt a chill when the idea came to him. Recounting everything he'd discovered about the Mayan calendar and the Age of Aquarius, about dolphin ultrasonic communication, the 11:11 phenomenon and the Naval Observatory's solstice projection, he realized there was only one way he could share such incredible information.

He awoke with the dream imagery still vivid in his mind. Bolting up in bed, he leaned over and took a small tablet and pen from the nightstand. Then, as had become his habit whenever he was inspired, he began to write.

Days later, he was transferring the information into notebook-sized binders.

Weeks later, as he transcribed his notes and wove them into a narrative on his computer, he imagined the people who would not only read his story, but also feel aligned with its message of hope for the future. He did not know if there were two hundred or two million of them, but he knew they were out there.

And it was for them—the people already envisioning an era when peace would guide the planets and love steer the stars—that he named the book *The Aquarians*.

Every new beginning comes from
some other beginning's end.

Ancient Roman Proverb

Author's Note

Dear Reader:

I hope you enjoyed and were intrigued by *The Aquarians*. Although this book is a work of fiction, the story contains much factual information that you may wish to investigate further. More importantly, I hope you choose to become a proactive participant in the Age of Aquarius yourself.

Throughout history, many people have believed that they were witnessing humanity's last days on earth. Yet it is hard not to accept that we have arrived at a truly fateful moment in time. At one end of the spectrum, we are assaulted daily by apocalyptic headlines in the news, while at the other we feel a current of hope running through the world. You only need to tap into the online realm—Facebook, Twitter, YouTube—to realize that a true Aquarian shift is already well underway. Are you willing to play a role in creating a more hopeful future for this planet and its inhabitants? Now, more than ever, the need for compassionate caregivers and peacekeepers is critical. We have been around long enough now to see that acts of greed, oppression and violence only perpetuate more of the same. At some point, the cycle must be broken.

Peace,
Eric Rankin

Search Ideas

You may want to launch some Internet searches of your own regarding the information contained in The Aquarians. Here are a few keyword suggestions to get you started:

Mayan calendar
Mayan ajk'ij daykeeper
Mayan Goddess Ixchel
December 21, 2012
Age of Aquarius begins 2012
The 2012 Shift
Dresden Codex, last page prophecy
11:11 Phenomenon
U.S. Naval Observatory season times
Dolphin evolution and physiology
Dolphin ultrasound
Dolphins capable of transmitting images
Dolphins healing autism
Dr. John Lilly
Newport Beach California dory fleet
Tortola British Virgin Islands

Contact Information:
Blogs, updates, new information:
www.AquarianAge2012.com

Email:
TheAquarianMessage@Yahoo.com

LaVergne, TN USA
19 May 2010
183280LV00003B/127/P